CHAMPAGNE SECRETS

www.rbooks.co.uk

Also by Amanda Brunker

Champagne Kisses
Champagne Babes

CHAMPAGNE SECRETS

Amanda Brunker

TRANSWORLD IRELAND

TRANSWORLD IRELAND
an imprint of The Random House Group Limited
20 Vauxhall Bridge Road, London SW1V 2SA
www.rbooks.co.uk

First published in 2010 by Transworld Ireland,
a division of Transworld Publishers Ltd

A CIP catalogue record for this book
is available from the British Library.

ISBN 9781848270510

Addresses for Random House Group Ltd companies outside the UK
can be found at: www.randomhouse.co.uk
The Random House Group Ltd Reg. No. 954009

The Random House Group Limited supports the Forest Stewardship Council
(FSC), the leading international forest-certification organization. All our titles that
are printed on Greenpeace-approved FSC-certified paper carry the FSC logo.
Our paper procurement policy can be found at
www.rbooks.co.uk/environment

Typeset in 13/15½pt Bembo by
Kestrel Data, Exeter, Devon
Printed and bound in Great Britain by
Clays Ltd, Bungay, Suffolk

2 4 6 8 10 9 7 5 3 1

Mixed Sources
Product group from well-managed
forests and other controlled sources
www.fsc.org Cert no. TT-COC-2139
© 1996 Forest Stewardship Council
FSC

For Edward, my walking talking teddy bear

1

I can get through this. I just need to relax. I'll be fine once
I don't make eye-contact – *with anyone* . . .

Initially the press junket to Germany had sounded pretty
fun. As I'd flicked casually through the itinerary at the airport, I had read about trips to casinos and perfumeries, but
somehow missed the page that said, 'You'll have a chance to
get naked and humiliate yourself in front of fellow freelance
journalists, some of whom you've known previously on a
formal basis for years, and some of whom you've just met.'

Although I was chanting prayers inwardly for the world
to open up and swallow me whole, my pleas were not being
met, and I was growing weaker by the minute. I had never
been to a Turkish bath before, but though I was only at stage
three of what we had proudly been told were twelve stages
in total, I was already feeling faint from the hot steam and
the heat, not to mention the extreme effort it was taking to
keep my stomach sucked in. And while I was trying my best
not be prudish, the sight of old women's breasts drooping
on to their laps was proving too much at such an early hour
of the morning.

It didn't help matters that the night before I had sampled

far too many varieties of German beer; starting with the light ones, and building in bravery to the murky darker ales as the evening progressed. Our host had been an enthusiastic middle-aged man by the name of Hans Biermann, who, by the stroke of twelve, had turned out to be quite literally the beer-man who *was* all hands. He had looked like a character straight out of a children's fairy tale, complete with handlebar moustache and touristy lederhosen kit. Yet there was no confusion over the games he wanted to play when he bluntly suggested we try Hide the Frankfurter.

Although I'd been flattered by the attention (I'd been going through a man-famine of late), not even the gallon of sickly sweet free beer he had plied me with would have made me drop my standards that low. OK, well, also the killjoy PR woman who was in charge of the trip noticed the inappropriate behaviour and called time on the night snappish. It was hard to tell if it had been my *Coyote Ugly* impression – dancing on the bar – or my no-hands approach to drinking chasers of Jägermeister that had pushed her over the edge, but she'd refused to allow me to stay and follow her back later. I suppose I should probably thank her now for such a lucky escape – all I'd given her in the taxi last night had been the silent treatment. But any thank yous would have to wait, because I could hardly bear to look in her direction. She had a scrawny white body, and her giant collarbones protruded through her skin and threatened to poke me in the eye. Instead of too much flesh, this poor woman wasn't sporting enough meat on her bones. Indeed, there'd be more meat on a butcher's apron . . . or maybe even on a vegan supermodel's pitta-bread sandwich. If ever there was a woman to buck the saying you can never be too rich or too thin, it was her. Not even if Mr Biermann tracked me down and came in and sat beside me could this flesh-fest get any worse.

Averting my eyes, though, meant coming face to face with more matters fleshy. I began to amuse myself with counting nipples, well, boobs really — not in a pervy way, but in a more factual manner. Call it journalistic research. I knew my friends Parker and Lisa would ask for these details, so I collated in total seven pairs of droopy diddies, two big breastfeeders, five fried eggs, three fairly perfect funbags and me.

I was just musing over my own perkiness, or should I say lack of, when a bell sounded and everyone stood up and headed in the direction of the next door. Before I had time to avert my gaze, a tide of breasts large and small swished and swayed past my face, causing mild nausea. Closing my eyes didn't help — the horror was almost worse, as the slapping and squelching of women's body-parts was so loud. I'd only had my eyes closed for a few seconds when beads of sweat began to roll down over my eyelids, forcing me to bend over to reach the small facecloth of a towel that was barely covering my sacred bits. Though if the truth be told, I didn't possess sacred bits, just neglected and unloved-by-the-opposite-sex bits! When I opened my eyes again I saw I was being surrounded by another group of women, butcher and hairier than my own crowd, so I made a sprint for the safety of my companions, doing my best not to let my big Kim Kardashian bum slap off anyone on the way.

'So have you sweated all the booze out of you yet?' asked my skinny PR person, without a hint of a smile, as I re-joined the posse. I had lost the piece of paper with her name on it, and after the evening we had shared I thought it too late to ask her again.

'Ah, nearly there, thanks,' I mumbled. 'I feel about as fresh as an out-of-date bag of fish.' My PR chaperone just looked at me bemusedly. 'But I'm thrilled to be away. So thanks for having me on the trip. Felt like I was going batty at home. I've had serious cabin fever the last few months. Everyone I know seems to have caught swine flu or bird flu, and the recession has killed the fun out of most of my rich friends – and even a few of my poor ones, too.'

I didn't get a response, but I didn't care. Maybe I was still drunk from last night, but I needed to talk, and now seemed as good a time as any. I slipped into a warm pool of crystal-clear water and, feeling even chattier now that I was less exposed, I turned to the middle-aged woman beside me.

Joyce was a wild-haired travel journalist who, I had so far worked out, had very little time for personal grooming, yet a big love for cigarettes and the lonely existence of the road. 'Fancy a game of I spy?' I asked. After all, I couldn't be the only one uncomfortable with the view.

'P.' Her lips barely moved, and for a moment I wasn't sure if I had imagined a response.

'Excuse me?'

'You heard me,' answered Joyce abruptly. 'I spy something beginning with P.'

I let out a little snigger, flashes of naughty words firing off in my head. Penis? None of them in here. Pubic hair? Possibly, considering Joyce's ran practically halfway down to her knee. 'Ummm, pimple?' I asked, spying a large boil on a nearby German woman's back.

'No.'

'Pedicure?'

'No.'

'Ponytail?'

'No.'

'Ah, psychic . . . psycho . . . psychiatrist . . . ah, I don't know, paedophile . . . eh, party-pooper . . . I give up. What is it?'

'Piercings.' Once again Joyce's face barely moved. Instead she just signalled to my ears, which indeed had empty holes in them, where beautiful diamonds had once lived.

'Ah, well now, Joyce, there's a story and a half behind those.' I winked and began my sorry tale. 'In a former life, my soon-to-be ex-husband Michael bought me a gorgeous single solitaire diamond engagement ring. Marriage swiftly over, it lived at the bottom of my sock drawer until my second – or should I say fake – husband bought me a thank you gift of another diamond, and made them into stunning earrings for me—'

'Fake?' Joyce interrupted, her face moving for the first time as her eyebrows lifted in disbelief.

'Yep. The diamonds were real, the husband was fake – about a year ago I pretended to marry my gay friend Alistair George in a staged wedding because his ninety-year-old mother Agatha was about to evict him from the family home and give the proceeds away to her various animal charities. It had been his father's dying wish that Alistair marry, and although his mother knew that Alistair was most definitely gay, and not even in the slightest bit bi-curious, she'd demanded he make a full and public display of straightness, so as not to embarrass the family further.

'In the end the homophobic George family got their dream arranged marriage. Alistair got to keep his fancy mansion in Dalkey. Many out-of-work actors pocketed a handy few euros as pretend guests at the pantomime, and yours truly got a pair of sparklers just like Victoria Beckham's. Well, until the recession kicked in, my real hubby Michael kicked me out of the house I couldn't afford to contribute to, and some robbing thief in Essex paid three thousand, three hundred quid on eBay for them. They were easily worth closer to six thousand, but I needed a deposit on a ground-floor flat, and, well, now that I'm a single parent, I need all the spare cash I can get my hands on.'

Joyce's expression had frozen again. Her eyebrows remained in the raised, 'surprised' position – clearly my romantic life story so far was as good as a free shot of Botox for the unprepared. She muttered her excuses and floated off to check something with the PR lady, who was looking really uncomfortable in her own skin. She was surveying an older, more rotund type, who seemed to be completely at ease with herself as she laughed her way through a funny story. I wondered why the PR lady was so skinny. Did she have an eating disorder? Was she actually genuinely sick? Or maybe stressed out? It was as I began to feel sorry for her that I realized how much better I felt about myself. Was that wrong of me? Of course all of us have our own problems, but suddenly my newly acquired poverty – and singleton lifestyle – didn't seem so bad after all. My circumstances would improve with something as simple as a great first date. But could hers be turned around by a feed of drink and a calorie-filled meal? Methinks possibly not.

The next eight stages of the baths, especially stage ten, the scrub-down, were much more enjoyable once I had unshackled my fears. As I lay like a starfish on a hard bed while a woman who looked like Arnold Schwarzenegger took the top ten layers of skin off me with a yard brush, I decided this was going to be my year. It was only the second week in January, and although many of my New

Year's resolutions had already fallen by the wayside I felt that literally shedding my old skin could really help, if only symbolically, in starting over afresh. While my new home's address – 12 Park Avenue – looked good on paper, the reality was somewhat different. Yet it was becoming a home for me and my two-year-old daughter Daisy, and that was the most important thing.

It was a disastrously slow exit from the hotel the next day, due to four members of the entourage going missing in action. Two slept through their repeated wake-up calls, one never even made it back to sleep in their bed at all, and then Joyce went walkabout, claiming to have totally forgotten about the call time. 'I began meditating at the riverside and just zenned out. Sorry.'

Forty minutes later, the panicked search-and-rescue teams had returned to the minibus with all the tardy journos, none of whom looked the least bit remorseful, and the driver had taken off at great speed – urged on by our now desperate PR friend. Our journey should only have taken twenty-five minutes. In theory, that is. It wasn't to be, though. A large pile-up on the autobahn just outside the airport made the route almost impassable, so after a lengthy, frustrating and claustrophobic journey, we were told in no uncertain terms that we had missed our flight back to Dublin. Although we were given options, neither included a later Dublin flight home. Instead we had the choice of staying another night at the nearby Hilton or flying home via Heathrow, and much to my relief the group unanimously agreed that they were all sick of the sight of one another, and that the second option was the only alternative.

It was only when we arrived at our departure gate an hour later that things started to look up. As if I had walked into a special-edition copy of *Heat* magazine, there stood in front of me about half-a-dozen English WAGs that I recognized, engaged in what could politely be termed a heated debate. There were Page 3 glamour girls screaming at reality TV stars, and a soap actress pointing her over-accessorized finger at a very chavvy looking young woman who, I vaguely recalled, usually had a microphone in her hand. I just wasn't sure if I'd seen her in my local Lidl store calling special offers or on a pop video.

Needless to say their dramatics made quite a floor show, and numerous passengers from neighbouring flights had crowded down to watch — including a giddy group of flight attendants who seemed highly amused, and not the least bit interested in breaking up the catfights.

'This nose was done by the best surgeon in the world,' screamed one WAG. 'He also did Angelina Jolie's, so what do you know? You've the worst boob job ever. They're so mad lookin' you look like you're smuggling a bag o' cats down your top. They're all spilling out in different directions!'

Utterly riled by this outburst, another WAG let out a high-pitched scream that sent out frequency waves strong enough to burst her silicone implants. Then she pounced on her rival and pulled at her hair. 'You stupid bitch, how very dare you—'

'Get off me!' the other howled as she struggled to hang on to her locks.

'I'll rip those ugly extensions out at the roots,' growled the first.

The other women dropped their own arguments to form

two teams goading the squabbling divas on. The situation was beginning to get out of control.

'Yeah, you show her, Tanya,' screamed one.

'Rip her eyes out, Issey,' screamed another.

'Tanya, she's only a wannabe.'

'Don't mind 'em. You've more class in your little finger, Issey. You're better than her. Her fella's gonna be relegated next season. She's dead to us.'

The insults were coming thick and fast, but it was only when the two women fell to the floor and started to knock over their matching Louis Vuitton carry-on cases that security arrived to break up the duelling duo. Instead of applause, there was a symphony of boos, which was followed by a fair bit of pushing from nosy passengers trying to get a better glimpse of the spectacle. While I think we all secretly wished one of the ladies — if not both — would be carted off in handcuffs, both feuding foes were allowed on to the plane after a short cooling-off period, a stern talking-to and, from what I could see, an impromptu autograph-signing. It wasn't quite a rumble in the jungle — more an at-loggerheads in Lagerfeld — but it was certainly entertainment enough to get us disgruntled journos back on talking terms.

'Which one is married to the gorgeous striker, you know, the one who's meant to be gay?' asked my skinny PR friend excitedly as we queued up to board the plane. 'Is it the blonde with the really large breasts?'

'They're all blonde and they've all got inflatable boobs,' I mused, pretending I wasn't the least bit interested in celebrity culture.

'Yeah, but the cartoonish-looking blonde with the breasts that look like they're going to topple her over . . . Her. The one who left several hair-extensions on the floor, and who's wearing the boob-tube as a dress. She's with the gay foot-baller. I'm nearly sure of it.'

Before I got a chance to reply, one of the older gentlemen on the trip, Clark – renamed Clark Kent after pulling a little disappearing act earlier – chipped in. 'No she's not. She's married to one of the Liverpool players. Or is it United?' He continued, frowning, 'No, it's Liverpool . . . oh gosh, no, I'm getting confused. I actually think she's married to one of the lads from Spurs. Oh, forget I said anything, I don't know who she is.'

'Thanks for that.' Our PR friend sneered. 'We're in a recession. My brand's survival depends on individuals like you endorsing the company and providing informed write-ups with accurate details. And it's only now, at the end of your all-expenses-paid weekend, that you reveal that you're clueless. Cheers.'

Clark shrank back into the shadows, muttering to himself, leaving the hard-nosed gossip queen tutting at me in disbelief. As she renewed her debate about which WAG belonged to which footballer, my attention was distracted by a beautiful Indian girl on the other side of the glass partition in front of me. She was already on her way to board the plane, but somehow, through the mass of busy people, her eyes seemed to find mine, and both of us got locked into an extended gaze. I couldn't help feeling she was important, somehow, but despite travelling in the same group as the boisterous celeb wives and girlfriends she had an inner peace that told me she wasn't famous. Did I know her? And why was she looking at me? It was almost getting uncomfortable when a commuter behind her bumped her forward, and the connection we had was broken. Despite her managing a small smile, which I'm nearly sure I reciprocated, she became lost in the bustling crowd, leaving me with a strange feeling that I might have met her before.

Hyped up from the drama at the gate, the passengers were collectively in party mood as the air crew tried without much success to settle them quietly into their seats. The women were whooping and texting, and the men giving congratulatory high fives to one another as if they'd just scored a winning goal – and then scored one of the pneumatically enhanced blonde babes right after.

Even though I felt a bit odd, almost stalker-like, looking for the beautiful Indian woman I had seen earlier, she was nowhere to be found. So I collapsed into my aisle seat, excited that I was finally on my way home to see my daughter. It had only been two nights, but I missed her so much. She had looked so cute asleep in her cot when I had left her that I had had to resist the urge to nibble at her soft chubby little legs that stuck out the side of her blanket. Being a single mum, I felt a great weight of responsibility on me to provide for and nurture her, and because she was a two-year-old with Down's Syndrome, albeit in a mild form, I couldn't afford to take my role as sole parent lightly.

My thoughts became lighter, and I got the giggles as I stuffed my boarding card into my handbag. My seat was 34B, which was depressingly also my bra-size. I had always wanted to be larger, but even though I had previously been offered a freebie boob job through *YES!*, the magazine I worked for, I had declined their kind offer with a definite NO! Sure, big boobs would balance out my naturally big bottom, but I was too squeamish for elective surgery. One of my best friends, Lisa, had had enough artificial enhancements for the pair of us, so any curiosity I might have had about cosmetic surgery had been satisfied by her misadventures in the bizarre and impractical. Whether it be G-spot enlargements or a buttock lift, Lisa had sampled it all, and she had even recently taken to injecting herself with Botox.

'I get it in the post now,' was one of her most recent revelations. 'How fab is that?' I questioned whether it was entirely safe to be injecting herself with nerve toxin, but she claimed her actions were totally sane. 'Fifteen years, sweetie. That's how long I've been a Botox junkie. So I've learnt a few tricks along the way. And anyway, I only use it on my feet and under my arms. I rarely do my face myself. And it's cheaper. This is my way of saving Daddy money during the recession. DIY, baby. I've felt an enormous sense of empowerment since I've taken it up.'

Unable to argue my way out of any situation with 'Princess' Lisa, I just had to be gracious about the fact that she was born with money and I was not. I secretly consoled myself that I was blessed with a somewhat prettier face, not that I would ever say so, and I figured that, to balance things out, Lisa had been given plenty of Daddy's boom-time builder money to correct whatever she wasn't happy with.

An hour into the flight and I was lost in *Sex and the City* heaven, laughing out loud at the classic episode which sees the girls at a tantric sex class. Munching my way through large packets of Maltesers and Jelly Tots, I was distracted from my creature comforts by angry screams coming from the front of the plane. As I pulled out my earplugs and peered down the aisle I could see our old friends Tanya and Issey rowing again. And, just as before, they weren't holding back on the insults. Although I was finding it hard to understand their accents from a distance, I did hear Issey hiss at Tanya, 'And Jordan thinks you're a slapper, too.'

Although I had occasionally done celebrity interviews and been branded a celeb reporter during my freelance days, I told myself I had no interest in getting involved in the saga. I was now a feature writer, and that's how I liked it, away from drama and storms in DD cups. But the hack in me couldn't help but be curious. And of course, my PR friend was also keen to get an eagle-eyed view of the WAGs at war. 'Je-sus Christ, this is unbelievable,' she squealed. 'Where's a feckin' video camera when you need it?'

'I've got a camera,' I said, thinking out loud.

'Well, then, take the bloody thing out and start filming. This could be your big break! The *News of the World* would pay a fecking fortune for this scrap. What are you waiting for?'

It went against the grain. I hated the idea of shopping these women, even though I knew they were acting like trailer trash and would possibly love the press attention that would follow. But I wasn't sure if I was brave enough or reckless enough to go through with it. I remembered the hurt I had felt after being exposed in the Irish papers a few years previously for kissing a very married man in public. He had been a well-known Irish publisher, and our clinch had been caught at a press launch on CCTV and leaked to the press. Those images had devastated his marriage and lost me my job, home and family for an extended period of time. Could I expose these women to the same thing? My PR friend soon snapped me out of my anxious thoughts. 'Don't start to feel bad.' She nudged me as she spoke, sensing my reservations. 'Quick, quick, you're missing it. They're beside the toilet, look over there.' Although panic had started to build up inside me, so had adrenaline, and before I knew it I had grabbed my camera out of my bag and bounced to my feet. 'Listen, a toilet punch-up never stopped Cheryl Cole making it big. If anything, it helped single her out from the Girls Aloud crowd. Now get up there and seize your moment.' By this stage, my PR friend looked like she'd just been plugged into the mains. Her eyes were bulging in their sockets, her teeth were grinding, and her hair looked almost to be standing on end. 'It's like we've just been dropped on the set of *Footballers' Wives*,' she squealed. 'I can't believe this shit actually happens. It's unreal!'

I moved out of my seat and crept steadily up the aisle, zooming in on the fighting women like a paparazzo hiding in the bushes. Just as at the airport, the cabin had now erupted into cheers and laughter, and it was a struggle to push past the voyeurs. Abandoning my manners and, all things considered, my common decency, too, as I captured these women letting themselves and their country down, I edged closer to the eye of the storm, careful to keep my head low and not make eye-contact or disturb them. I was like a tigress stalking my prey. They were no longer people with feelings or families to get upset, all I could see was a paycheck. Maybe five figures? If I was lucky, it might even be six. Just as I got close enough to have both women clearly visible in the shot, several air hostesses descended on the feuding pair, and, as they stretched in to break up the fight, an extremely angry Tanya lashed out, pushing one of the hostesses to the wall and smacking her fully across the face. Everyone gasped in horror.

'Get off me, you stupid bitch,' cried Tanya as she dealt the damaging blow. 'You people never learn!' As if the situation wasn't bad enough, a male passenger stepped in to rescue the distressed air hostess and he, too, got a slap from Tanya. 'You bastard!' she cried, almost demented with anger. 'Take your hands off me. It's me you should be protecting. She's scum, I tell you. Scum!'

By now Issey had been wrestled back away from the scene and brought to the front of the plane. Tanya was manhandled to the floor, the male passenger shouting, 'This is a citizen's arrest,' as he pulled her hands behind her back. My hands were shaking and it was taking a great effort to keep my camera steady. I just couldn't believe what I had captured. But I wasn't the only one shaken by the brawl. The plane had fallen silent, apart from the abuse and complaints from Tanya, pinned to the floor. As if gripped by the horror of a car crash, no one could speak, yet no one could look away. This hadn't been a glamorous girlie squabble. This was hardcore stuff.

I was just about to stop filming when I caught Tanya's eye. 'What the fuck are you looking at? Get that camera off me. I'm gonna smash you and that stupid thing.' Terrified of what I had just done, I immediately backed away and scurried to my seat, crashing into people as I went. Was I mad? Did I have a death wish, picking a fight with a wealthy footballer's wife?

As soon as I was seated my PR friend pounced. 'Did you get it? Did you get her slapping the head off the guy?' For a moment I couldn't breathe. I felt I was having a panic attack. My whole body began to shake, and the walls and ceiling of the plane seemed to press in on me. 'Let me see,' she demanded. 'Remember that's gold in your hands. Be careful not to delete it. And don't forget the little people when you've made your fortune.'

'Can I just have a minute please?' I pleaded.

She ignored me. 'Give it me here. My friend Sheila will spit when she hears that I was in the thick of it. This truly is the best gossip ever.'

After handing over the evidence I continued to sink into my hard, uncomfortable airline seat, my mind racing with crazy thoughts and my breathing becoming increasingly more erratic. I had done a horrible thing by recording that girl's behaviour. Clearly she must have been in a dark place emotionally. Wasn't everyone allowed a meltdown at some point?

'I can see the headline now.' My PR friend chuckled, her face stuck in my camera. '"Wags Gone Wild." Yes, congratulations, Ms Valentine, you've just put food on your table for the next six months. Nice feeling, eh?'

The lump that had formed in my throat meant I couldn't answer. Could I really flog this footage? Could I?

2

'OK, I'm just going to put you on hold. Ben will speak to you in three minutes, after the commercial break.'

I was sitting on my suitcase, which was still in the hall, with one hand clutching my house phone, the other covering my face. One of my best pals, Parker, stood beside me for support. It was 7.05 a.m. and I was moments away from speaking on *GMTV*, Britain's top-rating national breakfast TV programme. It had been organized by media mogul Cassis Ripley, and I felt like I was having an out-of-body-experience. It was the first of many interviews lined up for that day, and I wasn't sure how I would cope with the pressure.

'Are you still there, Eva?' asked a voice at the other end of the line. 'Hello, Eva?'

'Yes, sorry, I'm here. I'm ready – are you ready?'

'One minute to air, stay on the line, please.'

After the white-knuckle flight with the WAGs, I had used my between-flight time at Heathrow yesterday and immediately rung Parker – who worked in the film business and had plenty of contacts in the luvvie world of meeja. It took less than thirty minutes for Parker to haggle out a

£27,500 deal with Ripley, and by that time a courier had been sent to collect the SD card out of my camera, and in return the biker had handed me an envelope with legal forms that I was apparently meant to read through, sign and fax back before 10.30 p.m.

'OK, speaking on the line from Ireland we have journalist Eva Valentine, who witnessed this brawl between Tanya Cruze and Issey Blaze – good morning, Eva.' I tried to respond, but terror had made me mute. 'Hello, do we have Eva on the line? Good morning?' With one eye firmly on the TV in the living room, Parker realized I wasn't answering my call and kicked me with his size 11 Prada loafer to get me to talk.

'Yes, eh, g-g-g-good morning,' I stuttered. 'This is Eva.'

'Thank you for taking our call, Eva. Now, I understand this is your footage, which was taken on-board the Ryanair flight from Baden-Baden Airport to Heathrow, which we are about to show for the first time.'

'Eh, yes. Yes it is.'

'OK, then. Now if you could just fill us in on a few more details of what exactly happened. From what the papers are saying today, the fight originally broke out in the airport, and then continued again once airborne. Is that correct?'

Even though I tried to elaborate on my answer, all I could do was reply, 'That is correct.'

Parker gave me another kick. I looked up, and he almost growled at me. 'Speak, woman,' he whispered with a snarl while rustling his fingers as a sign of money. 'Make a bloody impression. Just do it.'

'Emm, sorry, Ben.' I picked up confidence for fear of losing one of my cheekbones at the end of Parker's shoe. 'Actually, yes, I was there when the girls first started arguing, but they weren't the only ones rowing. From what I could see, a gang of about six, um, footballers' wives and girlfriends were screaming at one another in the airport at Baden-Baden, but it was Tanya and Issey that eventually let it get physical.'

'Really, Eva? That must have been scary for you to watch?'

'Actually it was intimidating for all of the passengers present. The language that the girls were using was extremely vulgar, and then when the fight itself broke out, I could see many of the older passengers looking terrified. I'm just surprised they were let on the flight at all, to be honest, Ben. But then I suppose many of the young, famous and rich feel they are a law unto themselves most of the time.'

Parker, delighted, punched the air with his fist and gave me the thumbs up, which boosted my morale.

'And what were the two reality stars fighting about, Eva?'

'Boobs.'

'Excuse me, did you say boobs?'

'Yes, it seems laughable really, Ben, but Tanya told Issey that her boob job was so bad that it looked like she was smuggling a bag of cats down her top.' I wasn't sure, but I thought I heard sniggering down the line, so I thought it best to continue making light of the situation. 'Yes, it wasn't what you'd call a highbrow debate, Ben. One minute Tanya was bragging that she had the same rhinoplasty as Angelina Jolie – wasn't that a stretch? And before I knew it Issey pulled a Catherine Tate and screamed, "How very dare you," and started ripping out Tanya's hair extensions.'

'I presume the situation was calmed down by security,

but tell me, Eva, how did the altercation on the plane come about?'

'Well, Ben, it was a classic storm in a double-D cup. It appeared to me to be nothing more than a jealous squabble between two girls who didn't like each other.'

'OK, Eva, stay on the line. We're just going to show our viewers at home the extent of the drama on board yesterday.'

Peering around the corner to see the TV, both Parker and I stared at the screen like two of the three wise monkeys – Parker covering his mouth with one of his hands, and me pathetically covering my ears. The section they played was only seconds long, but showed the most shocking scenes: from when Tanya lashed out at the air hostess, to where she was pushed to the floor herself by the male passenger. Although most of the sound through the telephone was quite muffled, I could clearly work out the end piece of Tanya screaming, 'What the *beep* are you looking at? Get that camera off me. I'm gonna smash you and that stupid thing.' It sent a shiver down my spine.

The presenter quickly picked up the conversation again. 'It's Ben here, Eva. That's pretty scary footage. Were you worried for your safety?'

'Emm, yeah, and just listening to it back there again, well, yeah, I was scared, and probably I still am. But you know, I'm glad I've made this video public.'

'Why is that, Eva? Do you not feel you're invading people's privacy?'

Gathering my confidence, I took a deep breath before unleashing the pent-up anger that I didn't even realize I had. 'Well, firstly I'm a journalist, and it's my job to report.

Secondly, I feel duty bound to expose such scandalous behaviour. How dare those girls subject other people to their violence? It was frightening to watch. I just feel they really let themselves and their footballing husbands and boyfriends down.' I quickly glanced at Parker, and saw he was now holding his chest in the dramatic fashion that only he could carry off. I knew I had to continue. 'But also, we live in a celebrity culture that allows young women like Tanya to act in such a low-grade manner. I don't think that's right. I feel very strongly that this kind of behaviour is shameful. And I believe there should be consequences.'

Interrupting my train of thought, Ben asked, 'What do you think should happen to Tanya?'

'Emm, I'm not sure, really, but I think she should pay some penalty, otherwise it'll just encourage this sort of behaviour. It's not healthy that today's kids want to be footballers' wives or reality TV stars instead of doctors or teachers. Glamorizing unruly behaviour is wrong. And that's why I made this public.' Out of breath, I listened to the presenter wrap up the item and thank me for taking the call. Before I knew what was happening he had cut me off. I didn't get a chance to say goodbye, but I wouldn't really have had the energy to do so anyway.

Feverishly darting his gaze from the TV to me, Parker asked, 'Well?'

Unsure how I felt, I sighed. 'I've done it now.'

'Oh yes, you have, girlie,' screeched Parker excitedly as he fell to his knees to join me. 'You're a proper heartless tabloid hack now. You'll be selling your granny next. Oh-my-God! I better watch my back. You'll be selling stories about me.'

'Shut up!' I moaned, uncomfortable with the idea that I

was now a bona fide guerilla journalist. But Parker had only started his teasing.

'So what's your next crusade, Ms Valentine, now that you've exposed the Brits as fame-hungry junkies? Gonna expose their royals for the Diana murder conspiracy? Or maybe pick a fight with Simon Cowell? Because, let's be honest, the British people love being slagged off by the Irish, don't they?'

Knocked off my moral high ground, I released some stress from my shoulders and fell into Parker's chest looking for a hug. Putting on a pretend-Quasimodo voice, I snuggled my face up under his, pulled my best girlie smile and growled, 'Am I a monster?'

Unable to take me seriously, Parker pushed me aside with a wave of his hand, doing his own little impression of a diva WAG. 'I can't be around you.' He smirked, trying to keep a straight face. 'Now that you've gone to the dark side, I'm not sure I can trust you.'

Continuing my monster voice, I laughed. 'It's true. I'm not sure I can trust myself any more . . . maw . . . maw . . . maw . . . maw!'

Twelve hours later, I had just finished my final interview with a Liverpudlian radio station when my phone started to ring again, flashing up another UK phone number. Tempted to let it ring out, since I had completed all the requirements of the deal that day, a pang of guilt hit me and I felt obliged to answer. 'Hello?' I croaked, my voice worn out from all the interviews.

'Hello, is that Eva Valentine?' It was a male voice at the other end. 'I'm looking for Eva, please, if she's about.'

Weary after my long day telling the same story over and

over again, I let out a mini-diva moan. 'Yep, this is she. Whaddya wanna know?'

'Oh, right,' came the reply, sounding a little taken aback. 'Well, it's not something I can go into in too much detail on the phone, really, but I just wanted to touch base with you over a little idea I had.'

'Would this request be of a personal or professional nature?' Slightly stroppy with the hunger, I walked into my kitchen and started making myself a sandwich.

'Oh, I'm sorry, I haven't even introduced myself properly, I'm such a plonker. My name is Bradley Brady, and I'm a producer for a film and documentary company called Brady Reel Time Films.'

Stuffing a biscuit into my mouth as I buttered some bread, I managed an 'Umhum' to let him know I was still listening.

'I'm working on a little project at the moment, which I unfortunately can't say too much about, but after listening to several of your interviews today, I really feel that you have the right personality to come on board with us. Have I lost you yet?'

'Ehhh.' I swallowed to clear my throat. 'No, I'm still here, but with all due respect, Mr Bradley . . .'

'It's just Bradley, though you can call me Mr Brady.' He laughed. 'It makes me feel very important sometimes.' He continued to giggle at his weak joke, and I did something I never do, and hung up the phone. The phone rang a further three times, but I managed to ignore it and went to join Daisy and an extremely drained Parker, who had spent most of the day taking care of her.

Devoid of the power of speech, I spent the rest of the evening in relative silence, just snuggling with Daisy until it was time for both of us to go to bed. As always Parker had been my rock throughout the day. Although he'd said he'd had work commitments, he'd done his best to divert any guilt I might have had over his babysitting service with a casual, 'Listen, it was only a lunch thing. George Clooney can wait!'

The next morning I arrived into the office at *YES!* and was pounced upon by everyone – even the MD of the magazine, Nigella Hartigan, who never showed her face around the office unless there was an audit or a big advertiser needing a guided tour. Today I was treated to a gruff bear hug that almost left me speechless. 'I've always liked you, Eva,' Hartigan grinned. 'This is your time. Continue to search your potential.'

The rest of the staff prodded me for details and gushed, 'Oh-my-God! You're famous. We're not worthy!'

After an overly excited morning meeting I was finally able to escape to the local Hughes & Hughes to get myself the papers and to Starbucks for a decent coffee – skinny latte, hazelnut splash – and have a moment's peace. The office only had a small staff of about five people, but I was exhausted from the constant attention and, feeling like I had jet-lag, I sat on the stone wall of a nearby bank, switched my mobile to silent and watched the world go by. It was only after my bum had started to go a bit numb from the cold cement beneath me and I'd dribbled the last drop of latte out of my paper cup that I had built up the energy to open the bundle of newspapers I had bought.

Despite seeing her photograph on the front page of the *Sun* back in the newsagent, I had ignored the headline 'Issey Loses Her Knickers', a story explaining how she'd lost some lucrative lingerie contract after being exposed as a brawler. The *Mirror* was running a story on Tanya and how she had gone into hiding yet was suspected of checking into rehab, while the *Mail* and the *Star* claimed that both Tanya and Issey were fighting over John Mayer after an insider claimed that they had both separately been spotted in London nightclubs hanging off him. I tried to enjoy a daydream inspired by John where he described *me* as his 'sexual napalm', and thought about how I wouldn't mind getting up close and personal with him myself – but my bum had reached its limit of numbness.

The rest of the day I struggled to write up my German holiday weekend feature while trying to resist the urge to punctuate it with silly references such as, 'Great for sight-seeing, but try Baden-Baden for WAG violence.'

By 5.29 p.m. I was home at my none-too-salubrious Park Avenue flat, just in time to relieve my amazing new child-minder, Alice. She had only been with us since the end of November and had been recommended to me by Down's Syndrome Ireland, but even though it hadn't yet been a full two months I could already see a huge improvement in Daisy's alertness and development. Lumping Daisy on my hip and showering her with kisses as I headed for the kitch-en to grab myself some food, I hit the flashing voicemail button on the landline and busied myself with dinner.

'You have six new messages,' sounded my automated American female friend. Off the top of my head I couldn't think of six people I knew with my home number, but I was hungry, and nothing made sense to me when I was without food in my belly.

'*Beep* . . . It's Parker. Clooney wants to know if you could set up a date for him with the WAGs as he's not getting any publicity for his new movie, and they're hogging all the column inches. Oh, and he says if you ever cancel one of my lunches with him again he'll hunt you down and talk politics at you all evening. OK, call me.'

'Beep . . . It's your mum here.' Her voice sounded despairing as she let out a long sigh. 'Well, Eva, another scandal for the neighbours to talk about. I'm not happy. I don't know when your father will be able to mow the front garden again. It'll be weeks before this dies down and we can leave the house. You can't ignore me for ever. I'll be expecting your call.'

'Beep . . . Hi, it's Lisa. I fucking love it. Rehab, love trysts, sounds like my kinda weekend. Call me, I want ALL the gories.'

'Beep . . . Eva, it's Bradley Brady here. I'm not sure what happened last night, but I'd like to talk with you about a really exciting opportunity I have and, well, I'm not very good talking into these things, can you call me? My number should have registered on your phone. Emm, please call me when you get a chance.'

'Beep . . . OK, it's Bradley Brady here again.' This time his voice had a more urgent tone. 'I'm not a stalker, but I need you to ring me. I've got a job offer for you. I'm going out on a limb here because I reckon you think I'm mad. But I want to offer you a job as an undercover reporter. I think you're made for it. It's highly secretive, so I need you to keep this tight, but it's a genuine offer, and you'd be handsomely paid. Emm, OK, so call me, if we can get you on board, we'd need you in London by the end of next week to get things started. Thanks, talk soon.'

Gobsmacked, I just stood in the kitchen staring at the microwave as Daisy tugged at my blouse and slobbered all over my shoulder. Undercover reporter, was he mental? London? Not in a million years could I consider it.

'*Beep* . . .' Not wanting to hear another message, I was just about to switch on the microwave – which contained a depressed-looking low-fat quiche – when I heard Bradley's voice again. 'Hi, Eva, I know my last couple of messages might have sounded a little nutty, but it's all above board. I'd been pulling my hair out trying to find the right guy to do this project, and then I heard you on the radio yesterday and it just clicked. We need a woman's touch. Call me and let's make this happen. Bye for now.'

Doing my best to stay calm, I went through my routine of eating, playing with Daisy, bathing her, and singing her favourite bedtime song several times over until she dozed off to sleep with her bottle tucked up under her arm. I had become slightly calmer since becoming a mother. Being flighty had previously been the norm for me, but when Daisy came into my life I had learned to control my emotions and show restraint. Well, *some* restraint – the second she had drifted off into the land of soft pink bunnies I was generally straight on the phone to Parker with a glass of Pinot Grigio in hand.

Forty minutes and two large glasses of vino later and Parker had worked out my interview wardrobe, which he decided must be all-black Prada like his, only with a feline touch and a cape something similar to Halle Berry's in *Catwoman*. And that I would need to adopt a Russian accent and say things like 'KGB' at random moments to give me a sexy undercover-agent edge.

I was just in the middle of practising, 'My name is Valentine . . . Eva Valentine,' when Bradley Brady's number flashed through on my phone. 'It's him, I'm gonna take it,' I said, hanging up before Parker had a chance to stop me. Putting on my best sober voice, I answered in what I thought would be a calm yet sultry tone. 'Helloooo, Bradley,' I gushed, no doubt sounding exactly what I was – piddly drunk. 'How are you this evening?'

'Not as good as you, I gather,' he chuckled.

I thought about continuing my smooth telephone voice, and then decided to hell with it. 'OK, Bradley.' I sat up on the couch to compose myself and placed my empty glass on the coffee table. 'Let me put all my cards on the table, so as not to waste anyone's time.'

I could hear him take a deep intake of breath before he spoke. 'OK.'

'All right then, Bradley, I'm a single mother, what do you think of that?'

'That's not an issue, Eva,' he answered back smartly. 'The job will mainly require you to work within office hours, with an occasional few hours in the evening.'

'And what sort of contract are you offering me?'

'Six months, possibly only five, but the fee is a hundred thousand pounds.'

'Fuck off!' I blurted it out without thinking.

'No, straight up, that's the fee.'

'What do I have to do for that money, kill someone?'

I could hear him chuckle at the other end. The frantic tone in his voice had faded away. 'Not this gig, Eva. Maybe in future projects. But what we need from you are eyes and ears, Eva. Someone on the ground who can blend into the crowd and deliver concise video reports about what they see.'

Almost too nervous to hear the answer I asked, 'And what will I be seeing, exactly?'

'Dodgy dealings. Sex. Rock 'n' roll.' He paused to get my reaction, but I needed to hear more. 'You'll be working in a restaurant, Eva. We'll get you a job as a hostess or waitress or something, and you will report back what you see.'

'Are you mad? Do you want me to expose the mafia or something?'

'No, not quite, but it's a corrupt business that needs to be exposed and shut down. This is a documentary for TV4. We have most of the evidence already in place, we just need to put the final nail in the coffin – and that's you.'

'But you haven't even seen me, how do you know I'm not some hound that has bad waitressing skills?'

'Well, are you a hound? And do you have bad waitressing skills?'

'Eh, no, I'm top class on both, actually.'

'Well, then,' declared Bradley, 'I take it you're in.'

'Hang on, hang on.' I started to get flustered. 'There's no way I'm doing it for a hundred thousand.'

Unfazed he asked, 'Well, how much then?'

Getting carried away with myself I barked, 'Two hundred thousand.'

'No chance,' came the reply. 'I can push to a hundred and fifty K all in, no expenses. When can you fly over to London to meet with me?'

'Eh . . . Saturday?'

'OK, Eva Valentine, I'll be back in touch with details for your flight later in the week. Don't let me down. I have faith in you. Make sure you have it in yourself.'

The following few days in work dragged. I couldn't concentrate on writing, and everything annoyed me – from the time it took my computer to switch on to the dodgy M button on my keyboard that had been threatening to give up the ghost for over six months now. Every time I hit the M it would wobble. It was weak and flaky, just like my husband Michael had been, and it was a constant reminder of the M tattoo on my ankle that I had picked up on our honeymoon and still hadn't gotten round to getting lasered off.

I hated Michael, but hated myself just as much for getting hitched to a man I barely knew enough to trust. For legal reasons we had to be separated for two years before we could get divorced. I would have to remain married to the cheater for a while to come; that sort of foolishness would never happen again. Yes, I wanted to find true love. And there were plenty of nights when I would cry with the loneliness, but friends were for ever, and if I desired male attention, well, non-committal one-night stands always served a purpose.

By Friday evening my nerves about my upcoming interview had sent me over the edge, and crabby didn't come close to describing my mood. So when I dropped Daisy off at my parents' house, pretending I was heading to a wedding in Kilkenny early the next morning, I didn't hang around for friendly chit-chat. It was now standard practice that my mother showed more interest in my daughter than me, and today it suited me down to the ground. I always felt she was scrutinizing Daisy for signs of neglect so she could criticize me afterwards, and I wasn't in the mood to cope. A quick, 'Thanks, Mum, here's her bag, talk to you Sunday,' a kiss and a hug for Daisy, and I was back out the door, no questions asked.

Once in the car, I cranked up the music, rotated my head a few times and released some stress from my shoulders. With Daisy in safe hands I instantly felt a weight of pressure lift, so I pulled off down the road, warming myself up on a cold January evening by singing along to U2's 'Get On Your Boots'. I had just walked back in the door of the flat when a text beeped through from Lisa. 'Hey, babe, I'm bored, can U get babysitter?'

Although I had planned my night-before-the-interview evening in detail while sitting in the heavy Friday-evening traffic home – soaking in the bath, ironing my clothes while watching *The Late Late Show*, and early to bed – all this was immediately dismissed. I texted back right away. 'Sorted. Any ideas?' And I made a shallow Cinderella promise to myself to be back in bed by midnight at the latest.

By 1.30 a.m. I was sitting in the back of a people carrier swigging from the neck of a bottle of champagne, en route to a private party in the Haven Hotel, and trying in vain not to spill alcohol everywhere. All my best intentions had gone out the window after Parker had joined me and Lisa in Krystle nightclub with a couple of young Aussie actors, Blake and Blair, who were in town on a recce for a surf movie. After spending a couple of days riding the waves of Bundoran and Long Strand the guys were crudely keen to 'get a gutful of piss and hook up with some hotties', according to Parker.

Despite the fact that Lisa and myself were probably the wrong side of twenty-five, not to mention thirty, for their preference, it was clear that aside from their crassness they were well-brought-up young men. They remembered their manners by not being ageist, and by getting their tongues stuck down both Lisa's throat and mine. By the time we got back to their hotel suite I had begun to repeat the catch-phrase, 'Respect your elders,' which, for some crazy reason, I found hilarious.

My young friend Blair somehow also found it funny, and kept falling to his knees in spectacular fashion while flailing his well-toned arms in the air and begging, 'Please can I disrespect you tonight? I promise to respect you in the morning!' Looking down at this handsome, fit young man begging me for sex, I couldn't help but give in to temptation. It wasn't an everyday occurrence any more, and he was making me feel so desirable and sexy.

'I first need to judge your champagne kisses before I sleep with you . . .' I pronounced matter-of-factly, as I swung my companion bottle of Moët teasingly in his direction.

'Here she goes again,' chimed Parker and Lisa together.

'Beg yours?' asked Blair with a puzzled face.

'It's her party trick.' Lisa giggled, before planting another slobbery kiss on Blake's open mouth and whispering, 'And this is what is called the Princess kiss.'

Bemused, Blair continued to look at Parker for advice, obviously in case he thought it involved a risky practice. He might have been a dude, but, thinking about it, I realized he couldn't have been older than twenty-two.

Parker, of course, was on hand to reassure his pet project. 'Don't worry yourself. It involves nothing illegal. She just wants you to knock back some champagne and then transfer it into her mouth by kissing her.'

'But you've gotta do it well.' I took Blair's face in my spare hand and shook it around as I spoke. 'You don't pass the champagne kisses test, then you don't get any more Eva lovin'.'

Back in his comfort zone, Blair took my hand in his and kissed it quickly several times. 'I'm good with making a splash. That's what I do.' And he wasn't lying either.

Not wanting to waste time, he pulled me and my bottle of champagne into the bathroom and began to strip me of my clothes. 'I'm gonna turn you into a Blair witch and make you scream with pleasure!' purred my bleached-blond plaything as he pulled down the zips of my black, knee-length fuck-me boots.

With a little wriggling and giggling the two of us soon ended up in the shower with soothing warm water streaming down over our skin. Although my body wasn't in the most amazing shape, I somehow felt empowered because I was older than him, and took confidence in pretending to be a worldly-wise woman. Of course, he was totally ripped. His abs looked like they'd been carved by some master sculptor, and he even had that sexy defined muscle just above his crotch that you only see in extra-buff men. I wasn't sure what it was called, but even below the tan-line of his shorts, his skin was sallow and smooth and, to my surprise, completely hairless!

Although it seemed like for ever since I had been in a serious relationship, shaving there was something I did like to ask a man to do. A hairless man was so much more fun to play with, without the worry of stray curls catching in the back of your throat. I wasn't sure if Blair had done it to make his penis look bigger, but it looked pretty damn good to me. So, trying to regain some control, I pushed him back from kissing my nipples and posed the question, 'Whatever happened to my champagne kiss?'

As the tip of my nipple fell out of his mouth with a pop, he stood back against the wall of the shower, and declared, 'I'm a champagne virgin. Will you go easy on me?' He flashed his pearly whites in a cheeky grin.

Taking direction, he grabbed the bottle from outside the shower and quickly swung back, pushing me firmly up against the shower wall to steady me. Holding my face softly but securely with his left hand, he began to pour the champagne over my chest with his right hand. Then, keeping his mouth at my belly button, he drank up the bubbles after they had filtered down over my breasts. As his alcohol-drenched tongue crashed against mine, I felt a wave of pleasure ripple through my body, my imperfect, cellulite-covered physique. But did I care? Heck no, I was about to have unconventional sex with a boy who looked like a catwalk model. So what if he shuddered with the fear the following morning as he recalled my childbearing, age-ravaged mass? I wasn't planning on hanging around to witness his meltdown.

All I required was validation. A quick fix of lovin' that would satisfy my womanly urges. Tomorrow's reality could wait. I just wanted him to boomerang his tongue around my erogenous zones and . . . 'Oh-my-God . . . that is so fucking good.' His tongue had moved to my neck. It was always one of my weak spots. 'Oh yes, thank you. Thank youuuu.' Before I knew what I was saying, I had somehow begun to praise him like he was a child. 'That's it . . . right there . . . ohhh, stay there.' Or, worse still, maybe like a pet.

He wasn't fazed. If anything, he was inspired to concentrate his efforts on further arousing me with his tongue-teasing while also busying himself on stimulating my clitoris with the firm tips of his wet fingers.

Things were moving at dizzying speed and the alcohol in my system was now fully working its magic. This was just the kind of passion and illicit excitement that I had missed.

Blair chuckled with delight as my body started to contort with the pleasure, then announced, 'Prepare for entry, I'm comin' in . . .' One of my last memories was the feeling of his rock-hard dick pressed against my leg as he released a mouthful of champagne into my mouth. What rude and lewd acts happened next was anyone's guess.

The next thing I knew, there was a mobile phone ringing. It was mine calling me from across the room . . . What the fuck? I rubbed at my eyes to open them and tilted my head up slightly from where I lay. At first I couldn't make out my bearings, but after a few seconds I started to focus. The first person I saw was Parker, looking like roadkill splattered across a white couch, all lanky legs and lifeless long arms. Amid a pile of jackets and coats I could make out two handbags. One was mine and the other was . . . Lisa's. OK, it was all starting to come back to me. But there was no sign of Lisa. Looking down my body, I could see that I had my clothes on, but something didn't feel right. My hair was damp. Oh-my-God! Flashbacks of my shower antics raced through my head. But where was my Aussie? Dropping my head back on the bed with pain I noticed the digital clock on the locker beside me. Through the black-and-white spots that danced in front of my eyes I read: 8.08 a.m. I didn't even know what day it was yet. OK, I really needed my brain to start working. I wasn't with Daisy, so it had to be . . . Saturday. Fuck, it was Saturday. My brain kick-started with panic. My meeting was in London today. What time was my flight?

Fuck.

Fuck.

Fuck.

Jumping out of the bed, I struggled for several minutes as I gathered my belongings and stuck my feet back into my FMBs, thinking that they really had done their job. I was hitting Parker to wake him up when it hit me: 10.40 a.m. That was when my flight left. Time was running out. Tripping over a misplaced jacket, I ended up on the floor and caught my reflection in a glass side-table as I climbed back into an upright position. I looked a wreck. My previously well-blow-dried bob was matted and wavy, like I'd taken to the sea with my surfer dude instead of the shower.

Although I wasn't sure I wanted this job across the water, there was something in me that also didn't want to miss the appointment under any circumstances. 'Parker, wake up,' I yelled, needing some guidance. 'Help me! I'm gonna miss my flight. Wake up and say something!'

'Ms Cou-gar . . . Valentine,' mumbled Parker, barely moving a muscle and looking scarily like a victim at a *CSI* crime scene.

As an opener it stopped me in my tracks. Mortified at what I could and couldn't remember I covered my face with my hands and began to laugh. He was right. I had been a cradle-snatcher the night before. Not having the stomach to look into the adjoining suite and see what state of undress Lisa was in, I signed a short note to my vanished surfer, saying, 'Thank you for a fun night, I hope you enjoyed popping your cherry! Eva xx.' Then I ran off to the lift, chuckling at what a slapper I was. I might have been a cougar the previous night, but I still wasn't sure if I had the makings of a hard-nosed undercover journalist who could hunt out a good story.

As the lights on the walls of the padded lift circled, I decided that all I needed to concentrate on was stalking down a taxi that could get me home to pick up my passport and deliver me to the airport on time. If I could manage that, well, anything was possible.

3

'Well, good afternoon, Eva, come in and sit down – hell, you look like you need to . . .'

As first impressions went, it was clear I wasn't making a good one. It was 2 p.m., I had just stepped into the conference room of Brady Reel Time Films in London, and my plans to wow the producers were not going well. Although I had been waiting for the true hangover to kick in all morning, it had held off until I arrived at the company offices, so just as I began to see a potential new life for myself in the UK, I also started to sense a black cloud hanging over me, rendering me weak and lacking in charisma. Feeling like one of the feebler contestants on *The Apprentice*, I had looked around the smart penthouse office space as I had waited in reception and had seen good-looking staff. I hadn't been sure if I would fit in, but I'd known that, despite myself, I was definitely excited at the prospect.

My telephone buddy Bradley might have wooed me single-handedly as far as London, but he was joined today by a stern-looking woman who introduced herself as Billie. While she was hard from the tip of her nose to the straight cut of her knee-length black pencil skirt, Bradley was softer in appearance. He was expensively dressed but slightly unkempt – as if lacking in the love of a good woman and her fashion eye. And his hair was a badger grey, and curled a little too much off the back of his neck and around his ears. Also, a large scar across his cheek suggested he was a man with a past. Could it be an old battle wound? Secretly I hoped it was, until my brain snapped back to thinking sensibly and I realized it wouldn't be a good plan to do business with a street-fighting crook.

'Well, Eva,' Billie said hesitantly, 'can you tell us a little bit about yourself?'

'Oh, absolutely. Well, as you know, my name is Eva Valentine, and I'm from Dublin in Ireland.' Billie nodded sarcastically as Bradley just sat back in his chair looking worried. 'And, well, I've been a freelance journalist for as long as I can remember. Mostly writing for magazines – features, reviews, celeb interviews, that sort of thing. And, umm, I'm a single mother to one daughter, Daisy, and, umm, my favourite colour is green!' I pulled a face and let out a nervous laugh, but neither of them seemed too impressed.

'Fond of a drink, Eva?'

Stunned at Billie's question, I could only respond with, 'Excuse me?'

'I said, are you much of a drinker, Eva?' asked Billie again gruffly. 'How many days a week would you partake in a few tasty beverages, exactly? Five days a week? Seven?'

Trying to make another pathetic joke, I mumbled, 'Listen, I know I'm Irish and I've shared a few pints with Colin Farrell, but we're not all dipsos.' But they didn't seem to get the humour.

'Well, Eva, personally speaking, I think you look a mess,

and frankly we're looking for a professional, not some flake who needs a mouthful of vodka to get them out of bed. Do you understand where I'm coming from here? You smell like a brewery. And, well, I'm insulted that you didn't take this meeting more seriously.'

I looked at Bradley hoping he'd save me, but he remained tight-lipped and gave me a disappointed look that meant: she's speaking the truth.

Mortified, I felt my eyes well up with tears. It took me three attempts before I could swallow the lump in my throat and find the composure to talk. 'Bradley, Billie, please let me apologize for my performance today. I'm seriously embarrassed. And I know I look like shit, but this is not the norm.' I paused, waiting for a reply, but they left me hanging. Forced to continue, I morphed into a sniffling idiot pleading for forgiveness. 'Listen, I'm truly sorry, it's just one drink led to another last night, and, well, it's a real novelty that I had an all-night babysitter so . . . well, I just took advantage of the situation. I'm so sorry.'

'Yeah, that's all very well, but this is my pet project, too,' Billie said. 'And just because my friend Bradley here made a half-brained decision to invite some random piss-head over from Dub-a-lin, doesn't mean I have to play along with it.'

Bradley gave Billie a meaningful look, then very calmly turned back to me and said, 'I apologize for my colleague's passion and forthrightness, but I think what Billie is trying to get across here is that she's a little disappointed by your lack of enthusiasm for this meeting. And, well, if I'm honest, I suppose I am, too.'

Desperately trying not to let Billie's harshness upset me, I swallowed my pride and chose to ignore her piss-head comment, while thinking to myself that what she really needed was a good shag – and forged ahead with some more begging. 'I may not have sold myself well so far, but since I have come a long way for this chat today, I must ask you not to make any rash decisions. And since all manners seem to be out the window, and I probably will be shortly after, let me tell you—'

'Please do, Eva,' interrupted Billie in a snide tone.

Feeling like I had nothing else to lose, I blurted out, 'OK, I got laid last night. I'm single. It doesn't happen often. You don't have any rings on your fingers, Billie, so I don't know about your status, but I wasn't prepared to miss out on that . . .'

Both looked a little shell-shocked by my statement, but once again Billie found the words to ask, 'At the expense of missing out on this job?'

Much as I wanted the chance to explain myself properly, I knew that I had no real excuse and that I'd blown the gig. So I decided my best plan of action was just to flee the room. I made a few more pathetic apologies and gathered up my coat and bag. Racing to the door, I thanked both of them, wished them luck in the future and bolted for the lift to transport me out to safety. As the lift rang down through floors 5 to G, the image of the two of them mockingly waving goodbye burned in my mind.

They must have thought I was totally cracked after my mini-confession of sexual frustration. What did I think I could achieve by telling two strangers – possible employers – that I badly needed to get shagged? As I stepped out on to the cold streets of London once more, a wave of self-pity hit me and I gave into my frustrated feelings and cried into my hands until I realized that my mascara clearly wasn't waterproof.

*　　*　　*

I must have walked aimlessly for thirty minutes, trying to find a cab. Eventually I managed to hail one just as a juicy blister erupted on the heel of my left foot. Though my return flight wasn't until 6.30 p.m. I hadn't a clue what to do with myself, so I instructed the taxi-driver to take me straight back to Heathrow and be done with it.

Rooting in my handbag to text Parker my drama, I had just found my phone when it lit up with a familiar-looking UK phone number. Dropping it with the fright, I fumbled to pick it up off the taxi floor when I noticed I'd answered it by mistake. I thought about hanging up, but said a cautious hello instead.

'Hello, Eva,' came the reply. 'It's Bradley here. Are you OK?'

'About as awful as you might expect,' I admitted.

'Yeah, Billie is pretty much a tyrant, I'm afraid. Sorry about that. But we've had a chat about things, and, well . . . we've come to an arrangement that she buggers off and looks after the editing side of the documentary, and I stick to the human resources side of things.'

I tried to work out what he was saying, but none of his words made sense to me.

'What I'm trying to say, Eva, is that I still want you on the gig. I admired your honesty, and it is the weekend after all, so everyone can be forgiven for a few after-work drinks, can't they?'

Rubbing my face and even more mascara on to my hands with frustration, all I could manage was, 'Really?'

'Yeah, please forget that meeting ever happened, will you? Can we start again?'

'Eh, does Billie know that you're speaking to me?'

'Yes, she does.'

'And she's happy for a piss-head like me to be working in the company?'

'Don't mind Billie, she has a few issues with alcohol herself, so you'll learn to ignore her little rants. So, whaddya say, are you on board?'

Totally disorientated, I mumbled some gibberish about not needing the hassle, but Bradley wasn't having any of it.

'Eva, I'm being serious here. I want you to be part of the team. Yes, Billie gave you a hard time, but you stuck it to her. We need someone with your kind of feistiness, and even if you do need a mouthful of vodka to get out of bed in the morning, that's OK as long as you turn up.'

Quickly I barked back, 'I'm not an alcoholic,' which distracted the taxi-man from his erratic driving and made him giggle. Mind you, I was beginning to question the claim myself, as all I now wanted were another few drinks to settle my nerves.

Bradley played pacifist and cooed, 'Hush there, now, where are you? I need to take you for a Bloody Mary to celebrate.'

After several short minutes of browbeating, Bradley convinced me to turn the cab around and meet him at a neutral location otherwise known as the Red Lion. With the intention of being a good sport, I supped on two Marys for the craic, discussed a bit of business – though how much of it made any sense was another matter – and made it for the 6.30 p.m. flight slightly tipsy from the top-up, smiling all the way home.

The following Thursday, Lisa and I headed up to Parker's Docklands apartment, just like old times, to have a cheeky bottle of bubbles. In case I felt the urge to disclose my new job, I had brought my contract with me as proof. Well, I wouldn't believe me if I was them, and it was the only piece of paper with my name on it that wasn't a bill, so naturally I wanted to show it off – to everyone! While neither Lisa nor Parker knew about my decision over the job offer yet, I was a little worried about breaking it to them, in case they thought I was mad. The three of us had shared many a boozy evening at Parker's down through the years, though it still felt a tad empty without the presence of our other old model friend – now foe, husband-stealer Maddie.

Keeping the numbers up on this occasion was Parker's very handsome husband Jeff, who, after six weeks in Dubai, had returned looking mahogany and, in Parker's eyes, 'Extremely straight.' Although they had been married several years, sometimes happily, like most hetero relationships they endured many stormy times, too. And since Jeff was not your stereotypical gay man, and normally preferred to be one of the boys rather than one of the girls, he usually kept himself busy with his building business – which was struggling but still solvent – along with his vast amount of charity work, and left Parker and us to our frivolous girlie chats.

Maddie, on the other hand, had been most definitely one of the girls. She, probably more than anyone, had been my best mate. But unfortunately our common interest in clothes and fun times had spilled over into our love for the same man, and, committing the worst best-friend sin, she'd stolen my husband in a poisoned affair that had so far, amazingly, lasted longer than my marriage.

Maddie had been my world since we had been teenagers,

but even though she had ripped my heart out by breaking up my family and starting her own with Michael – they now had a son together – I still dearly missed her friendship, and every time I called up to Parker's place, where Maddie and I had once squatted rent-free during our poverty phase, I was reminded of what a hole she had left in my life.

Not that I would ever allow her back into my world: I might have loved her, but her ultimate betrayal had robbed me of a future, Daisy of a father and both of us of a home. I'd been disgusted when Michael had finally booted us out on to the street after selling our house for the first stupidly low offer that had been made for it, just so he could afford to buy another new home for *them*. It was bad enough that he had abandoned his daughter emotionally, but I felt it was unforgivable to leave her homeless.

Despite old memories sending a chill down my spine as I stepped into the lift on the ground floor, I was determined to enjoy my evening. So with that in mind I eased my bum on to Parker's stone-coloured suede couch and blanked out all the bad feelings that I harboured. After all, I had a glass of pink champagne in my hands, a tray of pastel-frosted doughnuts that I had picked up at the local Shell garage, and no babysitting duties till ten o'clock. So, like any other single parent, I relished the freedom of a hands-free evening and settled back to enjoy the view and entertainment provided by my childless friends.

Typically the Princess was on great form, though today for a better reason than ever before. As soon as all of us were seated together, she demanded a toast, and said, 'Good news, everyone. I'm in remission. Yes, you heard right, I'm cancer-free. So, I'd like us all to drink to me, please.'

The rest of us immediately put down the glasses we'd

been holding in the air and tackled her to the couch for hugs, with whoops of joy. Just over a year earlier she had been diagnosed with cervical cancer and put on an emergency course of chemotherapy. Thankfully, she had responded well to treatment, and, assisted by some complementary healing by some fella from Wicklow who could talk to horses and had magical hands, she was back to normal relatively quickly. But hearing news of remission was the best thing that any of us could have wished for. Her cancer was never mentioned unless Lisa brought it up, and since she never talked about it, her condition had preyed on our minds.

After a short love-in, she shoved us away, saying, 'I'm sympathy allergic.' She ordered us to bugger off so she could drink her champagne in peace before it got warm, and asked Jeff to grab another bottle she had left chilling in the freezer. Pretending to act normally, Parker and I tucked into our doughnuts, while secretly winking at each other with delight. Embarrassed by the attention, but clearly delighted with herself, too, Lisa fussed with her phone, muttering, 'I told you you'd never get rid of me.' She ignored us for less than two minutes before blurting out, 'Ah, crap. I can't believe I've lost him again.'

Curious, I asked, 'Who?'

'The new guy I'm having sex with. I've lost him.'

Instantly Parker's ears pricked up. 'That's a bit careless, don't you think? And where, pray tell, did you lose him? On a bus, or did that huge man-eating vagina of yours swallow him up whole?'

'Ha! Ha!' Lisa chuckled, trying in vain to keep a straight face. 'Actually I've never even met him—'

'Is he imaginary? Or is it a telepathic thing?' interrupted Parker, over-eager as usual.

'He's a boy I'm having phone sex with. I've lost him a few times now – his number, I mean, if you must know.'

'Oh, I must,' cooed Parker, while rubbing his hands together with glee. 'Tell all, please. I feel like I'm the only one not feeling the love these days. If Captain Sensible pleads a headache one more night, I swear I'll trade him in for a younger model.'

'I heard that,' came a cry from the kitchen.

Clearly dying to tell us, Lisa continued her story while continuing to fiddle with her iPhone. 'Well, what I like about him most is that he has a filthy mind. It's not often I meet someone more sexually corrupted than me, and I have to say I appreciate it.'

Worried for her safety, I put on my mother hat and asked, 'What do you know about him, exactly?'

'That he's a pervert, and when he's not getting me off he plays darts in his free time.' Momentarily glancing up, she smiled the dirtiest smile before quickly returning her attention to her phone with renewed urgency.

'Wow, darts, eh?' Parker sniggered. 'There's a turn on. Could this guy be more exciting? I wonder, does he still live with his mother, too?'

'Eh, no,' answered Lisa, a tad sheepishly. 'He shares with a few lads.'

'In a squat?' heckled Parker.

'Nooo. In the nick.'

In complete synchronicity Parker, myself and even a re-turning Jeff screamed, 'Excuse me?'

'He's currently doing five to ten years for grand theft auto.'

'Ten years is a lot of time for stealing cars. How many did he steal?' As always, Jeff had his eye on the practical.

'I think there's a charge of GBH and some other stuff, too. I'm not one hundred per cent.' Her mood quickly changed from jovial to defensive.

'Delightful.' Parker cheered. 'So, when are you starting the conjugal visits? Eva, you've been looking for an idea for that book of yours. I hope you're taking notes. You won't get a juicer plot-line than this!'

'Steady on,' Lisa grumbled, 'we haven't taken things to that level yet.'

'Ahhh,' hissed Parker sarcastically.

'But it is a kinky idea.'

Although I was trying my best not to be judgemental, I couldn't help but moan, 'Maybe, in your polluted mind.'

But Lisa chose to ignore my sniping. 'No, it's strictly phone sex. He's working up his credits, though, to get time on the house computer. And then we'll step things up a bit and start having Skype sex.'

'Nice.' Jeff smiled before planting a big kiss on Parker's forehead. 'Just don't you be getting any ideas, all right?' Not wanting to distract Lisa, Parker chose not to reply to him, and smiled at Lisa, hoping she'd continue.

'Judge me if you like.' She looked directly at me as she spoke.

I chose to do my usual shaking of the head, which then morphed into a nod, and then back to a shaking, while whispering, 'Nooo . . . yes . . . nooo.'

'Well, I like being a gangster's moll. It's only a phone thing, and these cold dark nights are lonely for a single girl. Ever since I broke up with Francis last year, I've felt incredibly needy. No jokes, thank you very much. I brought the champagne this evening, and I might just leave with it again if this continues.'

Dismissing her idle threats, I asked, 'So how do you get to have phone sex with a criminal? Please tell me you haven't turned into one of those wackos who stalk men in prisons and then end up marrying them.'

'I'll ignore that, thank you very much. I dunno. He texted me by accident, and it just went from there. It's been happening every night now for about nine days. I suppose you could say we're going steady. Are you impressed?'

Jeff's jaw was now hitting the floor with the shock, while Parker and myself did our best to fake some support and gushed, 'Absolutely.' And, 'I reckon it's the real thing.'

'OK, enough about me. You're all annoying me now, so let's talk about you, Eva. I can tell you're hiding something. You've got that funny look you always get when you've got something on your mind. So spit it out. What's new with you?'

'Well, I don't have a character out of *Snatch* to call my lover. But I do have news.' Still recovering from Lisa's disclosure, the group just sat in silence, waiting for the next bombshell. 'OK, well, the thing is I've been offered another job.' Showing their manners, all three congratulated me formally. 'And it's to work on a documentary. For TV.'

Once again, they all showed enthusiasm and stepped up the compliments with mini-statements like, 'Wow. That's really cool.'

But everyone's pleasant chatter soon halted as I revealed, 'But the job is in London – and, well, I leave next week.'

Parker already knew, but Jeff and Lisa sat motionless, as if frozen in time. Swallowing nervously, I tried to get things back on track. 'Congratulations, Eva?' I suggested. 'That's wonderful news. Next week, you say? We must celebrate!'

Jeff looked uncharacteristically confused. 'I don't mean

to rain on your parade, petal, but have you thought this through? Can you really do this? What will you do with Daisy?'

'Daisy is coming with me, and, yes, I can do this.'

'But where are you going to stay?' asked Lisa, all flustered. 'What are we talking here? A month or two?'

'Relax, it's all sorted. More or less. I'm moving in with my auntie and uncle over there.'

'Don't they have kids of their own?' questioned Parker.

'Yes, they do. Three, in fact.'

'Cosy,' added Jeff.

I hadn't thought it through properly, in fact, and I stuttered, 'Well, y–y–y–yes, sort of. But we'll work it out. It's only a temporary thing. Five, six months, tops. I'll probably, I dunno, rent somewhere. Maura and John's is just a place to base myself from to begin with. Anyway, I think it'll be nice to be surrounded by family.'

'Maybe if you were a feral cat or a rabbit!' screeched Jeff dramatically. 'It's not healthy to live in such cramped conditions. This isn't sounding glamorous at all.'

'OK, thank you for your concern. But Daisy and I will have our own room, and I'll have plenty of spare hands to help out with her care. There won't be much room for a shoe and handbag collection, but I'm going to be work-ing as a waitress, anyway, so I'll have a uniform for every day.'

'Did you say waitress?' interrupted Lisa, echoing Jeff's surprise. 'I'm getting confused here. One minute it's a documentary, and the next you're waitressing from your auntie's box room.'

Feeling backed into a corner, I felt obliged to tell them the full story. I was just disappointed that it didn't sound as exciting once it left my mouth. 'OK, I don't want anyone to overreact, but I'm working as an undercover journalist in a dodgy restaurant.'

Jeff asked, 'How dodgy?'

'Ah, just normal dodgy, I think. Well the restaurant's not dodgy, it's just the people who work there who are. I'll be watching how the bar staff pocket cash without ringing it through the tills, and how managers hang on to certain bills as refunds, pretending there were complaints. Usual stuff, just that I'll be making secret video reports on what's happening, and then be pocketing two paychecks for myself. One from the production company and one from the restaurant. Not bad, eh?'

'That's it?' asked Jeff. 'How much are they paying you?'

'A hundred and fifty K.'

'To expose tea-leafing barmen, and managers with light fingers? That doesn't sound right. That's a lot of money, girlfriend. Are you sure there isn't something you're not telling us?'

'No, I don't think so. I've just been told I have to make friends with everyone and keep my eyes peeled for unusual practices.' Although I was saying the words, for some reason I began to question the deal myself. Maybe I was being too trusting because of the large amount of money that was being dangled, but it was more money than I could ever imagine making in six months. I'd be foolish to turn it down, wouldn't I?

'Eh, earth to Eva.' Lisa gave me a nudge to wake me from my daydream. 'I know you might have got a taste for the limelight after your WAG drama, but do you think you're up for this?'

Not wanting to show weakness, I did my best to sound convincing. 'Of course, why not? I'm capable of being discreet. Just call me Columbo from now on.'

'After your shower escapade the other week, I think we should nickname you T. J. Hooker.' Lisa sniggered as she refilled her glass with more champagne.

'Going by the way she scoffed those doughnuts I think she's more of a Chief Wiggum,' added Parker.

Doing my best to distract attention away from prying questions, I tried to keep up the lighter tone by poking fun at Parker's follicularly challenged head. 'Says Kojak here. If you lose any more threads you'll be able to play his doppelgänger.' Extremely sensitive about his thinning hair, Parker quickly closed his mouth. Although he regularly dyed what was left a bluey-black colour to match his entire winter Prada wardrobe, it only seemed to highlight the bald patches. But he couldn't be told, and he never listened to reason when the subject was brought up.

'Oh, oh, I've got another one,' continued Lisa, as she finally flung her phone on the couch. 'Maybe I should move over to London as well, and we could be a double act. We could call ourselves Cagney and Lesbian. Ha! Ha!'

Knowing that the latter referred to me, I complained, 'I'm not a lesbian.'

Only for Lisa and Parker to respond, 'Oh yes you are,' in perfect panto mode.

Defending my honour, I pleaded, 'Excuse me, a couple of snogs with a girl does not a lesbian make. That was just an experiment.' But my argument fell on deaf ears.

Putting his arm around me protectively, Parker pulled me in close and laughed, 'We love you no matter who you kiss. If you only want to be called a lesbian from the waist up, we'll make sure to use the correct term in future.'

Knowing I couldn't argue my way out of a paper bag, and since I actually had enjoyed a brief yet mild flirtation with another girl some years back, I killed the joke with a mannerly thank you and let them have their laugh.

I ended up leaving my UK contract in my bag and never showing it to them. Instead I headed back to the flat early, overcome by a serious bout of self-doubt, and needing to be alone and have a clear head to think things over. I gently lifted Daisy out of her cot that night and put her into the bed beside me. Like a giant hot-water bottle, her body heat had a calming effect on my nerves and, after much deliberation, I decided the London move was the best decision for both of us. I needed to provide for her future, and aside from winning the Lottery this was my only hope of saving money for a rainy day. I was just drifting off to sleep, thinking that good things came to good people, when Daisy jolted and belted me smack in the nose with her fist.

4

Moving to London was not just a scary prospect, it quickly became a frightening reality. I might have had a few wrinkles on my face, but that didn't mean my emotional age had progressed much past that of a nervous 17-year-old. Acting first and thinking later had long been a Valentine trait. But packing my life into black bags and stacking photo-frames of Daisy and myself into vegetable boxes from the local supermarket started me thinking far more than any therapist or Oprah Winfrey ever could.

Although I had thought that I had few belongings, it was only when I began to file them away that I realized that not only had I lived a full and busy life, it had been one filled with laughter and love, and that even without a man to hug and kiss every evening, all had been good. In fact, better than good. It had been great; and now it was about to change.

Now Daisy and I were about to encounter new people and new adventures in London. Lisa had joked about all the fresh blood that the city would offer me. 'London's a bit like New York. It's got millions of men with a swagger! Just be careful to steer clear of any old haunts we might have frequented. You don't want to be bumping into any old exes now, do you?'

Aside from having to avoid the Primrose Hill area for fear of bumping into an old boyfriend – whom I had actually forgotten about until the idea of moving to London became a serious issue – this was the fresh start I needed to kick me in the ass. For a long time now, I had been going through the motions of everyday life. I needed to put myself out there and shake things up a little. Get some of the old Eva da Diva attitude back. And this London job was exactly the motivation I needed.

Catching my reflection in a small mirrored plate from my upsettingly dusty bookshelf, I gave myself a cheeky wink and laughed out loud at the silliness. I disturbed Daisy from watching her cartoons, blew her a kiss and whooped, 'Here's lookin' at us, kid,' before leaping over to her, rolling her back on the floor and blowing bubbles on her belly to make her laugh. While a display of affection like this would normally have been greeted with fits of giggles, this time I was instead quite definitely pushed off in a huffy manner, so she could have a clear view of the TV again. Did it curb my enthusiasm? No way. But it did show me that change was not something that everyone embraced. And that if I wanted to make a go of this life, I would need to start be-coming a heck of a lot more charming in my approach.

My older sister Ruth had thought me mad to go to a cold and heartless city and leave the safety of my steady job at *YES!* Having turned into our mother, she had moaned at me, 'You'll regret it. And when you do, don't bother running back to me. Because I'll only tell you I told you so.'

I pointed out that she was just scared of change – after

all she was the one who married her childhood sweetheart, and wasn't exactly good at making decisions that involved anything bigger than choosing spaghetti or beans for the kids' tea! But, seeing I had hurt her, I stopped teasing and thanked her for her concern. Though I did subtly slip in one more jibe by texting afterwards, 'All I want is a little support, sis. Just because U've got your life all sewn up here, doesn't mean U should stop me from pursuing my dreams xx.' Clearly frustrated, she never replied.

As first days in a new job go, this was definitely proving to be a difficult one. For some as yet unexplained reason, Bradley hadn't turned up for work that morning, and with no sign of 'Brutal Billie', as I was privately calling her, I was pointed in the direction of a desk and told to make myself comfortable. All I knew was that I had to keep the nature of my assignment a secret from the rest of the office, and that, if anyone asked, I was nothing more than a PA to Bradley. Dressed in a formal black pencil skirt, a cream vintage-lace blouse and quirky coordinating cream and black heels from Schuh, I felt I looked the part of a sexy assistant. Going for the understated, confident look, my poise was soon crushed when I realized I was going to be left to my own devices for a few hours.

Instead of making friends in the office, I knew I was supposed to blend in and keep myself to myself, so, feeling like my wings had been clipped, I kept my head down and busied myself with some newspapers that had been left on my desk. Each of them offered a different sordid story about my WAG rebels Tanya and Issey. Naturally I felt responsible for every tale, but I did my best to fight the guilt and tell myself I didn't put Tanya in rehab, and I wasn't the person who checked her out early only for her to get caught snorting cocaine in the toilet of the aptly named Sir Charlie's nightclub. As for Issey, the papers were reporting that she had been put on suicide watch after splitting from her boyfriend, and had pulled out of a reality show that was due to start filming for Living TV.

After reading the quote, 'A close friend revealed, "She says she wants to die"', I came over all panicked and went in search of some caffeine to calm my nerves. It only took me a couple of minutes of snooping to find the kitchen, which seemed to be the epicentre of the whole place, as staff hurried in and out of the sliding kitchen door to the smokers' balcony outside. While I was struggling to find a clean cup, a friendly face made eye-contact, a pretty blonde asking, 'Can I help?'

For a moment I thought about walking away, but decided being rude would only make me more conspicuous in such a relatively small building. 'Oh, yes, please. Just wondering where you kept the cups? I've been gasping for some coffee.'

'Ahhh, cups. That's an issue around this place. Unless you grab one early, you might not score one at all. Here, have mine, I'm done for now.'

I took the cup hesitantly, but she misinterpreted my unease.

'Hey, listen, I'm Carol, by the way. I know I look like shit. It's because I've been sick, but don't worry, I'm not carrying any abnormal germs or anything.'

'I never said you looked . . . I mean, you look great. Are you OK, though?'

'Sure, don't worry, I'm not contagious or anything. I'm just a bit loopy because I haven't had a drink in eight weeks, and that, as you can imagine, is driving me a bit silly.'

'Ohhh.' My response sounded dismissive, but it wasn't meant to be.

'I'm not an alco, by the way. I'm just getting over hepatitis. Shellfish, would you believe? Yeah, I went away for a week to Miami with the girls. They whored themselves out every night, while I went to bed early pining for my boyfriend, and I'm the one who comes home sick with hepatitis from eating at a sushi bar. And not one of them bitches had the decency to come home with as much as crabs! I mean, where is the justice?'

Smacked in the face with her honesty, all I could say was, 'Wow. That's fairly crap.' But my new friend Carol hadn't finished with her stories yet.

'Oh, that's nothing,' she confided, leaning closer into my personal space to make her point. 'The real icing on the cake comes when I arrive back with my liver half-dead, and my boyfriend Titus informs me he's been sleeping with some tart who understands him, and dumps me. And there I was saving myself in the party town of unlimited sex. It makes me mad just thinking about it. So much for healthy eating. What a con.'

For a moment I stood back, waiting for her next rant, but, realizing my discomfort with the situation, Carol had stopped. Clearly embarrassed, she apologized for losing the run of herself.

Understanding the pain of being cheated on, I briefly explained my own story with Michael as I rinsed her cup with warm water, and she responded by giving me the strongest of hugs by way of sympathy. 'Oh-my-God. You poor thing,' she gushed. 'I'm sorry for moaning. Your story is much worse than mine. And here's me going on like a bipolar maniac. I'm Kerry Katona without the fame and misfortune.'

Not knowing if I really wanted to be the one with the worst story, I thanked her for the hug and the cup, and excused myself back to my desk with a nasty-tasting filter coffee and some pretend errands that needed urgent attention. I was only moments in my seat when a gorgeous man strode by, the spit of Tom Ford, leaving a blast of his scent in my path. He reminded me of an ex of mine, and I breathed in his musky smell, instantly feeling lonely. It was a bittersweet feeling – how good a man could make you feel, yet how devastated you were when they had gone! Lost in the memory of a past relationship, I was jolted back to the present by a girl at a neighbouring desk.

'He's cute, isn't he?'

'Who do you mean?' I asked, as if it wasn't obvious.

'It's OK, you know. Everyone fancies Peter. It's just a pity he's such a pig.'

Trying to sound nonchalant I whispered, 'Oh really?' while keeping my eyes firmly on my cup of bitterness, but it was clear my game was already up.

'Don't worry, I've thought he's hot for several years now. I just don't like him very much. All I'll say is: be careful. If you're stuck for a bit of company, go for it, he's a great lay. I know from experience. Just be sure to keep it covered. He's done more mileage than Jenson Button, that man. Oh, and watch out not to get cornered in the conference room when you sneak in to get the free biscuits. It's kinda his thing.'

Doubly shocked at how forthright the women in the office were, I thanked her for the tip-off and started shoving irrelevant pieces of paper around my desk in an attempt to snuff out any further conversation. Thankfully her mobile rang, and she turned away, whispering, 'You're such a shit . . . No, you are . . . Such a shit. I love you . . .'

By lunchtime I had received a call of my own from Bradley. 'So sorry, lovely, but I got held up. Why don't you go home? And we'll see you back in the morning. All right?' Bloody right it was. I was out of my seat before I had even hung up the phone and was at the lift with a discreet, 'See ya,' to the girl at reception. After a scandalous two hours trying to navigate my way through London traffic, I arrived back at my Aunt Maura's house stressed, sweaty, and cursing the fact that I had worn my best outfit to make a good impression and Bradley hadn't turned up to see me in it.

Maura's might not have been the fanciest of houses, but she'd made it a real home. When Daisy and I had arrived the previous evening, Daisy had been tired and I'd been a bit homesick off the plane, and we'd immediately been made welcome by the whole family, despite the fact that they'd only had a few days' notice that I was on my way. I had hardly set my bags on the floor before, like any good Irish mammy, Maura had had the kettle on and a pile of buttered toast waiting to be devoured.

The lovely atmosphere continued today. Walking into the Maguire living room was like stepping into a fairy tale, made even more idyllic by my daughter happily sitting in the middle of the floor, being fussed over by everyone, and loving every minute of it. Taking turns to show her a Malibu Barbie and a Spider Man were Kelly, eleven, Fiona, eight, and little six-year-old Jack. Unlike the two girls, who possibly were treating Daisy like a real-life doll, but in a caring way, Jack was boisterous like any little fella, but practical. He was paying close attention to the expressions on Daisy's face. Although none of the kids had ever met Daisy before this trip, she was fitting in quickly, and it was a relief to see they were patient and understanding when she grunted and screamed out loud in her own unique excited fashion. Standing in the hallway, I proudly watched the way she interacted with the other kids. I secretly wished that someday Daisy would have brothers or sisters of her own to watch out for her, and protect her against the cruel world that she would have to make her way out into.

Playtime was interrupted by the arrival of my Auntie Maura, and what looked like homemade scones. 'Oh, hello, lovee, didn't expect you back so early. Come on in, we're having a little tea party.' Daisy threw me one of her winning smiles, and I dropped my jacket and handbag at the door, kicked off my shoes and rushed over to pick her up and bring her to the dining table to have afternoon tea with everyone else. Maura claimed Daisy had been, 'A doll all morning. Nah bother.' It was obvious that she meant it, too, as Daisy soon put out her arms for Maura to hold her instead of me.

Making the most of it, I took myself upstairs to change into something more comfortable and left the girls and boy to their Ribena and scones. After sending some catch-up texts to my mum, Parker, Lisa and my editor at *YES!* – who had very kindly agreed to unpaid leave, since I had now become a superstar journo off the back of my WAG report – I sat down on my new bed and looked around my very compact room, praying that the walls, complete with Barbie wallpaper, wouldn't start to cave in on top of me. Parker was right, though, I had ended up in the box room, and I even prompted him to gloat about it in my text. But instead of feeling like a single-mother statistic, I felt lucky that I had a family who could take me in at such short notice, and even more blessed that they had not only opened their doors but also their hearts to me and my special little girl.

Being practical, I had already put the money from my WAG video nasty away for five years into a post office savers' account that I couldn't touch even if I had wanted to. Ever since Daisy had been born my natural self-preservation instincts had extended to cover her welfare, too, and I was determined to provide for her future, whatever that might be. So I was banking on this UK adventure to pay for itself and a lot more in the future. And although I had agreed to hand over a modest rent for the bedroom and some money towards the groceries and bills, Maura had said she would refuse to accept any money at all for babysitting Daisy until I found myself a properly trained professional or crèche.

'We're family,' she'd said proudly, which was true. But even though she was my father's youngest sister, I couldn't remember the last time we'd even spoken before this, and the only contact I could recall was a Christmas card from the 'London gang' posted to my mam and dad's house two or three years ago, with my name included on the envelope. That was the nice thing about the Irish. No matter where in the world they ended up, they always seemed to remember their roots, and how much they too had struggled when they'd first left the green isle. Helping others out didn't seem a chore to ex-pats, but just a way of passing on the goodwill, and no doubt somehow easing whatever Catholic guilt they might be living with, too.

That night I went to bed early, exhausted by a combination of emotional and physical stress from the move. Although Daisy looked so peaceful in her cot, I couldn't help myself, and selfishly lifted her gently into my bed so I could give her the usual cuddles. It was becoming a regular practice these days, but she never seemed to mind. If anything, making this big journey together had made me realize more than ever how much I loved her. Even though I knew I would still occasionally have feelings of despair over the challenges that might lie ahead, I adored the feel of her. Just her body heat and the sweet strawberry-shampoo smell of her hair was enough to calm me again. Back in my happy place, I drifted off to sleep the most contented mommy alive, blocking out any unnecessary worries about undercover work, or the fate of unstable reality stars who would blame me for their shameless and inevitable fall from grace.

Arriving at work the next morning, I was pleased to see the handsome Peter waiting by the lift. Busy chatting on his iPhone about some overdue edits, he didn't seem to notice my small self ogling the back of his head and coveting his nicely shaped bum. As soon as the lift opened, he quickly ended his phone call, stepped inside and bluntly asked me, 'Going up?'

Of course the filthy part of my brain screamed, 'I'm much better at going down.' But I politely replied, 'Yes, please,' while trying not to sound too eager. Surprised when I didn't press another button after he pressed 5, Peter did a double take in my direction and asked, 'Are you going to the top?'

That was it. In a fit of random giddiness I blurted out, 'That's where I'm going, baby. Stra–ight to the top!' As soon as the words had left my mouth, I wished that I could take them back. His sullen face said it all. He thought I was an idiot. But he wasn't alone. I thought I was an idiot, too.

We both stared awkwardly at the floor, numbers flashing

by, until the silence seemed to become too much for Peter. 'Are you new?' he asked, his questioning look only adding to his appeal.

Unsure how much information I could give away, I mumbled, 'Eh, yeah, sort of,' and hoped he wouldn't ask too many more questions. To my relief, he simply stared at me, though in a baffled way, kinda like I was some freak in a circus. Thankfully the doors opened at the fifth floor before I needed to ask what the hell he was looking at, and he marched off, his iPhone stuck to his ear.

Instructed to wait at my desk again by the pretty blonde receptionist, as Bradley was in a conference call and wanted to speak to me as soon as he was done, I'd barely been sitting down five minutes when Peter marched briskly up to me. Then, without fear of embarrassing me or himself, he pointed at me in a very definite manner, as if I was some sort of criminal, and said, 'You know, you're very familiar. Have you been on TV?'

Thankfully, I didn't get a chance to answer, as Bradley swiftly swooped in like Superman, batting Peter's accusing finger away from my face as he arrived.

'Can we help you, Peter? Running out of females to harass on your side of the department?'

'Good morning to you too, Brad. I was just welcoming the new girl to the office. I'm curious about her job.'

'That's of no concern to you, Pete,' snapped Bradley. 'OK, Eva, let's go to my office, fewer predators floating about there.'

Obediently, I followed him, leaving an insulted, yet super-sexy, Peter still standing by my desk. Once in Bradley's office I felt momentarily safe, but that feeling soon passed as he unveiled what looked like a victims' wall full of photographs of young people, with their names, occupations, and the list of offences that I was to look out for at the restaurant. As I quickly scanned the images, many of which seemed to be pictures of nights out swiped off Facebook, I read snippets such as, 'Helen Foley, assistant manager: pocketing cash from till.' 'Steven Ryan, barman: free drinks scam.' But when I laid my eyes on 'Jake Lewis, head of security: drug-dealing,' the alarm bells in my head started to ring.

'Eh, Bradley, what's the story with this Lewis guy?' I tried to sound casual, but inside I was trembling. Drugs were not something I was comfortable being around. Although I had once snorted some cocaine during a grim drunken evening while trying to impress a couple of people, it was something I was seriously embarrassed about and wished I could blank from my memory. So the thought of having to work closely with – and spy on – a drug-dealer was terrifying.

'What do you mean?' asked Bradley. 'He's a very slick operator. He runs the door, is in charge of the team, and, if our information is correct, he has most, if not all, of the security staff selling drugs for him.'

'Right.' My brain was racing too fast for words to form properly. 'And – it's my job to report on his activities?'

'Exactly.' Bradley smiled as he proudly gazed at his board, unaware of my reservations. Then he quickly went on, 'But what we really need from you is to catch some of these transactions on camera. Think you can manage that?'

'Oh gosh, Bradley, I don't think . . .'

'You'll be great,' he gushed. 'We'll provide you with everything you'll need. You'll have the tiniest of hidden cameras, that will fit in a buttonhole, for your surveillance work, and a high-definition mobile-phone-styled camera to film your reports. And the rest is then up to you.'

'I'm . . . I'm not very good with drugs,' I replied, being as truthful as I could.

'Don't worry,' cooed Bradley. 'I'm not asking you to take them. I'm just asking you to catch them being sold on tape. There's no danger involved at all.'

After a very one-sided discussion with Bradley I was sent home early again, but this time with ample homework. Aside from having to familiarize myself with the profiles of each of my new work colleagues, I was given sample scripts which I was to memorize, rehearse in front of a mirror and then record on a small video camera to get me used to doing so at the restaurant.

By 3 a.m. I still hadn't switched the video camera on. It didn't matter how many times I read the lines on the page, the second I saw myself in my vanity mirror I clammed up and lost the power of speech. Disappointingly, this wasn't as easy as I had at first thought. My career as an undercover TV journalist seemed doomed to failure before it had begun. So I reasoned that maybe it wasn't such a bad thing to catch a few hours' sleep, just so I could allow my brain to rest before Daisy woke me up, demanding my undivided attention.

At 6.45 a.m. I woke in a sweat, panicking about my pieces to camera. I couldn't possibly arrive at Brady Reel Time Films with the excuse that my dog ate my homework, so I called Parker for some pointers, and prayed that he'd pick up the phone at such an early hour.

'You are sooo lucky this is a shoot day, missy,' he scolded when he eventually picked up. 'Now what can I do you for?'

'I need tips on becoming a TV diva.'

'Well, you are a diva, so you're halfway there, petal.'

'PARKER! I'm serious. I'm in big trouble here. If I don't go into work today with four segments recorded, I might as well pack up my bags and head back to Dublin.'

'Mmmm, OK, as much I would love to see you back home, I'll help you out. But I'll need a sweetener.'

Thinking on my feet, I promised to send him some gay porn that he wouldn't be able to buy back in Dublin, and pleaded with him to hurry.

'OK, OK, firstly you need to imagine yourself as the person you want to be. In this case a bad-ass reporter who takes no prisoners. Forget being Eva Valentine, and think of this as an actor would. You need to put aside any inhibitions you may have and mentally become this character. Do you understand?'

'Yes, but no. I mean, how do I actually do that?'

'A lot of people find meditation good for clearing the mind—'

'Oh, give me a break. I haven't got time for bleedin' meditation. We're up against the clock here, Parker.'

'Keep your knickers on, it was just a suggestion. Right then, the quickest way for you to do this is to pretend you're mimicking someone.'

'What do you mean?'

'Exactly what I said. Pretend that you are taking the piss out of someone, in this case a TV reporter, and deliver the piece to camera as if you were poking fun at them. Methinks that's your best bet.'

'That's genius,' I squealed, stupidly disturbing Daisy from her slumber. 'Gotta go.'

After nipping down to the kitchen to grab a bottle of milk for Daisy, to keep her in her cot, I ran into the family bathroom, covered myself up with one of Maura's spare towelling bathrobes, and in minutes had all four pieces to camera on tape.

I felt very pleased with my work as I arrived in the office, homework done. For future reference Bradley suggested I actually look at the camera lens rather than the reflection of the view-finder in the mirror. (Which I could have turned round, and so seen myself directly.) But, considering it was my first attempt, he told me, 'Not bad at all – and your pieces to camera weren't rubbish, either!' Of course, that gave me a much-needed confidence boost, and from that grew a desire to succeed.

Not wanting to lose momentum, Bradley shooed me out of the building again mid-morning to swot up on more scripts, only this time I would have to come back to his office later that day and record them under his direction. Feeling like I was auditioning for *Britain's Got Talent*, I paced the aisles of a nearby Marks & Spencer's repeating my lines over and over, and instead of trying on any clothes in the dressing-room cubicles, I performed each of my pieces to the full-length mirrors, becoming more expressive and energized each time I did them – or so I thought.

Back at Bradley's office, though, I was told I looked like Ross Kemp playing a pantomime dame, and that less was definitely more when it came to TV presenting. He said, 'You're over-acting, like Darius.' And, like Darius, I needed to start listening to heavy metal rather than Britney Spears. Seemingly that would start showing through in my delivery. That evening I was sent home with another batch of scripts and the video camera again, and told, 'You're under pressure now.' As if I wasn't already aware of that.

The next morning Bradley's verdict was, 'Third time

lucky.' And that even though there was some room for improvement, I had pretty much nailed the task. Over the next two days we moved on to master classes in how to work the cameras: from using the best light to film, to disguising my pinhole surveillance camera in either clothes or a handbag. We also did hours of role-playing to learn how to set up 'stings', as Bradley called them; and I continued to learn more about the dodgy dealings of my future workmates.

None of my new knowledge could have prepared me for the next bullet, though. I was just walking out the door on Friday evening when Bradley revealed the location of my new workplace. 'It's Sir Charlie's,' he said casually. 'I've a map and some directions printed out. You'll need to be there Monday morning at 10 a.m. Your contact is Helen Foley, and she'll show you the ropes. You can call me on your progress when you get your break.'

Remembering the newspaper story about Tanya, I asked, 'Are you sure? Isn't that a nightclub?'

'Yes, it is.' Bradley smiled, his eyes widening at the recognition on my part. 'But it's also a restaurant by day. I'm glad you know it, but I didn't tell you about it before as I didn't want you to fret about bumping into any of your old WAG friends. On that front, I think you should come up with a new name.'

Totally taken aback, I joked, 'Would you like me to change the colour of my hair, too?'

But that only seemed to spark an idea in Bradley's head. 'You know what?' He was now talking to himself rather than me. 'That's spot on. OK,' his attention quickly snapped back to me. 'How do you reckon you'd look as a redhead?'

Laughing at the idea, I joked, 'Is that not a tad clichéd for an Irish girl?'

'You're dead right,' replied Bradley. 'Blonde it is.'

Stuffing £200 in dirty twenty-pound notes into my hand, he whooped, 'That's perfect. Text me later when you decide on a name. But nothing too Oirish. Think more Melinda Messenger than Danielle O'Donnell, all right?'

Fighting against the temptation to respond with a smart comment like, 'So would you like me to get my boobs done as well?' I bit my lip and charged out the door before he came up with any other ways to upset me.

Having been a brunette all my life, the thought of going blonde was as scary as getting cosmetic surgery from a surgeon who credited himself for working on Katie Price, Jodie Marsh and Leslie Ash! But after remembering how Lisa had bravely cut off her own long blonde hair when she first started chemotherapy, I thought *what little sacrifice* and bought myself a couple of cheap packets of hair dye at the local pharmacy. With extra cash in my back pocket after choosing to bleach on the cheap, I was happy that I could hand more over to Maura as a thank you for caring for Daisy. I would need to give Maura a much-needed break from her that weekend anyway, so a trip to the hairdressers was just not a workable option.

Saturday morning and several bleached towels later, Maura was wishing she'd paid me to go to the hairdressers herself, after the mess I'd made in her bathroom. Despite following the instructions to the letter, my hair had turned out peach with the first natural medium champagne blonde kit I had tried, before turning platinum, and then a less scary ash blonde, thanks to Clairol. Worried that it would fall out completely, Maura ordered me to massage a full jar of Hellman's mayonnaise into my newly destroyed hair as I sat watching back-to-back episodes of *Hannah Montana* and *Spongebob Squarepants* all afternoon with the kids.

After washing the gunk out, I blow-dried my bob, feeling like Marilyn Monroe, and took a photograph of my new image on my phone, to send to Bradley. Tagging it with, 'Codename: Alice', I also sent it to Parker and Lisa, and sat by the phone with my fingers crossed. As if waiting for exam results, I hesitantly opened each of the messages that beeped through, praying for a positive reaction. On cue, both my buddies responded, 'Who the fuck is Alice?' I received nothing back from Bradley. Clearly bored, Parker spent the rest of the evening sending me stupid blonde jokes along the lines of, 'What do bleached blondes and jumbo jets have in common? Black boxes.' And, 'Why do blondes wear underwear? To keep their ankles warm.' But still there was no reply from Bradley.

That night I went to bed feeling a renewed sense of confidence. I had never dreamed of dyeing my hair before, but I actually really liked it. Pouting in my vanity mirror, I pretended I was Scarlett Johansson and gushed, 'Cause I'm worth it,' several times over. I finally went off to sleep with a smile on my face, wondering: as a blonde, would I really have more fun?

5

It was hard to believe I could have made a bigger mess of Maura's bathroom than I had during the brown-to-blonde incident, but my ability to apply St Tropez was always dodgy at the best of times . . . and with my auntie plying me full of booze, things went from streaky to downright manky.

Once Daisy was in bed, Maura's husband John gave her the night off from all parenting duties and ordered the pair of us upstairs to do whatever women do, with the warning, 'Not too much male-bashing, or else I'll try this tanning business meself, and mortify you both in front of the neighbours tomorrow!' Locking ourselves away from the last-minute Sunday-night homework chaos that was unfolding downstairs, Maura and I bonded with our horror stories of childbirth and stretch-marks, as I prepped myself to become body-beautiful for work the next day, helped along by not one but two bottles of Sancerre. I did more talking than blending, and I looked like I had fallen into a river at Willy Wonka's Chocolate Factory when we were finally evicted from our safe haven, so the kids could wash their teeth without fear of being heckled.

Taking refuge in the master bedroom with the last of the

vino, Maura took it upon herself to show me her and John's goodie drawer, which had to be opened with a key she kept hidden on top of a picture frame. She proceeded to list each mechanical device in order of preference, crediting them with adding years on to her relationship with John. 'Well, how else do you expect to keep a twenty-year marriage alive?' She asked this in all seriousness, before breaking into one of her dirty laughs and gasping, 'Who am I asking? Sure, I might as well be asking you what a macrobiotic diet is . . .'

In between the nipple tassels and the furry handcuffs, they had a different-coloured vibrator for every day of the week: the large black one acting as their favourite midweek treat, and a small ugly finger-type purple one being, as Maura put it, 'John's personal pleasure-finder!' Grossed out, and terrified I'd never be able to look the poor man in the eye again, I abandoned Maura, who had now become suitably horny, and promised to send John up to her just so he could get his 'Sunday service'.

The next morning I felt like a novice soldier going into battle. Even with my new blonde do, my patchy fake tan didn't ease my terror about the people I was going to meet, and my fear that they would suss me straightaway as a fraud. Advised not to take any cameras with me on the first day, I was very relieved I hadn't wired up when Helen – the assistant manager I'd learned about from my list of profiles – handed me a skimpy black dress and told me, 'You look great, but this is our uniform. We've all got to wear them.'

Instead of giving me some privacy, Helen ushered me into a small, run-down staffroom cluttered with duffle bags and oversized winter coats – in total contrast to the über-cool, modern restaurant she'd walked me through – and insisted on discussing the plan for the day as I struggled to slip out of my grey trouser suit and into the flimsy dress she'd given me.

Although I wouldn't normally wear Spanx under trousers, that morning had been particularly cold, so I had justified them as an alternative to thermals. And even though I was a tad mortified when I caught Helen trying not to stare at them, I thanked my lucky stars I had pulled them on when I saw myself in the dress. Trying to defuse the tension, I joked, 'They don't leave much to the imagination, do they?'

Helen bluntly retorted, 'If I was you I'd try and lose a few pounds. Craig doesn't hire staff over a size 10. If you don't fit the dress, you don't fit in, full stop.'

Patting my belly and throwing my eyes up to heaven, I said, 'I have my period, and you know yourself—'

Helen interrupted, 'It's my job to keep an eye on these things. You need to know there's a standard to be kept.' While I was still struggling for a comeback, a beeper in Helen's pocket went off and she was quickly out the door. From the hall she yelled back, 'I'll see you outside in a few minutes,' and then she was gone, and I was left in the stinky staffroom, feeling frumpy and inadequate and wishing I'd never had that hangover cooked breakfast which Maura had so kindly made me.

For most of my life I had been a size twelve, and if anything I had felt great about being a small twelve, or, as I had more appropriately described myself to Maura the night before, an eleven and a half. Until Helen's cutting comments I had felt sexy and womanly, but I was in a fragile state of mind already, and her advice was missing the sugar that might have made it easier to swallow. And, as if it hadn't been enough, I walked out on to the floor just in time to hear an extremely stick-like member of staff ask, 'Who's the fat chick?'

I could have pretended not to hear, of course, but I chose instead to confront my critics face on. 'I'm the new girl. My name is Alice. But I'll answer to any derogatory fat names, such as Porker, Salad Dodger, Lardass, Muffin Top, Tyra Banks, Busted Sofa, Omega Mu, Forgetful Bulimic, Great Personality. You name it, I've heard it. So I'd appreciate a little inventiveness in future, thanks.' Humour seemed like the best route – after all, I wanted these people to like me, or at the very least respect me for having attitude.

Momentarily flummoxed by my brazen manner, my skinny new nemesis just looked me up and down before walking off without even making an excuse. She clearly thought me mad, or maybe just plain dangerous. Her comments had cut me like a knife, but I was determined not to let her know that, so I simply asked Helen to start showing me the ropes.

The rest of the day was pretty uneventful as regards further confrontation. With business frustratingly slow in the restaurant, I spent my time folding napkins, polishing glasses and shadowing a waitress called Naomi, who took a grand total of seventeen covers to the kitchen, with the most calorific meal ordered being a prawn piri-piri. It was becoming painfully clear to me that the city crowd were different beings, and not big into eating. Forget Kansas, I most definitely wasn't anywhere near Grafton Street now.

Despite keeping my eyes peeled for unusual activity, the only person I became suspicious of was the kitchen porter, and that was just over his hygiene standards. After seeing the way he used large trays of salad to prop open the freezer door, I knew I could never order it again without visualizing it resting on the floor beside a mop and bucket and a sign that read 'Staff Toilet'. On my way home I rang Bradley to say that so far any scams or rackets were corruptly well hidden, and the only thing exposing itself was me. He apologized for the skimpy dress, but said if I wanted an honest opinion on it, he'd be happy to give me a babe rating out of ten on receipt of a picture message. I told him to use his imagination instead, and so he generously scored me a fifteen!

The next few days were a mixture of terror and exhilaration as I began to take chances with filming pieces to camera. While each location was carefully chosen to reveal the behind-the-scenes grime and disorder, my dialogue was sensational, bordering on full-on conspiracy theorist. Unless I actually started to witness some action soon, the entire project would look more like a spoof than a true-life documentary. More David Attenborough than Donal MacIntyre, I would crouch beside the bins to deliver my impassioned pieces to camera. Today was no different.

'It's Friday of my first week at Sir Charlie's and the mood in the restaurant is pretty bleak. There is an obvious lack of teamwork among the staff. The bar guys seem to be up to something. They're giving the waitresses the total silent treatment. The management are being extremely shifty when cashing out bills, and I've also noticed the head chef asking for bin money out of the till a couple of times this week, so I'd be curious to find out if and what that could be code for.' Slipping my camera back into my locker safely, I returned to the floor and had a big shock.

There, sitting propping up the long bar, were my two lunatic mates, Parker and Lisa. Unsure whether to acknowledge them as friends, my heart skipped a beat as I wondered how I should play this. Or, more to the point, how they would. I didn't have to hold my breath for long. The minute Parker saw me, he winked slyly, while maintaining his cool and collected composure, and spoke to me like I was a member of staff.

'Eh, hello, sorry.' He put his hand on my arm as he talked. 'Do you know where my friend and I can score some drugs, please? We badly need some.'

Frozen to the spot, as one of the barmen was in earshot, all I could respond with was, 'Pardon me?' while forcing a large smile that said *Don't fuck with me here, or else I will have to break your legs.*

Signalling to Lisa, who was also pretending to be a stranger, he spoke again with a strange quasi-South African accent. 'My girlfriend here has a headache. She was wondering if you could provide her with some painkillers.'

I was just about to offer some weak response when the barman jumped in with, 'Sorry, mate, we're not allowed to hand any out for legal reasons. There's a Boots just a couple of streets down. Won't take you longer than five minutes max.'

'Fuck it, then,' blurted Parker. 'We'll just have to get you pissed, darling. That'll get rid of your headache just as quick.' Parker then said to the barman, 'A bottle of house champagne for the little woman, please.' So I took it upon myself to walk away and leave them to their boozing. But it seemed Parker was only getting warmed up. 'Excuse me, miss?' He called after me. 'Can you sort us a table when you're ready? What station are you working? I like the look of you. Can you serve us?'

I was in the process of giving him another of my frosty

smiles when Helen strode up and took control of the situation. 'Hello, there,' she gushed, signalling for me to run along. 'You're looking for a table for two, is it?'

'Yes, please. And we'd like that gorgeous girl to serve us,' said Parker defiantly. 'Can you arrange that for us? We're planning on spending a lot of money on champagne today.'

Following the motto that whatever the customer wants, the customer gets, the odd couple were seated in my section, all the while loudly gushing, 'This is great! This is going to be a fun afternoon.' Once other staff members were safely out of earshot my friends quickly let their guard down. 'Surprise!' they both chimed proudly.

Slightly annoyed at the lack of warning, I growled back at them, 'Yeah, just a pity it wasn't a nice one.'

Thrilled with himself, Parker kept poking me in the arm to make his point. 'You shoulda seen your face. It was priceless! I thought you were going to faint.'

'Yes, thanks for that. Ouch. Now behave, or else I might actually have to faint on you.'

By 5 p.m., my drunken friends had polished off two bottles of champagne and had started up a friendship with the table next to them. Despite my begging them to keep their afternoon low-key they had cosied up to these two other couples, who appeared equally jolly, and kept loudly asking, 'Isn't this girl great? A credit to the establishment. Join us for a glass of bubbles.'

Something seemed a little odd about the other table: the guys were immaculately dressed in expensive silver pin-striped suits, with almost forties-style greased-down hair, while their companions were slightly less than groomed, and looked as if they had street-walked all the way from the opposite side of the Thames. Not that I was any great expert on class, but in this instance manners were in scarce supply, and fake tan and badly backcombed hair was in abundance. Thinking that she was saving me from the rowdy bunch, Helen asked if I wanted to swap tables with one of the other girls, but I thanked her and laughed my customers off as just a temporary pain – especially as I would be handing over my station at half five anyway.

By 5.42 p.m., Ms Alice had left the building, with tables six and seven following swiftly after me. I felt terrible about calling Maura to ask her to babysit at the end of such a long week, but I knew I'd feel even worse getting the Tube home and having an early night while my pals went on the lash without me. So, after some grovelling, and promises to take the whole gang out from under her feet for a few hours on Sunday, the deal was done.

With the green light to party, I put aside any reservations I might have had about the boys with marbles in their mouths (it turned out they were investment bankers) or the easy women who were hanging off them, and decided to put my suspicious mind to bed for one night and enjoy being a young, free, sassy singleton in London. Desperate to play catch-up, at the next bar we hit I knocked back two Mojitos and two Jäger shots in the space of five minutes, and instantly felt more relaxed and in party mood.

I was just settling into some man-spying when out of nowhere a drink came splashing over me, leaving me looking like I'd just completed a circuit on *Wipeout*.

I'd got in the way of an all-out war between the bankers' not-so-high-class lady friends. They had both been drinking all day, and were now screaming obscenities that clearly made sense to them and them only. While Parker sorted out the squabbling divas with our banker friends, Lisa came to my rescue, or so I thought, with a fresh outfit that she had in her overnight bag. We retreated to the bathroom, but it was only after I had stripped out of my wet uniform, and soggy and now ever-present Spanx, that Lisa handed me a pair of black wet-look leggings and a sparkly boob-tube over the cubicle door.

'No way! I can't wear that! I'll look like one of those hookers who threw the drink over me!' Although Lisa pretended to be insulted, she was always striving for the sluttish look and loved it when people noticed her bad taste. 'Ah, Jaysus, Lisa,' I went on. 'Were you thinking of auditioning for *Grease*? Neither of us are exactly Olivia Newton John material. This is just too much.'

'Shut up and put them on. You're not in the Four Seasons now. You're in London, baby, where nobody gives a shit who you are or what you look like.'

Having already thrown my wet clothes on the toilet floor, I didn't feel I had any other option than to put on Lisa's fresh outfit. So, with a heavy heart, I slipped into my disco costume and bounced out to Lisa, trying to feel upbeat. Waving my jazz hands for extra effect I struggled with a pathetic, 'Ta da!' But despite my enthusiasm, Lisa's concerned face spoke volumes. Needing to see what she could, I pushed her out of the way to get a proper look at myself in the mirror, and nearly fainted with the shock. 'OH-MY-GOD! I've got a fucking camel toe . . .'

Trying to salvage the situation, Lisa attempted to ease my stress with a weak, 'Not a big one,' before the two of us fell about the place laughing.

'Ah, Lisa, I can't go out like this. They'll start calling me Big Foot!'

'Shut up, you'll be grand. Come on, let's get back outside.

If you hang around here too long people might think you're a vending machine and start expecting you to spit out condoms!'

'Nice. That's just lovely. Remind me never to hang around with you again after tonight.'

No doubt dying to parade me like I was her own life-size Slapper Barbie, Lisa pushed me out the door and into the path of a drunken Parker, who even when sober was possibly the most sarcastic man on the planet.

I was doing my best to conceal my modesty with my overloaded handbag when, back at the table, Lisa proudly announced, 'Eva's got something to show you all.'

'Excuse me?' The shock of her statement almost made me pass out on the spot with the fear.

'Yes,' declared Lisa proudly. 'Eva's brought a little friend out to play.'

Hopeful that she was just winding me up, I asked, 'I did?' But then unfortunately got the answer I was dreading.

'Look.' Lisa quickly whipped my bag out of my hands. 'Eva's brought her camel toe out to play. Say hello, everyone.'

Unable to fight the unfolding joke at my expense, I thought best to go with it, and pointed both my hands towards my crotch, before taking an over-exaggerated curtsey to a rapturous round of applause. Having taken all the attention I could bear, I asked, 'So who's gonna buy me and my little friend a real drink? I think we need it.'

At which one of the banker boys stood up and ordered, 'A bottle of Moët et Chandon for the good sport.' While Lisa and I had been in the toilet, the lads had finally given the two slappers their marching orders after their tiff over who got to shag Jason, the better-looking of the two bankers, spilled over – literally – on to me. It seemed the boys had picked them up while walking down the road outside Sir Charlie's and simply offered to take them for lunch because of the short skirts they were wearing. But they'd tired of them when they'd kept asking for cash for special favours.

With the women gone, the evening became less stressful, and after we finished off the champagne we moved on to another private VIP club around the corner, which the lads said they had membership keys for. As we arrived at a closed iron-gated door, I felt a tad concerned that we might be being led into some whorehouse, especially going on the lads' previous track record, but Jason assured me, 'This is one of the coolest clubs in town.' So, after he spoke a code into the intercom, we were buzzed through the gates and climbed into a waiting lift.

Once upstairs it was as if we had stepped into another world. Dimly lit with deep red lights, the club wasn't a whorehouse but a gentleman's club that allowed open-minded ladies. It was full of Friday-evening suits, just like our banker friends. As the boys were regulars, we were all ushered to a table beside a stage area and told by the pretty blonde hostess, 'The usual, coming right up.' Pretty soon afterwards an ice bucket with vodka and cans of Red Bull was put on our table. The music in the room changed, and the lights dimmed further as the bottom of a black woman pushed itself out from behind a curtain. As the audience of mostly men began to whoop and cheer, I could see Lisa's face fill with excitement.

'Having fun?' I asked.

'This is the best. I'm so glad we came over.'

Delighted that my friend was so pleased with our night out, my happy buzz was slightly dented when she pointed to the bikini-clad black woman and whispered, 'I have always wanted to be a dancer. Do you think they'd let me up?'

Although I told her that this wasn't a karaoke night inviting punters to perform, Lisa was no longer listening to me. She was lost in adoration for the young dancer, who was by now doing lewd things to an innocent chair. Determined to get in on the act, Lisa started pulling tenners out of her purse, and reaching in and cheekily stuffing them through the dancer's diamanté bikini thong. Willingly accepting Lisa's notes, the dancer began to concentrate her gyrating in our direction, for which we were all exceptionally grateful.

A few dance routines later and this Valentine was fully up to speed. I'm not sure if it was the drink finally kicking in or just the energy from the lustful crowd around me, but before I knew what I was doing, I was standing up, dancing around my own chair, and putting on a show of my own. Clearly appreciating my performance, our new banker friends smiled and quietly watched me shaking my ass to Shakira, while Parker and Lisa attempted to wolf-whistle and knock back vodka at the same time. I was loving the music and the way it made me feel until I glanced over at the dancer on the stage beside me and I saw that she was mouthing something to me. Unsure if I was seeing things, I asked Parker, 'What did she say?'

He gaily replied, 'She said she'd like to eat your PEACH!'

Mortified that the dancer had also noticed my camel toe, I replied with a polite, 'Thank you,' and sat back down like I'd just been scolded at school.

Of course the rest of the table found it hilarious, and chanted, 'Eat the peach, eat the peach!' until one of the hostesses came over and asked them to keep it down.

Lisa no longer wanted to dance. 'You've stolen my moment, Eva, and why doesn't anyone want to eat my peach? I'm bored now. Let's move.' Assuring us that we had seen nothing yet, Jason took Lisa by the hand, who then grabbed me, who grabbed Parker, who grabbed the other guy, Jonathan, and we all walked hand-in-hand through the crowd to another closed door. After a few words with a mean-looking security guy, Jason handed over a couple of fifties and we stepped into a different room that had a small swimming pool and a woman in a bikini swinging over it. Unlike the mood outside, the music in this room was extremely chilled, and the bluey-green lighting just set off the vibe perfectly.

As we settled into a corner, Jason led an eager Lisa up to the bar and told us, 'We'll be back with drinks.'

I was curious as to how Parker was coping with such a hetero evening. He chuckled, then told me, 'I'm not sure if my hair is curling because of that, or just the dampness in the air.' He turned to Jonathan jokingly, 'Don't suppose you fancy a snog?' Before Parker had a chance to crack another gag, Jonathan had lunged at him and started kissing him passionately, like he was the only person in the room. Unsure what to do with myself, I glanced in the direction of Lisa and her banker only to see that they, too, were snogging the face off each other. I waited for the two boys to unlock their lips, but their embrace didn't seem to be slowing up, so all I could do was quietly laugh to myself and hope that someone would arrive with a drink for me soon.

Thankfully, I didn't have to wait too long. But it wasn't Lisa who came to my aid, but an extremely handsome man sporting a sexy two-day-old stubble, who, much to my delight, wasn't wearing a suit. Over several glasses of

champagne I learnt that Rory Baxter was a TV cameraman for CNN who was just back from Uganda, and that
he regularly travelled to war-torn countries to film their
famines and civil wars. Looking into his eyes as he spoke of
the extreme poverty he had witnessed, I had to wonder how
the hell a supposedly decent guy like him had ended up in
a den of iniquity like this. No sooner had I questioned how
genuine he might be, when I caught a glimpse of myself in
a smoked mirror, and instantly felt cheap and tacky in my
outfit.

Sensing my discomfort, Rory asked me, 'Are you OK?'
Before getting a wave of paranoia himself, and questioning,
'Sorry, am I boring you? Would you like me to leave you
alone?' I glanced quickly over at Parker and then Lisa, but
it was painfully obvious that both of them were still busy
with their bankers, so I reassured Rory that I was intrigued
to hear his stories, even if the woman swinging half-naked
over his shoulder was just a tad distracting. He apologized
for being such a serious drone – which he claimed he always
was for the first few days after one of his trips – and promised
to lighten up and turn the conversation all on me.

Not usually the best liar in the world, I amazed myself
with the tall tales I told him. How I was loving training for
the London marathon, where I was hoping to raise money
for Amnesty, and how I wanted to study photography, as
working in Sir Charlie's was just a means to an end for the
moment. Firmly sticking with the name Alice, I shamefully
failed to mention my precious daughter, or the fact that
I was about to have a little TV career of my own. What
was the harm? I reasoned. After all, I was meant to be
keeping my new career a secret, and this guy Rory was
too wholesome to be believed – especially hanging out in

a watering-hole such as this. And it wasn't as if I'd ever see him again. We were just in the middle of tracing Rory's Irish roots when Lisa found her way back to the table, and in a true Princess moment demanded that I accompany her to the toilet. Disgusted that I had to abandon my chat, I tried to ask casually, 'Will you still be here when I get back?'

I was relieved when Rory's reply was a most definite, 'Of course. Don't be long.'

Hyper with excitement, the two of us practically skipped to the Ladies while screaming at each other, 'Oh-my-God! I've so much to tell you.' In the interests of an easy life I suggested Lisa kiss and tell first, in the hope that she might actually listen to me when it came to my turn, instead of going, 'Yeah, yeah, yeah, OK, my go,' like she usually did. Unsurprisingly enough, Lisa just wanted to ask my permission to head off into the night with her new friend and ride him senseless. It appeared the handsome Jason had an apartment close by, and if she didn't leave soon, she'd just have to shag him at the bar, she was so horny.

'Now, how's your own evening going with that bearded new buddy of yours who looks like Gerard Butler?'

Somehow the words, 'I've just met the man I want to marry,' popped out of my mouth without my even thinking it through beforehand. But strangely, I kinda meant it. Rory was a lovely guy, and even though I kept telling myself I would meet my Mr Right in the readymade-meal section at M&S, I felt I had met him here, this night, in between the Friday-night chaos of the gays, the gals and the scantily clad bikini lust-objects.

Having heard it all before, Lisa put her arm around me to give me a squeeze, before sarcastically saying, 'But you want to marry everyone, hon.'

'No I don't,' I argued.

'OK.' Lisa smiled, doing her best to *plámás* me. 'You might not want to marry all the boys, but you do marry more than your fair share of them.'

'Don't be right,' I pleaded. 'Not tonight. I just want have fun and fantasize about being happy. I deserve a future, don't I?'

'Yes, you do. And I deserve a ride. So with that thought, I'm out of here. At some stage remind Parker that he's got a husband at home, and that I'll see him back at the hotel later – or tomorrow. OK, sorry about running off on you like this. I'll phone you to get the skinny on your wedding bells. Let's hope this is third time lucky, eh?'

By the time I had fixed my make-up and returned to the table, Lisa and Jason had already left the bar, and Parker was still practising his tonsil-tennis with Jonathan, and, by the looks of things, fishing for gold. But there, just where I'd left him, was Rory, looking every bit as gorgeous as I remembered. 'That was too long,' he said smoothly, giving me a cheeky wink.

Delighted to be back in his company, I pulled my chair just a little closer to him as I sat down and apologized for the delay. 'My friend needed to say goodbye. She just wanted to let me know that she was going.'

'I saw her.' Rory smiled. 'She looked like she was in a hurry.'

'She's a very spontaneous girl. When she sees something she wants, she just goes for it.' Without meaning to be flirtatious, I had somehow done it all the same, so I stopped myself from saying more, just in case he wasn't interested.

Instantly taking the bait, Rory leaned closer, brushed my

blonde fringe gently out of my eyes and said, 'You're not like most women, are you?'

Embarrassed, all I could offer was, 'I dunno, am I not?'

'No, you're different. You've got soul.'

Trying not to sound too disappointed, I repeated, 'Soul?' Like any other red-blooded female in a nightclub at 1 a.m., I had been hoping for beautiful, or sexy — but soulful? I hadn't seen that one coming.

'You're deep.' Rory sighed, as he continued to play with my hair. 'You're clearly a dedicated follower of fashion.' He laughed, looking down at my crazy outfit. 'But I won't hold that against you. There's a lot more going on behind those gorgeous eyes of yours. And I'd really like to find out more about you.'

As a wave of giddiness rippled up and down my body, I took it upon myself to pay him a compliment as well. 'I think you're deep, too,' I said coyly. 'But I also, more im-portantly, think you're hot. What do you feel about that?'

Stalling for time, he looked up and mused, 'I think . . . emm, I think . . .'

I gently punched his chest and questioned, 'What do you think, big man? I might be a deep thinker, but I'm not a mind reader.'

Before I had a chance to say another word, his eyes swooped down to meet mine, and with a broad smile across his face he told me, 'I think you're the hottest babe I've seen in a long time. I've had two serious relationships in the last fifteen years, and after the last one I spent six months having meaningless sex with random women. That all stopped about a year ago now.'

A little taken aback by his honesty I nodded and said, 'OK.'

But he put one of his large hands gently over my mouth to silence me, and continued, 'I'm not finished yet. Sometimes I'm a little too serious for my own good. I need help with that. But I haven't chatted to a woman, a real person like you, in a long time. So forgive me, I'm a little out of practice. But I just wanted to be completely honest with you. Is that OK?'

A part of my heart sank after the world of lies I had told him, but I nodded again and decided to keep it simple. 'Kiss me.'

Holding my small face in his large hands, Rory pulled me in close and began kissing me. The bristles of his beard rubbed off my face, but they were somehow softer than I had imagined, and his masterful tongue made my body go weak as it bounced around inside my mouth, shooting waves of pleasure around my body. This wasn't just any kiss. This was a demonstration of what a good lover he'd be. He was strong and passionate and, most sexy of all, a real man – unlike the young naive surfer dude I'd last been intimate with. Possibly starting to enjoy the kiss too much, I pulled back to check his eyes and see if he was feeling the same way as me.

'I'm sorry,' said Rory, looking down at his feet.

Unsure what for, I asked, 'Why?'

'I can't help it. I find you incredibly attractive.'

Confused, I asked, 'And the problem is?'

'I want to make love to you. I desperately don't want to be the old me, but I can't help it. I think you're hot!'

Laughing off my nervousness, I grabbed his face and whispered in his ear, 'Well, let's do this. Let's do this now.' Looking around the room for inspiration, I could see a little light bulb go off in his head.

'I've got an idea.' He smiled, while pointing his finger upstairs. 'Do you trust me?'

'Ask me that tomorrow,' I cooed. And with that he took me by the hand and led me towards another door at the end of the room.

Just before we disappeared through it Parker miraculously noticed I was leaving, and stood up. 'Where are you going?' he yelled from across the pool.

Unsure, I just laughed back, 'I don't know, but don't leave without me.' Within seconds I had stepped into yet another world with Rory, a maze of corridors and endless stairs. Finding a door that opened, we discovered a storage room of stacked chairs and bags of laundry, faintly lit by street lights outside the window. It wasn't the most romantic of locations, but I didn't care – the danger of the situation made it sexy enough for me.

Closing the door behind us, Rory pushed me up against it and swiftly asked, 'Are you sure you want to do this?'

'Sure I do.' I smiled back. 'But do you have a condom?'

'I have one.' Rory smiled. 'But I want to taste you first.'

And with that he pinned my arms to the door and began kissing me from my wrists, down my arms, all around my sensitive neck area, before moving lower and lower down my body, across my breasts, over my belly button, and reaching the top of my leggings. Trying not to think about my embarrassing camel toe, I continued to pant with joy as he grunted and groaned while exploring my body with his mouth. He had just began to nibble on my hip bone when we felt a thump coming from the other side of the door. 'Open up!' said a man's voice. 'I know you're in there.' Quickly fixing myself up, I begged for five minutes more, but the voice on the other side wasn't in the mood for bargaining. 'I'm going to count to five, and by that time I want this door open. One . . . Two . . .'

By the count of three Rory had swung open the door and was full of apologies, but the guy wasn't interested in hearing them and just pointed his finger at the stairs. We did what he wanted, albeit while giggling like guilty children. As he marched us back out to the pool area we were told, 'Try that again and you're both out.'

'No way!' Rory argued. 'Apologies again, but you can't exactly blame me, can you? The woman is a doll.'

Amazingly, Parker was just drinking instead of snogging, and welcomed us back to the table with a hand-clap, while announcing, 'Well, that didn't take very long.'

I laughed. 'Coming from the man who spent the last hour holding his breath and making fish faces, I'm surprised you have any grasp on the reality of time whatsoever.'

'Touché,' whooped Parker, while retaking his seat beside Jonathan. 'What can I say? This man is the best kisser. Tomorrow I may be swimming with the fishes, but tonight I've been enjoying the greatest snog-fest a gay married man in London could possibly dream of having.'

That opened up a can of worms. 'You're married?' Jonathan snapped, my cue to move Rory and myself back over beside his friends. As a conversation began between them, I searched in my bag for my phone to check the time. It was 2.45 a.m., and the sight of Daisy smiling back at me from my screen saver didn't help with the guilt. Deciding it was most definitely the right thing to do, I stood up and announced to both Parker and Rory, 'Sorry, lads. I've got to go.'

'Why?' they both asked in unison. But I wasn't for turning, and I wasn't offering up any explanations, either.

Through smart comments like, 'What, will you kick me into submission with your third foot if I don't comply?' Parker eventually gave Jonathan his final kiss, while thanking him profusely for, 'The best non-sex evening of the year.' As we gathered up our coats, I turned back to Rory, who was now looking a small bit lost.

'Was it something I said?' he asked, all sorrowful.

'Not at all. I've just got to go. Thank you for a great night.' As I looked into his face, I wanted to ask to see him again, but I couldn't break my own rule. I had broken it too many times before with disastrous consequences. So unless he asked, I had to hold my head up high and keep walking.

I was just starting to edge away with a polite wave when Rory grabbed my arm and asked, 'That's it? You don't give me your number?' Of course my initial reaction was one of relief that he wanted to see me again, but something told me to play hard to get, even if we had already passed that point after our previous antics upstairs.

So, pretending I was a woman in control, I replied, 'No numbers, Rory. That's too clichéd.' And then confidently kissed him on the cheek and whispered, 'If it's meant to be, it will be.' And I spent the entire taxi-ride home giving Parker hell over how he could have allowed me to be such a stupid, clueless idiot.

6

It wasn't until I went to withdraw money from the bank machine at the local shops that weekend that I realized my wages hadn't gone through.

Still feeling fragile from my big night out on Friday, my Monday morning meeting with Bradley sent my head in a spin. Bradley had fobbed me off on Saturday with, 'There must have been some mix-up, I'll get it sorted next week.' On Monday he had no other option than to tell me the whole truth, once I arrived up to his office first thing and looked him in the eyes.

'I'm so sorry, Eva. The company is having a few solvency issues at the moment, but as soon as things are sorted you'll be the first to know.'

Though I kept asking more and more questions, the answers came back the same. 'When we know, you'll know.' Eventually Bradley snapped. 'We're currently being sued . . . some idiot reckons they were stitched up. Anyway, the bank has temporarily stopped the overdraft. Happy now?'

Due in the office anyway to go through my footage of the previous week, I found the atmosphere an extremely frosty one, partly due to the fact that we were joined by my old friend Billie. So between the company's lack of funds and my lack of dodgy findings, the two hours spent watching me on tape exaggerating the smallest of details could barely be heard over Billie's childlike huffing and sighing.

My final report over, Billie picked a stapler up off the desk and flung it against the wall. 'Utter shite,' she screamed as the stapler fell to the ground. 'We spent months trying to get someone into Sir Charlie's, and then after ALL our background work, this is what you deliver?'

'In my defence, Billie—'

'SHUT UP!' Billie had risen to her feet. 'You can't defend this — it's complete crap. I could have uncovered more simply by looking in the window. This can't go on. Bradley, we need to talk. Alone.'

Shooed out to sit at the same empty desk I was always sent to, my mind raced to try and make sense of the situation. I was just in the middle of questioning my abilities when Carol, the chatty girl I had met on my first day, bounced over to me and asked, 'Hey, what's up? Did you not get your coffee fix yet?' Startled, I jumped up off my seat before I realized who was talking to me, knocking a bundle of envelopes out of her hands. 'Easy does it, girl.' Carol laughed sympathetically. 'You'll do us both an injury.' I made some weak excuse about expecting an important phone call, and Carol chose to ignore my jitters and ask, 'How's London going for ya? Meet any nice men yet?'

I thought about excusing myself to the loo to escape getting into conversation, but decided what the hell, I badly needed a distraction. 'Emm, yeah, I did, actually. I met a very nice Londoner at the weekend. But I never got his number.' Feeling myself slipping back into a confused and depressed state, I quickly added, 'Not to worry, sure. It's nice to know there's someone out there somewhere, I suppose. How about you? Adjusting to single life yet?'

'I'm so glad you asked me that.' She beamed cheerily. 'Because it turns out that I'm no longer single. Well, sort of not. Unofficially, like.'

'Oh, congratulations. In an unofficial kinda way. Did you get back with your ex?'

'Eugh! No way. As if? No, I met a beautiful man by the name of Rory, and, well, I'm smitten. I think he feels it, too. Hey, are you OK?'

Desperately trying to swallow the lump that had skipped into my throat, I probably coughed up one of my lungs before I was able to speak again. 'Sorry . . . about that,' I spluttered in between coughs. 'I don't know what happened there. So eh, Rory, yeah? Unusual name. When did you meet him?'

'Saturday night.' She beamed proudly. 'So as you can im-agine, we're still in the honeymoon period.' I felt ill at the thought of Carol having sex with Rory. *My* Rory. After all, how many Rorys could there be in this city? I decided it was best if I walked away from Carol, just in case my body turned violently uncontrollable. Turning towards the kitchen, I continued to cough as I edged away from her, but instead of leaving me be, she followed. 'Oh, let me get you some water. Sorry, I don't know what I was thinking. I must be dizzy in love. Would you believe he's Irish?' Carol chirped, reaching the water cooler. I swallowed from the cup she thrust at me.

'How Irish?'

'Oirish Irish. Well, he's Northern Irish. From Derry. I can barely understand his accent, but who needs good diction when you've got the language of lurve, eh?' Released from my torture, I burst out laughing as my body relieved itself of stress. 'Yeah, his name is Rory Gallagher, just like the singer. And he's got a big mop of red hair. He's like a shagging cliché, I know, but Christ is he a superstar in the bedroom. He had me at "hello" – and then again at "over here!"'

I was just about to share some of the details of my own Rory love story when the gorgeous blonde receptionist found me and told me that Bradley wanted to speak to me again. Congratulating Carol one last time, I turned on my wedge heels and, like a dead woman walking, dragged myself in the direction of Bradley's office. I took a deep breath the second I heard Bradley call me sternly to come in.

I could see as soon as I entered that Billie wasn't with him, so that instantly took some pressure off. But from the tired look spread across Bradley's face, it was clear that he still had some bad news for me. Trying to make light of the situation, I swiftly breezed in, sat myself down on the seat opposite and told him, 'OK, then, let's do this. Let's get it over with. Am I fired? Do I continue to work for nothing? Hit me.'

Refusing to make eye-contact, Bradley stared at his computer and hit some buttons as he began to talk. 'Well, it's like this, Eva. I like you. You've got great potential—'

'But?' I asked, interrupting.

'But nothing,' replied Bradley, now staring straight at me. 'There are currently some money problems, but that should be sorted out by the weekend. And as for your reports, all they are lacking is newsworthy detail. It's obvious that we're not going to uncover the information we need during the day, so I think we have to get you swapped to working evenings.'

Without thinking I blurted out, 'NO WAY!' before correcting myself with an apology and a quick explanation. 'Sorry, what I mean is, well, evenings are not really suitable for me. With my daughter, you know? I need to put her to bed. She's fine generally, but she's used to me being there at bedtime. I told you she was special needs, didn't I?'

'OK. OK,' snapped Bradley. 'It's not a runner, is what you're trying to tell me. Fine, then. We'll just have to try and get you working nights, then. By that time young . . .' He paused.

'Daisy.'

'Yes, with night shifts you can put Daisy to bed. OK, you'll just be extremely tired when she wakes you up the following morning. But them's the breaks. So tomorrow when you go to Sir Charlie's I need you to put in a request to work nights immediately. Is that understood?' Still in shock, all I could do was nod to acknowledge his request. 'We need to make this documentary happen yesterday,' he continued, 'or else I'm gonna have to listen to Billie bitch about what a bad decision I made hiring you. Is that understood?' I nodded and he continued, 'Come back in five minutes and I'll have some new scripts for you.'

On my way out of his office, my power of speech only returned when I stepped into the path of Peter, who seemed to be charging somewhere in a considerable hurry.

It caught both of us off guard. Peter let out an almighty roar before realizing who I was – and then he pushed me to one side to speak with me in private. 'I've been looking for you,' he growled in a menacing tone. 'Where were you last week? I thought you were playing assistant to Bradders. Did you get lost on the way into the office?'

Feeling like I had been pushed about enough already,

I snapped back, 'Listen here, *Peters*. What's bugging you? I'm not quite sure why you're so fascinated by me, but I don't really have the time for such trivial quizzing, so if you don't mind, I've things to do.' I tried to push past him, but not wanting me to, he firmly stood his ground. Springing off him back to the wall, I could see a mischievous glint in his eye that softened his appearance and, though I tried to ignore it, made him look immediately more attractive. 'Excuse me,' I said, trying to keep a straight face, but my mean look melted as I caught his devilish eyes scanning my face and body.

'You're very sexy when you're angry.' He smirked, un-dressing me very obviously with his eyes. 'I've always wanted to do a mad Irishwoman. Maybe you could tick my box, and I'll lick yours.'

'That's extremely crude talk for a Monday lunchtime. It's not even one o'clock yet.'

'I could have you naked and screaming for mercy by ten past,' returned Peter, elated.

'As much as the idea of begging for freedom sounds, well, interesting, I think I'll pass, thanks. For someone to, emm, lick my box, as you say, there is a protocol. The woman attached to the box needs to be wooed. Manners are everything to us mad Irish, so if you don't mind, I've somewhere to be right now, and it doesn't involve getting sloppy with you.'

Admitting defeat, Peter obediently stepped back and bowed to let me by. He managed to simultaneously give me a mini royal wave and produce a business card out of his back pocket. 'The city can be a lonely place for a Celtic cub like you. I'd hate to think of you out there by yourself, especially when I could be helping to keep you warm.'

'How very generous of you,' I flirted back. 'But who says I don't have someone to warm me up already?'

'Whoever it is, they're not doing a very good job of it,' said Peter confidently. 'I know what a woman looks like when she's getting it good. And your face looks needy.'

Slightly uncomfortable again, I took his card, crumpled it in my hand and threw it over my left shoulder. 'Not interested. Now go annoy someone who hasn't heard this type of bullshit before.'

Not dissuaded, Peter just laughed at the sheer sport of it. Pushing past him, I brushed off his broad well-toned arm and let out a small sigh of appreciation. 'You'll be back,' he said defiantly. 'I'll tame you yet.'

I was twenty minutes pretending to be busy on the internet before Bradley had my new sample scripts prepared and I could leave the building. With Bradley feeling that my pieces to camera were edging on repetitive, I was to go off and learn new ways of saying the same thing, and make provision for my new night-time working schedule.

I must have been a bundle of misery that whole week, as both Helen and Frankie, one of the barmen in Sir Charlie's, told me to smile because I was starting to make the customers feel depressed. Although Craig, the manager, had easily agreed to let me work nights – and set up for me to do Tuesdays, Wednesdays and Saturdays – my mind wasn't on the job, just Rory. Despite my best efforts I couldn't erase him from my mind. All I thought about was his fabulous tongue, and how he had made me feel as he had swept it across my body. How the soft bristles of his beard had tickled my tummy, and how the sincerity in his eyes had made me pine for a relationship. I sorely missed being in a twosome. I always worked best as part of a couple; I just seemed to have problems when it came to keeping a man.

Each day I made a quiet wish that he would walk through the doors of the restaurant brandishing a large bouquet of flowers, proclaiming his love for me. But he never did. Instead I served food to the rich men and women who lunched at Sir Charlie's: more bankers, plenty of cheaters, and hordes of skinny women who thought they were Victoria Beckham, and spent their afternoons pushing salad around their plates before complaining about something in order to avoid paying the bill.

I was like a love-sick teenager. Customers would ask me for salt and pepper and I'd come back with, 'You're welcome, have a nice meal.' If it hadn't been for Daisy finally saying her first clear word – 'Mam-may' – and me catching one of the kitchen porters blatantly swiping bottles of vodka and whiskey on camera, while laughing and saying, 'Fuck the establishment. They're nothing but gangsters who deserve to be robbed,' my week would have been an utter write-off.

Everything altered on Friday afternoon. I was at the end of my final day-shift and just in the middle of changing back into a pair of jeans in one of the female toilets when two blokes ran in and started arguing over a delivery that had fallen on to Craig's desk by mistake. They obviously thought they were alone as I hadn't closed the cubicle door, yet was still hidden inside it, so I calmly pressed 'record' on my ever-ready camera, just in case it might pick up their conversation. Terrified of making a sound, I stood frozen to the cistern, moving just to switch my mobile phone to silent.

'The bastard is refusing to hand it back,' continued the first guy.

'Well, how far do you want to take this?' asked the other.

'As far as we need to,' continued the first. The following ten minutes were possibly the longest of my life, matched only by the horror I had experienced during childbirth. During that time the men, who sounded like Londoners, discussed their terrifying plan of action. The first one went on, 'The only way forward with this idiot is hard-ball tactics. We've got to convince Craig to see sense – the brutal way. If he doesn't hand over the blow he'll be sorry when his bitch comes home with a knifed-smile across *her* face.'

Almost laughing at the sport of it, the second guy chuckled. 'Let's spook him till he cracks,' he said. And then, as quick as they had arrived, they abruptly left the bathroom – and me quaking in my boots.

Terrified to leave, I must have stayed there another twenty minutes, with several more staff coming in and out going about their business, before I plucked up the courage to bolt. Afraid to check my camera for sound quality, I stuffed it to the bottom of my bag and breezed out of the restaurant doing my best to look casual. If anyone had stopped me and asked a question I'd probably have passed out with the fear. Luckily, I managed to avoid everyone. I scurried up to the front door and looked at the new security staff throwing shapes to the crowd. Were they the thugs who had been in the loo threatening to cut up Craig's girlfriend's face? And who was his girlfriend, anyway?

Quietly acknowledging the men as I waved goodbye, I got an evil feeling about them as they looked me up and down with obvious disapproval, so I picked up my speed, hoping to get away as quickly as possible, and stupidly went smashing straight into someone as I turned my head.

But it wasn't just any someone. It was Rory. My Rory. He caught me in his two strong hands. The impact knocked him back a couple of steps, making him cry out, 'There she is!'

Not sure if I was hallucinating, I took a couple of moments to stare at his face before I knew for sure that it was him. He somehow looked a bit different to how I remembered him. Taller, maybe, and also friendlier, or sweeter . . . I wasn't sure yet. With my heart still racing from the stress of listening to a woman's disfigurement being plotted, I was having trouble finding the words to speak to Rory. 'What? Eh, how? Eh . . .'

'Slow down.' Rory smiled calmly. 'It's OK. I didn't mean to startle you.'

Not knowing my own mind, I mumbled, 'I can't . . . stay here . . . I need to go . . .' while struggling to get out of his grasp. Clearly disappointed by the lack of a welcome, Rory's face dropped as he tried to get my attention.

'I'm not here by accident,' he explained, trying to make my eyes look into his. 'I came here for you. I thought I had missed you – they told me you had finished over an hour ago.'

'I did. I just got delayed.' As I spoke I kept looking over my shoulder to see if the bouncers were looking at me. They weren't, but it didn't stop me from checking. Trying to regain my composure, I shook myself and coaxed Rory to walk away from Sir Charlie's by linking arms with him and walking towards the Tube station.

'OK, this is better,' teased Rory as he gently poked me

in the ribs. 'We're walking – together – that's something, I suppose. But are you not pleased to see me? I thought you'd be happy.'

Once we got walking down a different road, my pulse rate started to slow down and the reality of seeing him again made my heart skip to a different beat.

'My apologies.' I smiled, pushing him up against the hoarding of a rundown building. 'For being so scatty. You just got me at a bad moment.'

Smiling down at me with his piercing green eyes, his hands slipped to my waist, and he asked, 'Is there any way I could make this moment better? A kiss, maybe?'

'Gosh, you leave me hanging for a week, and now we're straight back to kissing. Some guys just can't make up their minds.'

'Hold on a minute, you're the one playing hard to get. I was just giving you some space to miss me. So – did it work?' As if we were magnetically charged, the two of us were now rubbing noses and giggling like we hadn't a care in the world.

Not willing to risk playing any more games, I threw caution to the wind and whispered, 'Yes, it did. Very much so.'

Taking that as his green light, Rory leaned down to kiss me. The first was a gentle one on the lips, but he followed it up with something much more passionate. He pulled back from me, and my eyes were still closed as he whispered, 'I missed you, too. Actually, I haven't stopped thinking about you all week.'

Stretching up to rub off his nose again, I cooed back at him, 'You're such a tease. You're a very naughty boy for leaving me hanging.'

'And what happens to naughty boys?' asked Rory with a hopeful chuckle.

'They get to walk me to the Tube, that's what.'

Confused, Rory tilted his head to one side and asked, 'Where are you going?'

Not knowing a funny way to play it, I just answered, 'Home.'

Thinking I was joking, Rory began tickling me again, 'Ha ha! Very funny. You're not getting away from me that easily. I won't let you go. I've reservations at The Wolseley, and I've a wallet full of money that I only want to spend on buying you champagne. And that's just for starters. It's Valentine's Day tomorrow, don't you want to be romanced?'

'No, I'm serious, Rory, I'm not playing. I genuinely have to go home. I'm sorry. Of course I'd love to be wined and dined, but I can't go for dinner now.' No sooner had the words popped out of my mouth than I made the decision to text Maura and see if I could pull a late one again.

Although I could imagine the questions on the tip of his tongue, I begged for silence as I pressed send on a text to Maura. I didn't have to wait long for a reply. The answer was a definite, 'No chance.'

Trying not to show my disappointment, I just smiled at Rory and made my voice sound upbeat. 'I'm sorry, but I've things to do. A girl needs advance warning. I just can't be expected to drop everything on the promise of champagne, you know.'

'But what about last week?' asked Rory with a serious face. 'Didn't you tell me your friends surprised you then?'

Starting to feel backed into a corner, I could only mumble, 'Yes, but that was a special exception. I'm sorry, I really am.'

Not waiting for a reply, I shook his arm and asked, 'Please walk me to the Tube. I'm sorry, it's just I'm really late as it is.'

Doing as I asked, we walked on soberly for several minutes before he asked, 'Do you have another date?'

'I wish. I mean, chance would be a fine thing. I mean, definitely not. I just have to go home. It's a family commitment, that's all. I'm just expected home.'

That was the last of his questions, other than what my mobile number was, and we walked arm in arm the rest of the way to Knightsbridge station, making plans to try again the following week, when, as he put it, 'You'll have plenty of notice to beautify yourself.'

As we said goodbye, we kissed again, but just on the lips, and I was sure the disappointment I could see in his eyes was reflected in mine. We were just about to separate when Rory asked, 'Can I come back with you? I'd love to meet your family.' Gobsmacked, I let out a tiny squeal, stuck for a way to get out of the bind I'd created for myself with my string of lies. Like a dog with a bone, he continued, 'Why not? Unless you'd be embarrassed to be seen with me – would you?'

I barely managed the words, 'Of course not, don't be silly—'

Rory interrupted, 'That's agreed, then.'

The frustration made me snap. 'You're not coming home with me. I mean, how the hell would I explain you? Oh, hey, everyone, this is the guy I pulled and almost shagged last Friday night. Is it OK if he stays for dinner?'

Unlike most men, Rory didn't argue back. Instead he just said, 'You're right. It's too soon. As much as it would be lovely to have our first milestone argument out of the way,

I agree that tonight is not the night. I'm sorry for pushing you. Forgive me?'

Relieved not to have to tell him the truth – just yet – I kissed him again, only this time like a lover, and each time his tongue touched off mine it sent teasing shocks of pleasure shooting across my body, which made me extremely horny and lustful for more. Bubbling with excitement as I walked away down towards the escalators, I found it hard to process the level of emotions I had felt, all within the last hour. I hadn't even boarded the train when I received my first text from him. 'Sorry for being cheesy,' it read, 'but I miss U already xx.'

My thirty-minute train journey was one of fun and relief. In between Rory's frequent texts telling me everything from how sweet I smelled to how he could still taste me, I listened to snippets from my camera, and was able to make out the men's chat perfectly. Things were finally on the up and up for my career, and in the love stakes. All I needed to do to take things a step forward was call Bradley with my latest news, but the idea of telling Rory that I had a daughter was a lot harder to come to terms with.

The thought of confessing this scared me. What if it frightened him away? The concept of spending time with another man's child was off-putting enough for most men. Add in the fact that Daisy was special needs, and I'd probably never hear from Rory again. Then again, why would I want to be with a man who wouldn't accept my daughter just the way she was? My brain was running too fast for me to concentrate and I missed my stop, so it took me another twenty minutes to get back. It was beginning to feel like the never-ending journey.

As soon as I had escaped the crush of the underground

I called Bradley, who enthusiastically congratulated me for being so brave, and then asked if I wanted to go out for a celebratory drink. My reply was interrupted by his speeding brain as he then quickly decided he needed someone to stake out Sir Charlie's immediately and hung up the phone to make arrangements.

Back home at last, I walked into the living room only to find Daisy already asleep and tucked up in a ball on the couch. Maura's daughter Kelly had her arm protectively around her and a worried look on her young face. 'She was crying for ages, so I sang her "The Climb" over and over to calm her down.' So much for my situation improving. While I had been off playing Miss Marple and flirting with a man I really hardly knew, my daughter had been crying herself to sleep. That night I was a little clumsy with Daisy as I carried her to bed, in the hope that she just might wake up and I could make amends. Despite doing her best Sleeping Beauty act all the way up the stairs, just as I lowered her under the duvet on my bed she finally opened her beautiful big eyes, softly said, 'Mam–may', and smiled, before closing them again and drifting off back to sleep.

With both of us at peace with the world and each other, I didn't feel guilty about spending the rest of the evening text-flirting with Rory. Of course I would have to come clean with him about everything eventually, but not yet. After all, he, too, deserved a little fun after all the stress he'd been through with work, and, well, I was a single woman and at heart a little bit of a diva. And there was no better stress–reliever, to my mind, than some sexy bloke to obsess over.

The next morning, I woke to the sound of a text beeping through on my phone. It wasn't Rory this time, though, but my boss. Bradley's text read, 'The stakes have just gotten higher. Turn on *Sky News*.' Disturbing all the early-morning risers from their daily dose of *Spongebob Squarepants*, I flicked the channel only to read the tickertape racing across the bottom of the screen: MAN SHOT IN LONDON NIGHTCLUB . . . POLICE CALLING FOR WITNESSES . . .' Unable to hear myself think, I changed the TV back to the cartoons and ran back upstairs in a panic to text Bradley, 'What the hell should I do?'

His reply said, 'Nothing for now. I'll speak with our lawyers and get back to U . . . Send your address again so I can send a bike to collect your camera. We need that asap.'

Chomping my nails to the stubs I sat at the top of the stairs and texted Bradley again. 'I'm scared. Should I be scared?'

Within seconds his reply beeped back. 'I don't know. But don't breathe a word to anyone.'

7

'Can you believe that Jeff has taken up knitting?'

'Translate that?'

'You heard me – KNITTING,' screeched Parker down the phone line. 'Yes, that's right, my butch husband has chosen to spend his evenings playing with balls of yarn, instead of my big juicy—'

'THANK YOU, thank you,' I interrupted, not wanting to be left with a graphic visual.

'And what's worse is he's become obsessed with it. When he's not knitting he's online chatting about yarn with other knitters, and he literally lobs it out wherever it takes his fancy.'

Chuckling to myself at the ridiculousness of the idea, I joked, 'But I thought that was part of the reason you loved him: his ability just to flop it out any time, any place, any-where, like a Martini barmaid.'

'Mmmm, indeed. The problem is I'm the only one turning floppy with this old lady business. This is getting serious, Eva. First he started off small, but now he's getting all sorts of shit delivered to the house. There are bags of it arriving.'

'Have you thought about combining the online orders with some hardcore porn? Then at least you'd have some chance of saving your sex life, and the postman won't think you're freaks.'

'Too late for that, methinks. So, any news with you?'

I was juggling Daisy on one knee and keeping a wary eye on the TV for any news on the Sir Charlie's murder. No doubt sounding absurdly defensive, I snapped, 'NO. No. Everything fine, dull, quiet, uneventful. Have you been speaking to Lisa at all? She texted me Wednesday, but I never got a chance to reply to her.'

Knowing something was up, Parker started his loud fake-coughing routine before asking, 'You've a salacious tale to tell me. What is it? You can't hide from me, my pretty, so just spit it out.'

It was now the Sunday morning, a full twenty-four hours since I had heard about a man being shot dead in Sir Charlie's, and I was like a cat on a hot tin roof, waiting for instructions from Bradley. As yet, I was unsure if the man killed was one of the gangsters I had overheard in the staff toilet, or if it was even Craig, for that matter. So it was taking all my powers of self-restraint to keep sane – and most of all to keep quiet. Back in my twenties I had been a massive fan of thrillers and horror movies, and those scary stories had taught me, above all, never to put anyone else's life in danger. Right now it was bad enough that I had overheard threats being made, but somehow telling Parker – or anyone else other than Bradley – felt like I would be burdening them with a death sentence. I knew I would have to lie to protect my secret, but it was near impossible to lie to Parker, since he knew me inside out – on occasions even better than I knew myself. Thinking quickly, I joked that the connection on the phone was really bad, so I could buy myself some time to think of a make-believe story.

Now more curious than ever, Parker demanded answers. 'Ms Valentine, start talking. What have you done? Or better still, what has been done to you?'

Good ol' Parker, always bringing the conversation back to sex. I straightaway thought of Rory. Thank Christ. 'OK, OK!' I pretended I was backed into a corner. 'If you must know . . . My cameraman Rory has been in touch. And we've kissed again.'

'Woohoo! Happy belated Valentine's Day to you. Any other bodily fluids?'

'Nope.'

'Liar liar, uncomfortable diamanté thong on fire.'

'Parker, that's the truth.' My throat constricted as I spoke. Although it was the truth, it was only one truth in a now growing list of secrets. 'He's even more lovely than I remembered him,' I gushed, while doing my best to sidetrack myself as well as him. 'And he's got really cute freckles across his nose, too.'

Instantly distracted, Parker teased, 'Keep me updated as to where else those cute freckles of his are hiding. I need naughty thoughts to entertain me while Bridie here sings out her knit-one, purl-one hymns. It's like I'm living with a ninety-year-old woman. All we're missing is the stinky old smell of mothballs – throw that into the mix and I might just have to die of a broken heart. Listen, speaking of a broken heart, when do you plan on coming back for a weekend? I miss you.'

'Ah, that's sweet. I miss you, too – some of the time. But I can't really come back.'

'Why not? Gotta keep your weekends open for the freckled boy?'

'No, don't be stupid, though I'm hoping things might develop that way. But no, I've managed to sublet my Dublin flat, so I'd have nowhere to stay if I came home. Anyway, I only saw you last weekend. If I was in Dublin, I might not see you from one end of the month to the next. Just goes to show that despite yourself, you really are just a typical man at heart really, eh? You just don't know what you got till it's gone.'

'God, I'm such a bitch for missing my friend. My deepest apologies for lumbering you with my inner thoughts.'

Parker was coming out with all the huffing and puffing sounds that would usually make me feel guilty, or at the very least a tad remorseful for neglecting him, but he was outgunned by the TV screen in front of me. 'TWO MEN SHOT DEAD IN CENTRAL LONDON: SUSPECTED GANGLAND REPRISAL' was running below the *Sky News* reporter's mike. The sight of it jolted me back to reality. Thank God Parker only followed *Xposé*. Speaking in the coldest voice, I said, 'Parker, I love you, but I really have to go. Talk soon, yeah?' I hung up the phone before he got a fighting chance to answer. I was desperate to speak to Bradley, but after fielding question after worried question from me he'd put a moratorium on calls. I texted him instead with the news that there had been two more men shot dead in the city, and asked, 'Would they be connected?'

Despite willing the phone to beep back a reassuring answer, nothing came. Over lunch with the Maguire clan I must have texted six more messages, ranging from, 'I'm worried for my safety,' to, 'If you don't settle my nerves quick, I might just have to quit!' But there was still no reply. I was halfway through an aggravated text blasting his silent treatment as unacceptable when I realized he hadn't replied to any texts I had sent him on a Sunday that I could remember. What was it that he did today that kept him from answering urgent messages? I continued writing my text to vent the frustration I was feeling but, by the time I'd finished, I thought it best just to delete it. If he hadn't replied to any of my earlier ones, I couldn't imagine he'd be interested in answering one of the none-too-seductive, 'You can go fuck yourself, and your documentary' variety.

After a tense day of snapping at everyone, and being no more the wiser as to where or by whom the latest men had been shot, a message from Bradley beeped through that made my heart sink further. 'Sorry, pls don't quit. My girlfriend sick. Been in hospital all day. No news on shooting. Talk tomorrow. Won't put U back in if 2 dangerous.' Although I tried to word a sympathetic text, I kept deleting it back to a simple, 'Sorry xx.' I then went around the house and apologized to everyone I had barked at that day before climbing into bed for an early night with Daisy.

I just wanted the weekend over. Tomorrow would be a new day, and I was doing my best to stay positive. I was lying in bed staring at the ceiling and listening to the random traffic outside the house when a text beeped through on my phone. Jumping up to catch it early so it wouldn't wake Daisy, I knocked it open to read the name MICHAEL CAFÉ. It was my ex-husband. For some reason the name I'd designated for him in my phone hadn't changed in the short time that we had gone from dating, to getting married, to complete disaster zone. Asking myself if this weekend had been cursed, I closed my eyes as I opened the text, only opening them when the suspense became too much. Adjusting my eyes to the screen, I had to squint for a couple of seconds before I could read the words, 'Hi. We need to talk. I'm sick.'

Probably not as receptive to his announcement as I should have been, I quickly texted back, 'Sorry. Who this?' just to send him the clear message that I was most definitely over him. Knowing my style, he quickly texted back, 'Eva. I'm not looking to play games. Can you give me a good time to talk tomorrow? It's about Daisy.' While I initially thought that he could be dying, and possibly thinking of leaving some money to Daisy, my imagination then started to get the better of me and flipped to terrible thoughts of genetic conditions. With images of Michael having passed something terrible to Daisy *and* to me running through my head, and with my heart thumping in my mouth, I somehow managed to text back, '8.30 a.m. pls' with the shakiest of hands. 'Thank you. Talk tomorrow,' he beeped back, finishing with not one but two xes.

I lay awake the entire night, experiencing every emotion from bad to worse, my worried tears eventually easing to gentle sobs. I suspected that whatever the outcome of my phone call with my ex the following morning, my life, and the life of my precious daughter, was going to be much worse off. I had spent many angry nights during what I called my 'former Eva years' wanting to smash Michael's smug face in, and until that night I had felt that I had moved on from the deep resentment I harboured for him and let go of all my abandonment issues. But this new threat my ex-husband was holding over me made all the revulsion and rage I had suppressed come flooding back.

My eyes were as sore as if they'd been attacked with wire

wool by the time I got up at 7.00 a.m. And sheer exhaustion made my body feel like it had swum the English Channel overnight. Thinking the worst was inevitable, I had tried to Google on my phone possible conditions that Michael could have passed on to Daisy. Despite being a journalist, I had never been great at navigating the internet, so after several stabs at it I gave up my search for information after I keyed in 'diseases transmittable between parent & child', and the links showed up: 'Why Do Teens Have Unprotected Sex?', 'Gum Disease Between Family Members', and 'Herpes From Sharing Dessert?'

Although I knew that obsessing over the possibilities wasn't going to give me anything other than high blood pressure, no amount of counting Barbies or reciting Leaving Cert poetry could clear my mind of ominous thoughts.

I kept my head down and I rushed in and out of the kitchen as the Maguire posse went about their usual manic breakfast routine. Scared of blurting out my fears, I shared minimal chat with Maura as I explained, 'Daisy is fine with her bottle, and she'll be happy listening to one of her CDs.'

By 8.01 a.m. I was out the door and on my way in to Brady Reel Time Films. Just like Bradley had promised, my wages had gone through by Friday evening, but such money matters seemed meaningless compared to the issues I would have to confront today, between the dead men and – well, I couldn't even contemplate any further illness or possible death until I'd spoken to Michael. Bang on half past eight he rang me. I was sitting on an overcrowded train, and even though I couldn't remember the last time I had actually spoken to him, the sound of his voice immediately catapulted me back to my old life. It suddenly felt like only yesterday since I had seen, touched and held him.

'How'r'ya doin'?' he asked casually, out of politeness as much as anything, I suspected.

'Shite,' I answered grumpily. 'I didn't sleep a wink last night trying to work out what you were insinuating. So what's up? How sick are you?' We may once have been very much in love, albeit briefly, but I couldn't allow myself to show any more emotion to the man. He had wooed me, married me, made me pregnant – and then abandoned me and our baby. Even though he had made himself another life with my former best friend, and didn't keep in any kind of regular contact, we were always going to be connected through Daisy. But that in no way meant I needed to be sympathetic or nice to him.

Narky back, Michael snapped, 'Nothing ever changes with you, Eva, does it?'

'Oh, nothing changes with me, Michael, except nappies, living arrangements, general stuff like that. I've got responsibilities keeping me busy, but of course you're not familiar with that term. So, tell me, Michael, what do you need to get off your chest? I'm all ears.' At the end of my rant there was nothing but silence at the end of the phone. Curious to see if he had hung up on me, I carefully asked, 'Hello. Anyone there?'

'Are you finished?' came his reply.

Not wanting to back down too easily I snapped back, 'For now,' and then held my tongue in anticipation. My heart and stomach were pounding in my throat, almost jumping out of my mouth. Panic was starting to grip me as endless medical conditions flashed through my head. Daisy had already been sicker than one little person ever deserved to be. I never wanted her to see the inside of a hospital again, other than to meet and greet a younger brother or sister. So all I could do, while armed with nothing but a mother's natural protective instincts, was to beg. 'Michael, just spit it out please. You're killing me here.'

Although we could have continued sparring at greater length, he generously ended the suspense with the news: 'I've got a blood-clotting disorder, Eva.'

Taken aback, I was confused. 'What's that? And why are you sharing this with me? I'm not the one who has to make you chicken soup any more.'

'It's a hereditary disease, Eva. Daisy could have hereditary thrombophilia. You'll need to get her checked out. I've got some V-Factor, and Daisy has a fifty-fifty chance of having it also.'

'You couldn't have the X-Factor, no? All the drama there's been in our lives and you decide to have the V-Factor. I've heard it all, now.'

'It's not a definite, Eva. I'm sorry, but she should be tested. Myself and Maddie are bringing the baby to see a specialist next week.'

'Oh, what an inconvenience that must be for Maddie! I hope she doesn't have to miss out on lunch with all the other husband-robbing whores who she probably hangs out with now.'

'Anger is a normal reaction, Eva, so I'm gonna understand that you're hurting.'

'That's big of you. Are you also gonna pay for the specialist, considering you've paid for nothing else for Daisy?' He seemed taken aback at such a request, and I could hear him mumbling with confusion at the other end of the phone. 'Well?' I asked abruptly. 'She's your daughter, and you're the one who gave her this. Are you going to do the right thing and pay for her tests and, God forbid, her treatment if she needs any?' Trembling with anger, I needed to get off the phone quick before I started to lose it completely on the Tube and someone had me committed.

His answer was a weak, 'Yes, of course,' but at that moment it was probably the best I could expect to hear.

Not able to cope with the logistics of organizing every-thing, I rushed him off the phone as I approached the underground part of my journey and the reception threatened to disappear. 'I can't focus properly right now. I'll call you later,' were my final words.

As if my world wasn't crashing down around me enough already, I ran all the way to the Brady Reel Time Films offices and went straight to the computer on that lonely desk to Google 'blood-clotting diseases' instead of asking directly to speak to Bradley. I didn't get much time for my research, though. Bradley was soon out of his office and calling over. 'Inside when you're ready please, Alice,' he requested.

Trying to buy more time, I shouted, 'Five more minutes, please, Bradley . . .'

But he wasn't feeling charitable. 'Now, THANK YOU very much,' came his sarcastic reply.

It was only as I walked through the door of his office that I remembered that his girlfriend had been extremely sick at the weekend. With all my own dramas I had completely forgotten to enquire about her wellbeing. 'I was sorry to hear about your girlfriend. Is she OK now? Are you OK?'

'Not really. She's still in hospital, some problem with the mechanics of her brain. And I'm pretty shattered too,' came his response. 'But undercover documentaries – with associated dead bodies – aren't going to make themselves now, are they?'

Choosing to ignore his obvious pain, I thought it best to continue our discussion all businesslike and stick to the facts of the situation surrounding Sir Charlie's. After all, up there with Daisy's possible health concerns were my own health and safety issues. 'So what's the latest on the deaths? Who was killed? Were those second shootings linked? And should I go to the police about what I heard?' With my mind already in a whirl from the morning I'd had, a barrage of uncensored questions came flooding out as soon as I opened my mouth. But although he looked shell-shocked, Bradley still managed to take it in his stride.

'OK, it's like this. As far as we can work out, the person shot at Sir Charlie's was not an employee. Our intelligence has told us it was a private feud, yes, drugs-related, but nothing, it seems, to do with our guys. It was just a coincidence.'

'Really? Pretty extreme sort of coincidence, don't you think? It might not have been a staff member who died. But who's to know it wasn't one of those bouncer guys I heard in the toilets? There's a smoking gun in the picture, and I don't want it to be pointed at my head. Do you hear where I'm coming from on this?'

'Don't start, Eva—'

'ALICE, please.'

'Sorry, Alice. Yes, I do understand, and let me reassure you, I don't want any more blood on my shirt this week. My heart's not able for it. Now, do you believe me when I say that? I would not, and will not, put you in jeopardy. But I do need you to go back to work this week.'

'With my body camera?'

'Very much so. You're gonna need it all the time, so I

suggest you organize some sort of decorative hairpiece or headband to put it in, since that dress of yours is too revealing. Busy up that blonde mop of yours, and keep the camera phone charged twenty-four seven.' Stressed at the thought of having to recreate some sort of Amy Winehouse beehive, and smuggle a camera into it into the bargain, all I could do was sigh heavily, which didn't seem to be appreciated by Bradley. 'What's the problem here?' His eyes burrowed into mine in a menacing fashion. 'Scared of a bit of work? This is the job, Alice. You are not standing in a cosy studio somewhere reading a fucking autocue, and that's reflected in your high salary. It's called danger money, honey. That's why you're on the big bucks. *Capiche?*'

With nothing to keep me in the office that afternoon, I cheekily texted Rory to see if he was about. I desperately needed something – or better yet someone – to distract me from my dire situation. Michael had graciously texted me again to say that the tests that Daisy needed didn't have to be done immediately as it wasn't an urgent threat. But, much as it shamed me to admit it, my heart couldn't deal with going home to look at my little girl's trusting face now I had learned what might be in store for her further down the line. The new man in my life was at least one area where something positive might be just around the corner.

Rory's reply was mercifully speedy. 'I'm about – R U?' Within an hour we had met up, and within another we were sitting cuddling at some art-house movie off Shaftesbury Avenue. He had had an afternoon of diving planned, seemingly his favourite activity when he had a break from work, but he cleared his diary, 'Immediately – if not before!' to spend a few hours with yours truly.

Since this was our first official – if last-minute – date, Rory wouldn't allow me to even buy the popcorn: 'I'd look like a cheapskate! If word got out I'd never get laid again!'

Although I laughed, I wasn't sure if he was treating our fledgling relationship seriously. I was sure I felt a connection on my side, I just hoped he was feeling something, too. I would have to take things slowly and not rush the situation too much. OK, so secretly what I wanted in the long term was a daddy for Daisy, and possibly another child also, but as far as Rory was concerned we were just two singles out on a spontaneous date, having a laugh. Getting serious too fast could be my downfall. It had been before. If only I was a better liar! I was useless at keeping secrets. And yet a big part of me hated myself for being as good at it as I had been up to now.

Trying not to over-analyse things, I ignored some of his frivolous comments about his pet hates, deciding that most of them were born out of nervous chitter-chatter. His remark that, 'All kids are brats under the age of twenty-four,' was, I felt, a little harsh. Not to mention his description of, 'Single mothers who drop off their sprogs to cinemas thinking it's a babysitting service, without any regard for people like us, who might like to do some canoodling in private.' Not wanting him to put me off any further, I planted a big kiss on his lips in order to shut him up. Unsurprisingly enough, it worked a treat, and before I realized it we were snogging extremely passionately, as if we were alone in the dark on our own.

For some reason, though, my brain wouldn't allow me to enjoy the moment for long. Yes, his manly tongue did taste sweet, and had the power to delight in places that probably shouldn't be delighted of a Monday afternoon, but images of my daughter playing with Maura kept flashing through my head, as did the gruesome faces of those bouncers standing outside Sir Charlie's. And then, for some reason, I started visualizing my mother giving out to me, complaining that I was once again letting myself down by not playing the game: the make-men-wait dating game. The sight of my mother, real or imaginary, was just too much to take, and I quickly pulled back from our marathon snog to ask, 'How much do you like me?' I immediately knew I had said the wrong thing. How stupid could I be? Did I never learn from previous mistakes? As a confused, pained look shot across his face, I made the decision to stop him in his tracks for fear he'd say something unbearable like, 'I like ya, but I don't like you that much when you come on all heavy.'

Quickly, I whispered, 'Do you like me enough to take me out again on the town, I mean? I'm working Tuesday, Wednesday and Saturday nights, but maybe we could have a little fun afterwards?'

Visibly relieved, his face lit up, and he said, 'I think I like you that much all right. In fact, I might even like you enough to take you out every night this week. If you let me?'

Doing my best to be non-committal, a tip Lisa always urged me to use, I seductively licked my lips, and after wiggling the tip of my tongue for a few seconds like an anaconda smelling its prey, I chuckled. 'Oh, I'm not sure I like you that much.' Then I smacked another kiss on his lips and teased, 'But maybe if you try a little harder you might win me over.'

Just as our kissing turned more serious, an usher came down and started shining her torch in our direction. 'If you don't keep it down, you'll have to leave,' she demanded. 'If you want to see a skin flick, take it down the road.' Apologizing through fits of giddy laughter, we eventually managed to make her leave with promises of good behaviour. Although Rory playfully teased that he had the expertise to film his own skin flick with just his trusty Nokia, while waving his mobile around in a very masterful fashion to show off his capabilities, we actually did end up watching the rest of the movie and snuggled throughout in a very loving way.

After pizza slices and full-fat Cokes, Rory walked me to the Tube, and the last thing he said to me as he left lifted my heart. 'This was the best afternoon delight I've had in years. Just being with you has made me so happy.' Although I tried not to read too much into his words, I must have sat on the train with a broad smile across my face the entire way home. I focused on his positive attributes – like his ability to kiss and make me laugh – and chose to ignore his dislike for children and his suggestion about making Paris-Hilton-style home movies; those issues were for another, less fraught, day.

Sure, I would have to return to reality as soon as I arrived home, and tomorrow would bring its own challenges with my first night-shift at Sir Charlie's, but for now I was happy. The bright lights seemed brighter, the big city no longer as cold. I was no longer just a lost little Irish girl, fading away into the background. My idle fantasies deemed me an attractive woman making her way in the big city, a woman who had a handsome suitor willing to drop his friends in order to spend an afternoon of quality time with her. OK, so I would have to cheat the crooks and hide a camera in my hair tomorrow night, but I laughed quietly to myself as I thought of the famous song: 'Bright Lights, Big City'. That would indeed have to become my theme tune . . .

*   *   *

Looking like a cross between Gary Glitter and Marge Simpson, I stepped out on to the floor of Sir Charlie's with a strange sense of confidence. I wasn't sure where it came from – it sure as hell wasn't from my appearance – but I somehow reasoned that this was a dog-eat-dog place, and unless I chose to embrace my task I would just be overwhelmed by it.

Unlike daytime, Sir Charlie's by night was a much noisier hangout. Although it still functioned as a restaurant, it was mainly a nightclub – with more people just drinking at the tables, and, of course, the occasional reveller dancing around them. Despite it being just an ordinary Tuesday, the place was full and showed no signs of being affected by the recession.

Although it was hard not to get caught up in the fun of simply working in a hip restaurant, I bounced back into reporter mode after overhearing two blokes walking to the toilets, one of them saying, 'I've picked up an 8 bomb.' Watching them return, I discreetly followed them back to their table to discover that my old pal Tanya Cruze was sitting among their group of friends.

Terrified that she would recognize me, I tried to walk away as quickly as possible, but had no choice but to acknowledge her presence after she clicked her fingers at me, demanding, 'Sparkling water, doll. And another round of Red Bull when ya get a chance.' Despite the fact that I'd eyeballed her for a moment too long, it was obvious that my appearance was in no way familiar to her. But my delayed response did make her a little stroppy. 'Can I 'elp ya?' she asked, looking bemused.

'No, sorry,' I replied with a big smile. 'I was just admiring your necklace. It's really pretty. Your drinks will be with you right away.' As I turned to head to the bar, I listened out to hear if there was any late recognition, but there were no unusual comments to be heard. It seemed I was utterly incognito. And so far, so was my camera. All I needed to do now was hang around and watch the party kick off.

I began to keep a guarded eye on Tanya's table and her 8-bomb pals, and it wasn't long before I started noticing neighbouring tables pop pills. Or at least, that's what I thought I was seeing. Without needing to stare at anyone, I was able to go about my business waiting the tables while my hidden camera, or, as I was secretly calling it, my third eye, did all the work. Feeling like some undercover vigilante, I was beginning to warm to the thrill of the chase. Everywhere I looked now, women were swallowing pills at their tables and men were busily walking to and from the toilets, feverishly wiping their noses. This was a total drugs haven. It was obvious now why Bradley had chosen this place to represent modern culture. And as the mood of the place became more excitable, the punters became louder and my job as a reporter a heck of a lot easier.

After witnessing Tanya scream, 'I've lost my bag . . . Who's got some more drugs?' I knew it was time for me to slip off and record a report. Checking that the coast was clear, I removed my high-tech camera phone from my locker and took myself out to my familiar base in the storeroom to record my monologue. Energized by my WAG-spotting, I nestled myself behind a mountain of beer boxes and started filming. 'It's Tuesday,' I began, with a smug TV accent. 'And there's no sign of cutbacks in Sir Charlie's. Everywhere I look the party people are popping pills, and even celebrities such as Tanya Cruze are on the hunt for drugs. The former

WAG was only caught snorting cocaine in the toilets here several weeks ago, yet despite being publicly outed in the newspapers, the glamour model has returned to the scene of the crime and is looking for more action. I'm not sure who's supplying the drugs here – that's if they are being dealt here at all. I still need proof. But I've my suspicions that—'

Hearing a noise behind me, I quickly switched off my camera phone. Jumping up I moved directly into the eye-line of Craig the manager. 'What are you doing?' His voice was gruff and he looked to be scanning the storeroom for any other absentee waiting staff.

'Ehhh, I was just on a call,' I offered weakly, while waving my fancy-looking phone around for effect.

Unconvinced, he barked a series of questions at me. 'What the fuck were you doing in here? Were you looking for some booze to hide in your bag? Were you looking to have a little private party of your own?'

With Craig growling in my face, and with no space for me to step back out of his way, I was sure the microphone in my backcombed fro would explode from the sheer volume of his voice. Amazingly, I remained extremely calm and smiled back at him, explaining, 'Of course not, Craig. I really was just talking on the phone.' For some reason I took strength from knowing that I wasn't totally alone. My hidden Big Brother camera made me feel strangely protected. Determined to put his mind at ease, I stressed the point again, 'I just had an important phone call to make . . . and, well, I needed some privacy, not booze. I'm sorry, I didn't mean to upset you. Listen, I better get back out there. It won't happen again during my shift.'

Moving as quickly as I could, I strode past Craig, and deposited my phone back into my locker further down the hall. The close call made my heart pump faster, and I was starting to lose my composure. It felt like I'd never get back out on to the floor. Checking around my neglected tables, I apologized for my absence and asked each of my customers if they needed any more drinks from the bar. One by one they all asked for water, and it seemed as if the mood of the room had changed. No longer the restaurant I was familiar with, it now felt like some sort of a hardcore rave club. Even the music had altered. It was harder and faster in pace. I was just working my way back up to Tanya's table, where the lovely lady seemed to be wiping something over her gums, when a heavy hand grabbed me from behind.

'Where do you think you are going?' As I turned around, I could see that Craig had turned from angry to furious. 'I wasn't finished with you.' He snarled. 'I think we need to talk out back – NOW.'

Convinced he had rumbled my hidden camera, I almost threw up with the sudden fright. I looked around the room to see if there was someone I could signal to and let them know I was in distress, but there was no one who cared. All off their faces with drink and drugs, the festivities continued for the party people and I had no choice but to follow Craig. As I solemnly turned towards the back rooms and pushed past the sweaty bodies, feeling like a dead woman walking, I suddenly began to feel dizzy. The corridors narrowed, my legs felt heavier, and my eyes widened as my surroundings became blurred. His mouth was moving, and the words came towards me slowly: 'You need to show me what you've got . . .'

8

'Parker, it was awful. I actually passed out with the fear – I'm still hurting in all sorts of strange places from the fall. But I really thought he was going to put a bullet in my head, or something.'

'Now, did you really faint, petal? Or were you just testing the law of gravity again?'

'Well, safe to say it still works. So much so that I now need a feckin' cap on my front tooth. More bloody money. And there's no way I can leave it as my roots have started to show through this stupid peroxide and I look like a total scrubber!'

'OK, so you've got a gap between your teeth and slightly dodgy hair. Get yourself some muscles and people will think you're Madonna.'

Although I didn't want to laugh, I couldn't help doing so. As always, my man-in-waiting was doing his best to show me the lighter side of life. No matter how dire the situation, Parker would always point out the humour and turn my grey clouds into, well, a slightly lighter shade of grey. 'Ah, thank you, sweetness. I love that you see shit and smell roses, but I'm not sure I'm coping very well over here. One minute I'm up, and the next I'm—'

'Down? Indeed.'

'Ha! Ha! And we're talking literally, now. I'm telling you, this undercover business is highly stressful. I know I wanted a career, but this is hard work.'

'Don't talk to me about hard work,' hissed Parker. 'It's as overrated as monogamy. And that's where my life is at right now. The only FUN part of my day is when my FUN-ny bone gets some action as I perform some DIY entertainment on myself.'

'OK, OK. Enough information, thank you. What's up between you and Jeff now? Is he still knitting up a storm?'

'He's really starting to freak me out. Honestly, it's got out of hand, and that's not meant to be a pun. Just this morning I asked him to make me a cup of coffee and he looked at me, said, 'Get knotted,' and walked off chuckling away to himself. It's not right, not even for a gay man.'

Trying to soothe his pain, I said, 'As far as I know Cameron Diaz and Winona Ryder are big knitters.' But my comments were shot down immediately.

'They don't knit. No one with any real star quality would be caught dead with needles and a ball of wool.'

'Well, has he made you any nice jumpers yet?'

'Don't be smart. Prada don't do knitting patterns. Well, as far as I know. But wait for this, he got a pattern off one of his blogging websites. Yes, you heard right, he BLOGS about knitting. Anyway, he got all excited about some Scottish woman who knits with her arms. The company's called Wool Fish, seemingly, and just one large ball of wool makes an entire dress. Wool Fish! I told him if there was anything fishy I liked I'd be straight, so he was to get that idea right out of his head immediately! Can you believe he wanted to knit a dress?'

'If it'll make him happy, I'll wear it.' I giggled, before changing the subject back to myself. 'Right then, forget I even mentioned Jeff. I need to talk more about me, please.'

'Nothing new there, really,' sniped Parker.

'Hang on a second. I was frogmarched out of the restaurant last night, I fainted, and then as soon as I woke up I was shouted at and had to acquiesce to demands to open up my locker!'

Finding it hard to show sympathy, since he was wrapped up in his own world, Parker bitched back, 'Yeah, but he just thought you were swiping booze. You'd nothing in your locker. So what's the problem? You weren't snared.'

'I thought he was going to kill me, Parker.'

'Over a bottle of vodka? I don't think so. At worst he might have touched you up and thrown you out.'

'That doesn't sound so bad, actually.'

'Amen to that, girlfriend. I might just have to come over there and hide out in the storeroom myself if that was what was on offer.'

Getting slightly frustrated at not being able to have a serious conversation about my situation, I made my excuses and promised to ring him later.

There was no one else I could discuss my latest adventures with, since the Princess was off skiing somewhere in the French Alps. So Daisy and I got ourselves wrapped up in full winter gear and went for a walk in the rain. As I pushed her through the nearby park, all bloodshot eyes and weary body, I told her about my worries, in a fairy-tale voice of course, and as she smiled through her plastic tent-covering,

135

my stress started to lift, and all felt well with the world once again.

I was as excited about going into work that night as a mail-order bride stepping off the plane to meet her elderly husband for the first time. I was convinced that I would be the talk of the club, but when I arrived out on to the floor, there wasn't one single staff member that I recognized.

Walking up to the manager's station I was greeted by Rosa, a statuesque Brazilian beauty with creamy, chocolatey skin, who immediately put me at ease. 'Ahhh, you must be Alice. Welcome to Wednesday night at Sir Charlie's. I'm your manager and I hope you're up for some hard work, as this is going to be one busy night.'

Unsure how much she knew about me, I did my best to seem keen, and answered in a preppy way, 'Bring it on.'

By 11 p.m. all replacement night staff were on the floor and the place was hopping. Although it had become obvious that only good-looking, slim-figured people could work here, tonight's employees were particularly stunning. They might be working as waiting and bar staff, but all of them would have looked at home on the catwalks of Milan or Paris. Despite feeling decidedly Irish and awkward, I found the girls were the most friendly I had met, and the boys behind the bar were just as hospitable. The first guy who caught my eye introduced himself by saying, 'Hey, newbie, I'm Harry,' before pointing in the direction of another radiant guy throwing bottles and explaining, 'And that bull over there is Blue.'

'Blue?' I questioned.

'Yes, as in the colour. But it also characterizes his state of mind – filthy.'

Hearing his name, Blue finished serving a customer and quickly bounded over to greet me. 'Hey, I'm Blue, welcome to the A Team. We're all slightly mad here, but in a good way.' As he spoke he extended his arm and gave me a quirky handshake, but I was only aware of his piercing bright-blue eyes. Sure, he had a winning smile, razor-tight black hair that showed off his beautifully shaped head, and shoulders that looked like they could wrestle a lion, but his eyes were so dreamy that I felt like I could dive right into them. Coming over all giggly, I averted my gaze so he wouldn't notice me blushing. He was movie-star gorgeous, and as I looked around the room it was obvious, from the legions of women hanging around the bar, that they had all noticed him, too. As soon as he returned centre stage and resumed throwing bottles of vodka and Triple Sec in the air, another of the waiting staff, Kris, whispered in my ear.

'You may or may not be aware, but Blue is in a new crime drama on TV. It's only been out three weeks, but already he thinks he's in Hollywood.'

Not able to hide my adoration, I gushed, 'And he deserves to be there. I didn't know they made men that gorgeous . . .'

Laughing in a knowing way, Kris chuckled. 'And you should see what he's packing underneath those trousers. It's pure artistry.'

Without saying a word, I looked at her, as if to ask: 'Did you go there?'

And with a nod and a wink, she laughed. 'Ohhh, yeah,' she said, before whisking a tray of drinks off the bar and towards her tables.

As my own tables continued to fill up, my energy lifted and the fear I had had about facing Craig disappeared.

Although he had told me that he was 'for ever omnipresent', Rosa told me that Wednesdays were his night off, so if there were any problems she was the woman to go to. As the night progressed, I found myself hanging around the bar hatch more and more to get an eyeful of Blue. But as the centre of all the gossip, it turned out to have other benefits, too. I witnessed some of the girls working the tables asking the bar staff for 'special coffees', for the doormen. They were also being told to double up on the cocktails on several bills, as the customers were too pissed to notice any different. Informed that I could share in the profits later, it was difficult not to feel guilty about filming them because they were being so nice to me.

By 2 a.m. I had pushed through a sleepy phase and was enjoying a second wind and a complimentary vodka and 7 Up, courtesy of one of my tables. Assuming that the evening was beginning to wind down, I got the fright of my life when Rosa rushed up to me and said, 'Clear everyone from tables fifteen and sixteen now. Trappim and his crew will be here in five minutes. Go do it.'

Unsure who or what 'Trappim' was, I tried to ask Kris what to do, but she was busy with her own customers. She just screamed back over their heads, 'Do him if you can.' Then she gave me a big thumbs up.

Fretting as to what I could say to shift my customers quickly, I ran back up to Rosa and asked, 'What do I do with the people on my tables? Can I offer them a free drink on the house or something?'

Clearly anxious and a bit tetchy, Rosa snapped back, 'Just fuck them off. And don't offer any of those losers free drinks. They should think themselves lucky to be in here at all.'

A bit taken aback, I agreed to get rid of them right away, but chanced one more question, hoping it wouldn't be the wrong thing to say. 'Sorry, Rosa, just one more thing. Who is Trappim?'

Making a disbelieving face, she snapped at me again. 'He's just one of the hottest music producers around. And he also drops on average about three thousand quid a night in here. So get him his tables now.'

As I expected, clearing people wasn't as easy as I wanted it to be. They cried out, 'Don't you know who I am?' as I persisted in ushering them towards the bar, and I had barely wiped the tables clean when Rosa walked over to me with a large posse behind her. Flanked, in true Hugh-Heffner style, by about ten generic blonde women, Trappim emerged out of the crowd like Moses parting the sea. He was dressed head-to-toe in white, including white baseball cap, white velour tracksuit, white trench coat and over-sized white runners. In absolute contradiction to his sporty leisure kit, he walked with a stoop and leaned on a white cane that looked like it was wrapped in albino snakeskin.

Within seconds of their arrival I was inundated with requests from the ladies for different branded vodkas, Hennessy cocktails and several bottles of champagne. Respectfully taking all their pernickety orders, I made my way through them all until I reached the pimp daddy himself, who by now had settled himself across the top couch with his pasty white, shrunken face glued to his iPhone. Being as assertive as I could, I gently touched his knee to get his attention, and asked, 'Can I offer you a drink?' I instantly knew I had done the wrong thing.

As if I had just clapped the Queen on the back, or asked Mariah Carey if I could borrow her lip-gloss, Trappim slowly raised his gaze from his mobile to meet mine, and snarled in an oddly primal way. 'Have we fucked?' he asked, eye-balling me.

Unsure if I was hearing things, I managed a 'Pardon me?'

'You heard me. Have we fucked?'

Letting out a short, nervous giggle, I ventured an answer, fearful that I was treading on eggshells. 'Emm, I don't believe we have.'

'Then why the fuck do you think you can touch me?'

Seeing a potentially big tip slipping out of my purse, I knew I had to mend the situation, and quick. Although my first instinct was to grovel, I looked around at his yes-woman dolly birds and thought that if I did that he'd probably only abuse me further. Instead I smartly retorted, 'Steady on, with talk like that you may never find out what a great lay I am. Now can I get you a drink or assist you in any other way?'

'What's your name?' he asked, an expression somewhere between interest and respect playing across his face.

Not wanting to give in too easy, I teased, 'Why does it matter? I can't imagine you can remember any more women's names.'

Breaking a smile, he quietly sniggered. 'Cheeky Irish. I like you.'

Although the women in his harem weren't threatened by me, nor had they even noticed me other than when I took their drink orders, they were beginning to stare in our direction. So, fearful of being lynched, I started to back away from the cloaked Trappim and asked, 'Champagne OK for you?'

'If you think so.' He smirked, looking me up and down in

a sleazy way. Feeling like I had bitten off more than I could chew, I retreated to the bar before I could say anything else that might land me in a sticky situation. As I walked away I felt a chill down my spine; I was sure his eyes were burrowing into my back.

The blondes kept me busy for the rest of the night by ordering each drink one at a time. It seemed that whenever I returned to the table with one bottle of champagne, or one Smirnoff and slimline tonic, another blonde would ask me to go back to the bar again. Even though they treated me like I was an insignificant skivvy, Trappim kept his eye on me the whole time, an experience which by 4.30 a.m. had become exhausting.

I escaped to the toilet for a quick break and to check out just how shattered I looked, and when I returned to the corridor the white prince caught me off guard. Backing me into a corner, he stood strong and silent in front of me, his now somewhat drunken eyes scanning every inch of my body. Fearing that he might discover my hidden camera in my headpiece – after all, the disguise was just a flimsy black flower pinned over my almost matted, backcombed hair – I did my best to keep things light. 'Lose your bearings, Mr Trappim? I think your ladies are back that way.'

'I like blondes,' he declared, slightly slurring.

'Really? I never would have guessed. Ehhh, sorry, excuse me, can I get past you, please?' I smiled, but was unsuccessful in trying to push my way back towards the bar.

Holding his ground, he replied, 'You've a lovely aura about you. I need to party with you tonight, girl.' All I could do was laugh tensely.

As I fretted that he might feel compelled to lift his walking stick and use it to penetrate me right there in the corridor, my prayers for help were suddenly answered when Tanya Cruze appeared out of nowhere screaming, 'Trappim, where have you been hiding? Mommy needs some happy pills.' Remembering me from the night before, she acknowledged me with a half-smile before throwing her arms around my captor and demanding his undivided attention. Although it was evident that he was annoyed at the interruption, she chose to ignore this and continued begging for drugs. 'Come on, baby. I need to keep the party going. Tell me you can help me out. You're my last hope.' Pandering to her demands, he reached inside his trench coat to an inner pocket and pulled out a gilded silver box that was full of different-coloured pills, paper wraps and small cellophane bags of what looked like cocaine. Although I desperately wanted to get away, I knew this moment was documentary gold, so I kept quiet and pretended to look at the floor in order for my camera to pan down towards his hands. Screaming with delight, Tanya made no effort to be subtle and jumped up and down excitedly. 'Gimme gimme gimme,' she whooped, while stretching her slender hand towards the box.

Angry with her impatience, he snapped the lid back and told her, 'Get some respect.' Obediently, she pulled back her hand, but still continued to bounce with anticipation. Looking back at me, Trappim coldly asked, 'Do you think if I throw my stick she'll go run after it?' But all Tanya did was start laughing like a horse and pretend to slap him across his chest. Glaring at her until she steadied herself, Trappim then slowly opened his pill box once again and picked two white ones out, before replacing it back inside his coat. 'OK, Irish, stick out your tongue.' His eyes widened as he made his demand. Feeling the heat once more, I weakly tried to refuse, but he didn't seem to want to take no for an answer. 'I said, stick out your tongue . . .'

'Just do it,' interrupted Tanya, all agitated. 'It's good stuff.'

Looking at Tanya, and then back at Trappim, it was obvious that I wasn't going to worm my way out of this situation without causing a scene. Reassuring myself that I could put it in my mouth and then hide it inside my cheek, I accepted with a casual remark of, 'OK then,' and slid my tongue out for both of them to see. As Trappim placed the pill on to it a nasty bitter flavour shocked my taste buds, so I quickly closed my mouth, pretended to swallow and then lodged the pill under my tongue for safe keeping.

I licked my lips to indicate that I had complied with his wishes, and he turned to Tanya, who was now shivering with the excitement, and simply handed her the other pill, saying, 'You're such a dumb fuck. Now get out of my space.' Happy with her lot, Tanya waved goodbye, and once more Trappim had me – well – trapped!

'So is this how you earned your name?' I asked in all seriousness.

'What you talking about?'

'This, here.' I waved my finger, pointing out the minuscule distance between him and myself. 'Is this a normal move, for you to trap 'em – trap the ladies?'

Pulling himself up straight, he stretched to elongate his height and explained, 'It's a music thing. I'm known for collecting the best rappers, the best crew, the best . . . I don't need to explain myself to you. I don't need to trap no woman. I've got a football team of them out there that are all waiting for me to take them home.'

Feeling like I had him on the back foot I decided to push

him further, and asked, 'So what's stopping you? I'm not.' And then I coughed into my hand to transfer the tablet, which felt like it was disintegrating in my mouth.

None too impressed at getting the brush off, Trappim thought for a moment before returning to his previous snarling manner, and grunted, 'Now that I see you in the light, I realize you're not that pretty. And definitely nowhere close to my standard.'

Trying to stifle a laugh, I asked, 'Really?'

'Yeah,' he confirmed, while nodding his head. 'And whatever look you were going for here,' he circled his free hand around my hair, 'you've missed the mark completely.' Feeling like he had done the dumping, Trappim slouched back off out the corridor towards his tables and declared, 'Get my fucking bill. This place stinks.'

Gathering my composure, I took a couple of minutes before stepping back out to the floor, and thankfully when I did the majority of people had already been ushered out by the bouncers. Heading straight to Rosa, who had Trappim's bill ready and waiting for me, I could see that she was tempted to ask if everything was OK, before thinking better of it. Glancing down at the bill, I saw that it totalled £2,385 for all their drink, with a tiny line running underneath it that said, 'No Service Included.' Figuring that I didn't stand a chance in hell of getting a tip, I decided to go for broke and place the remains of the tablet he gave me on the tray with his bill. It was mashed and slimy, though you could still see with painful obviousness what it was. Mustering all the courage I could, I strode over to him and presented him with the bill. Praying that my camera was still filming, I spoke extra-clearly, announcing, 'Your bill and your pill. Drugs aren't my style, so I would like you to have it back.'

The anger was instantly visible across his face. His precious male ego clearly dented, he loudly asked, 'Which of you bitches am I taking home tonight?'

A couple of them replied, 'All of us, Trap!' before collapsing into whoops of laughter. Determined to throw his weight around, he then flicked a black American Express card on to the tray and signalled for me to leave. Losing my bottle to return and see him sign it, I asked Kris if she'd do the honours – and fled for the relative safety of the locker room.

Terrified at the prospect of being caught doing another piece to camera, I took my bag out of my locker, grabbed my coat and hesitantly started to make my way back out to the floor. By the time I got there, the lights were up full, the music was off and everyone had left except for the staff sipping cocktails and beers at the bar. 'So what happened with Trappim?' Kris asked curiously, as she signalled the others to stop their conversation and listen.

Aware that I had the eyes of the A Team on me, I casually laughed, 'Nothing, why?' But it was obvious that none of them, especially Kris, bought it.

'Well, he told me to give you this.' She handed me £200. 'And told me to tell you thanks for the BJ.' As if on cue, the gang at the bar fell about the place laughing.

Mortified, I stuffed the money in my bag and said, 'I never went near him!' But all they could do was laugh. Not having the energy to protest my innocence, I offered a group wave and told them all to enjoy their drinks. With the sky already starting to get light, I felt blessed that there were still several cabs waiting outside Sir Charlie's, so I jumped into the back of the first, and with ample cash in my pocket asked the driver to take me the whole way home.

It must have been 3 p.m. before I woke up later that day, with the mother of all hangovers thumping in my head. After a range of weird nightmares – from being trampled by polar bears to being scratched and bitten by cats – I was sure that some of that pill I had put in my mouth had been absorbed into my system.

Still in my pyjamas, I slunk down the stairs into the living room to find all the kids and Maura staring out the back patio windows – at *snow*! 'Good afternoon, Auntie Eva,' called Maura. 'Good to see you're still alive.'

I barely got a few grunts from Maura's kids, who were too distracted by what was happening outside, but as I lifted Daisy up off the floor she gave me the biggest smile and the loudest, 'Mam–may', and the horror of my dreams started to slip away.

In bad need of a shot of caffeine, I walked towards the kitchen, bouncing Daisy on my hip, and asked Maura if there was anything that I could do to help around the house. 'I'm off the next couple of nights now, so use and abuse me. All I have to do is go into the office tomor-row.'

'Good stuff. Cause in case you've forgotten, your dad is here tonight for his trade fair.'

Maura looked at me, and I could feel my face drain of the little colour it had. 'Is that tonight? Ah, crap. The idea of drink is making me feel weak.'

'Ha! Ha! I've spoken to him already, and he's on super form. He says that crabby ol' sister-in-law of mine was moaning at him this morning to check that I've been looking after yourself and Daisy properly. She thinks I won't have been feeding you right.'

'As if!' I chuckled back.

That night we tucked into Maura's homecooked beef and Guinness pie prepared with, as she herself boasted, 'Actual homemade pastry, none of that shop-bought stuff.' And we reminisced about old times back in Dublin when my dad wore flares and Maura wore extremely short miniskirts. Several bottles of vino later, Maura and I were sitting at the front window watching the snow falling through the beams of the street lights, while Dad and John talked sporting greats and agreed that Pelé would have been no match for Keano.

Having restrained myself all evening, it was only a matter of time before I brought up the subject of Rory. We had been in constant contact since our last date, but the physical separation was killing me. 'I can't believe it's snowing,' I mused, building up to my boy talk. 'It looks so romantic. I'd love a snog right now.'

Giving me a big-sister hug, Maura then did her best to wind me up. 'I'll snog ya if you like. I've been told I'm quite good at it.'

Pretending to shrug her off, I chuckled, 'You're all right thanks. I was more thinking along the lines of Rory.'

'So call him,' suggested Maura, matter-of-factly. 'Call him now and invite him over.'

'But how can I? He thinks my name is Alice, for Christ's sake. And he also doesn't know about Daisy, who just happens to be sleeping upstairs.'

'So?'

'So . . . I can't ask him over. It'll only let the cat out of the bag.'

'Oh, relax,' bellowed Maura, topping up my wine glass. 'We'll all play ball. Sure, I'm dying to see him. Ring him now and see if he'll come over. Go on. It'll be a bit of craic.'

'But what about my dad?'

'Never mind him, he's in his element. Here, hang on – Patsy, Eva here has a new fella on the go.'

Temporarily lifting his head from his deep conversation with John, my dad asked, 'And?'

'Well, she wants to ask him over, but she has a problem. He thinks her name is Alice and, well, she doesn't want to let him in on the secret tonight. So will you play along, Patsy?'

Thinking for a moment, he ran through a couple of bizarre facial expressions before asking, 'Just remind me before he comes, will ya?' and then turned away from us again to resume his conversation with John.

'There ya go.' Maura smiled, all pleased with herself. 'Nothing stopping ya. So go and call him. This gathering could do with a distraction.'

Grabbing the bull by the horns, I picked up my phone and rang Rory before I could change my mind. His phone had barely rung twice when he lifted it up and said, 'I was just thinking about you. I wish I could see you to-night.'

In a giddy girlie voice I gushed back, 'Well, hop in a cab and come see me then. That's if you're up for a challenge?'

'What's the challenge?' His voice sounded cautious.

Laughing with the nerves, I coughed a few times be-fore explaining, 'Well, I'm at a bit of a family gathering. Small family gathering. Just Maura, John and, well, my dad. Who's half-cut at this stage, so he won't be annoying ya.'

I paused for a moment, but heard nothing. 'Well?' I asked again, pressing the point.

'Am I stepping into a minefield?'

'Absolutely not. And while I know it's bad weather out-side, it's extremely romantic too. And, well, I'd just really like to see ya.'

'Do you promise not to be asleep with the drink by the time I get there?'

'Promise.'

'OK, then, I'll hop in the shower, you text me the address, and I'll see you and your gathering as soon as possible.'

Melting with the thought of seeing him, all I could say was, 'Thank you.' Then I turned to Maura in a panic and asked, 'What have I just done? He's coming over now.'

The next hour and a half was possibly the longest in history. I must have changed five times before I got that casual, not-trying-too-hard-but-effortlessly-sexy image working. I finally stepped back downstairs in one of my trademark off-the-shoulder slouchy tees, with a cute pink bra-strap exposed, just in time to hear the doorbell. To the sound of which there was a rapturous round of applause from Maura and John, and a worrying wink from my dad.

'No one is to say anything about Daisy. SWEAR TO ME. And my name is Alice. OK? Now swear to me, please.'

'OK, we swear,' chimed the room, through coughs and giggles.

Although I was terrified that one of the three would forget themselves and drop a clanger, the idea of Rory calling around was thrilling, because I needed my family to meet him properly and give him their seal of approval. As I stepped out to open the door, a rush of adrenaline surged through my body, making me skip with a mixture of joy and nerves. Preening one last time in front of the mirror in the hall, I put on a quick blot of lip-gloss and I was ready for my close-up. Then, as if posing for a curtain call, I carefully composed myself and on the count of 'One, Two, Three', I swung back the heavy bolts to find – no one. Looking out on to the empty road, there was nothing but pretty sheeting snow to greet me. As lovely as the scene was to look at, it would have been far nicer with Rory in it, and the disappointment I felt was huge, which went some way to indicating just how much I had begun to like this guy. I'd been so looking forward to seeing him and parading him off to the family that the let-down was almost unbearable.

I snuck my nose around the corner of the door to see if there was any traffic around, and Rory suddenly jumped out from behind a bush, crying, 'I got ya!'

Despite being a shock, it was the most pleasant of surprises, and all I could reply with as he cradled me in his arms was, 'Yes, you have.'

Despite their taunts, Maura, John and Dad were on their best behaviour, apart from a couple of drunken jibes from Maura along the lines of, 'So, is this your next husband?' But all of them were ignored by me and, thankfully, Rory. Happy to drink whatever was going, Rory got stuck into playing catch-up, and before we knew where we were, John had pulled out an old, almost rusty-looking red-wine bottle with no label on it. 'This is poteen, Rory,' he explained, holding it up like it was an Academy Award. 'This stuff separates the men from the boys. It'll put hairs on your chest, it'll—'

'It'll make you sick,' interrupted Maura, cutting her husband down to size.

Intrigued, Rory leaned forward to get a better look at the

bottle, and took it from John to have a smell. He barely had the cap off the bottle when he let out a huge yelp. 'Fuck me!' he cried, before realizing where he was, and apologizing for his language. 'I'm sorry. I've heard of poteen, but what is it? An Irish version of arsenic?'

'Sort of.' Maura giggled. 'It's real liquor, brewed from potatoes.'

'You mean spuds?' asked Rory, in a put-on Oirish accent.

Somewhat drunkenly, my dad then reached around Rory's shoulders and in an uncharacteristic move kissed him on the cheek. 'Indeed it is, sonny,' said my dad, while shaking Rory's shoulders in a best-pal sort of way. 'Will you do me the honour of joining me in a shot?'

Quickly winking in my direction to let me know he was enjoying himself, Rory gave my dad a hearty pat on the hand and smiled, 'I would love to, surely.'

To which my dad smiled back, and answered with one of his oldest gags, 'I like you – but don't call me Shirley.'

Whether I wanted it or not, I was also handed a shot of poteen in a tacky glass that read, 'You lick it – you own it!' and told by my dad, 'Down in one, there's a good girl.' Feeling like a contestant off *I'm A Celebrity . . . Get Me Out of Here!*, I had about as much interest in swallowing it as if he had offered me up some kangaroo balls. But my protests about having an early start the next day were simply not listened to. Despite being as quiet as a mouse when sober, I knew how cantankerous my dad could be with a few drinks on him, so I thought it best for an easy life all round to just drink my poteen and be done with it.

So, as a group, we all clinked shot glasses, shared a giggle over Rory's – which read, 'What happens in my mouth – stays in my mouth!' – and in a great bonding moment, knocked back our shots together and howled at the moon like a pack of wolves. That night we pushed back the furniture and danced around the dining room to possibly every hit Elvis ever made. I melted as Rory crooned his way through 'Love Me Tender', and laughed till it hurt as my dad tried his best to dislocate his replacement hip with his moves to 'Jailhouse Rock'. It ended up being one of the most perfect nights I had had in a long time. Not only was it so great to see my dad let his hair down without fear of interference from my mother, but to see Rory blend in so well and just be utterly adorable was bliss. He was a total gentleman to Maura, and a man's man with my dad and John, but he also made it his business to frequently touch my leg or arm, and knowingly give me a gentle squeeze to let me know he cared.

By 2 a.m. he had made a big impression on all of us, but then he stunned us with his decision to leave the party so I could go to bed and get some beauty sleep. After he'd imparted many manly hugs to the men and compliments to Maura for being such a wonderful hostess, I reluctantly walked him out into the hall, not wanting the fun to end. Looking out the window, I could see it was still snowing heavily, so the two of us settled for a fumble at the bottom of the stairs, and began ravaging each other's bodies as if we had been starved a thousand years. Rory was just in the middle of telling me, 'If I don't have sex with you soon, I might just explode,' when a voice from the top of the stairs started calling.

'Eva! Eva! It's Daisy, she's coughing!' Jack yelled.

Startled, Rory looked at me and asked, 'Who's Eva?' before quickly glancing back at little Jack in confusion.

Not prepared to get into any explanations at this hour, I

quickly tidied up my clothes and told him, 'He sleepwalks. I'll have to go up and put him back to bed. He doesn't know where he is. Sorry, you'd better go.' As the tiny voice at the top of the stairs persisted in calling out my real name, I kissed Rory one last time and pushed him out into the snow, slamming the door behind him. By the time I'd shooed Jack into his own bed and checked on Daisy, she had settled herself back to sleep. Peeking out our window from underneath the blind I could see no sign of Rory, other than some footprints in the snow down the path. Scrambling for my phone, I hurriedly texted him. 'Sorry. U OK?' The reply was swift as always. 'Wonderful@I M fallen 4 U xxx.' Letting out a tiny squeak of delight that made Daisy stir in her cot, I lay down on my bed and texted back, 'Ditto xx', before falling asleep with all my clothes and make-up still on and clutching my phone like it was the most precious gift I owned.

9

'It's an eco-friendly clockwork vibrator. Genius, isn't it?'

'Thank you, Lisa. My, er, Earth Angel is a wonderful Valentine's present. I'm not sure when or where I'm actually going to get an opportunity to use it, but I thought I'd call to say it was very sweet of you to think of lonely ol' me.'

'What do you mean "where you can use it"? Take it to bed with you. It can't be as loud as a kango hammer.'

'Mmmm, nice image there, missus.'

'You know what I mean.'

'Yes I do, and thank you. It's just that although I could enjoy multiple orgasms without the worry of being hazardous to the environment, I couldn't live with the guilt of pleasuring myself within inches of my innocent sleeping child. We share a tiny box room, remember? It's just not right.'

Slightly miffed at my lack of enthusiasm for her postal gift, the Princess made excuses that she had a skiing lesson to finish off – more likely a skiing instructor to finish off! She hung up the phone on me abruptly. Lisa, as it transpired, was not the only person disappointed in me that morning. By the time I made it into the office, I had scripted an entire argument in my head as to why I didn't want to go – or why I couldn't possibly even think of going – back to work at Sir Charlie's. Of course, by the time I was sitting in front of Bradley in his office, the words coming out of my mouth didn't seem quite as convincing as those that had swum around my head. 'I'm sorry, Bradley, but I just can't go back there. You've got the footage on your desk now. I've told you what I witnessed. You've got enough to make your programme. So I'm out.'

I was waiting for a big angry reaction, but he didn't deliver it. Instead, he leaned over his desk and calmly explained, 'I own you. I own Eva and I own Alice. You're not going anywhere until this project is completed. Have you got that?'

'But I've delivered!' I pointed at my cameras and prayed that I could convince him to let me walk away. 'You've got druggie WAGs, a famous rap producer actually handing over drugs, violent drug-dealing bouncers – oh, and the tea-leafing staff as well. Surely that all adds up to a fairly impressive count – doesn't it?'

Sitting back in his chair, Bradley relaxed and conceded, 'OK, I'll give you that. You have done well.' And then, in a guaranteed Westlife moment, he stood up like a boyband wannabe. As if reaching the climax of a song, he punched the air to declare, 'But you're on the cusp of breaking something really huge here. I can't let you just abandon your post. It's taken us months to try and infiltrate Sir Charlie's. If you leave now we might never get anyone else in there. At this point in my career I need to be winning awards. This could be the one to do that for me.'

'But I'm scared, Bradley,' I explained, while thinking to myself how I was also now scared of him. 'I know you

spoke about danger money before, but it's not worth it to me any more. I was convinced that Craig had figured me out. I thought he was going to kill me or something.'

'But he didn't.'

'Well, he hasn't yet, anyway.'

'Listen, girl, you better hear me loud and clear. You're going back in: we've got a contract. And you're not coming out until you've got Craig or some of the doormen dealing drugs. Got that?'

Feeling my eyes starting to well up and my lip quiver, I asked, 'And what if I refuse?'

He looked like a man who was counting to ten in his head to control his anger, and I waited for him to unleash a tirade of abuse, but instead he settled himself down and said, 'I'm not going to make threats here, I'm not the bad guy. I'm just the guy trying to expose the bad guys. And you can't do this to me. I mean, if you pull out now we won't have a programme. We've already got financial problems. This will be the end. Surely you don't want to be responsible for throwing all these people out of work. Anyway, considering all that you've achieved in such a short space of time working nights . . . well, I believe you can finish this within a matter of weeks.'

'Weeks?' I shrieked, horrified at the thought.

'OK, maybe days. That's up to you. But I need management and or doormen dealing on camera. There is no walking away from this until you've nailed them. Are we clear?'

Furious that he'd talked me back into more shifts at Sir Charlie's, I stood up, grabbing my cameras minus their memory cards, then slammed my chair into his desk and stormed off before I could break down crying in front of him. Feeling like a total girl, I locked myself in the toilet and sobbed my heart out, occasionally muffling my cries as other women came in and out. I knew that I had made a commitment to Bradley and that I had no choice but to honour it. I just wasn't sure where I was going to find the courage to step back into Sir Charlie's. Even just the idea of coming across Craig or Trappim again made my skin crawl.

I was day-dreaming about doing a bunk back to Ireland when two texts beeped through to my phone one after another. Fishing it out of my bag, I accessed my messages to see one from DAD, and the other from RAVISHING RORY. Dad's read, 'Great night. Lovely to see U. On way home now. Fine bloke U got. Keep him. Love dad xx,' which of course brought another tear to my eye. Then I quickly flicked on to Rory's text, which read, 'Great night. Missing U sexy kisser. Sore head from that spuddy grog though. Can I see U later? xxxxxxoxxx.' Unable to stop myself, I allowed the tears to flow again at missing my father, and of course my life back home; but even more so over the exasperation of feeling like a fraud.

Although I was trying to fight it, the lying was causing knots in my stomach. Firstly, I was lying to my family, including Maura and John, about my real job. I vaguely remembered feeding them some bull that I was recording a lifestyle show that wouldn't be out till later in the year, and that my waitressing shifts were just to boost my income. But I had also lied to Rory about almost everything, and saw no possible way of telling him the truth without him running a mile. Maybe he could forgive me for lying about my job? But about my name? And, worse still, for not telling him I had a baby? Parker was the only one who knew the full truth, and that felt isolating. OK, so we had spoken to Lisa about it, but that wouldn't necessarily mean she would actually remember. I felt empty and alone in my deceit, and utterly petrified at the prospect of putting things to rights. In my moment of weakness I texted back my dad, 'I love U xx,' something I haven't told him sober in many years. And to Rory, 'Missing U sexy kisser xxx,' keeping my fingers crossed that he wouldn't ask to see me again that night.

With the rest of the house out on a family date to the cinema, Daisy and I enjoyed some quality time snuggling on the couch before her bedtime. Michael had texted to say that the first available appointment for Daisy to see the specialist was in six weeks, but that I wasn't to fret as it wasn't an issue unless she was in an accident or cut herself badly. A big part of me wanted to write back, 'I bet your OTHER child didn't have to wait six weeks for tests.' But after rewording the text several times over, I fixed on, 'OK. Stay in touch,' and patted myself on the back for being so mature.

By 8 p.m. I had a glass of white wine that was left over from the night before in my hand, and was settling down to watch *The Hangover* on Sky Movies. The house was peaceful for a change, and the idea of a night off with a few laughs was just the tonic I needed. All I could handle tonight was fictional drama, which offered a welcome break from my own real sex, drugs and rock 'n' roll lifestyle. I was in the middle of tucking a blanket up under my toes when a text beeped through on my phone. No longer in the mood to converse with anyone, I reluctantly opened the text to see RAVISHING RORY's name flashing up. Good news in theory, of course, but even though I fancied him like mad, all I wanted at this precise time was to be left alone.

'I want to C U tonight xxx', read the message. It was sweet and exactly the sort of thing women want to hear from hunky single men, but he got me at a weak moment and all I could muster was, 'Sorry, I'm tired xx.' Not willing to go down easy, he quickly texted back, 'I miss U xx.' So I tried to let him down gently, and texted back, 'I miss U 2. But I can't tonight. I'm 2 hungover. Nite nite xxx.' As if determined to aggravate me, he came back again, 'Hey sweet lips. What ya doing? xxx.' Not knowing what else to say I sent back, 'I'm watching a movie xx.' 'That's cool . . . Can I watch it 2?' And with that, this gorgeous guy who I had been fantasizing over the last couple of weeks started to really piss me off.

'Sure,' I wrote, while wondering if he would pick up on the sarcasm. 'If U have Sky Movies . . . switch it on ☺'. 'Wouldn't it just be easier to watch it with you? xx.' Now mentally exhausted, I wasn't able for the texting tennis he had started, so I decided to put a stop to it fast. And in a frenzied rage I drafted up, 'Not really. Stop messing, I've just sat down. I wanna watch this. Haven't seen it B4. I'll text U later xx,' hoping that I didn't sound too grumpy. Feeling a mini-diva moment coming on, I chose to put my phone on silent and stuff it under a cushion to concentrate on the movie. If I didn't I was in danger of sending him another, even grumpier, text telling him something stupid like shove off. Reasoning with myself that I would just tell him in the morning that my phone had been on the blink, I was literally seconds into drooling over the lead actor when the front doorbell rang. Then it buzzed again, and again, and then a fourth and a fifth time. Whoever it was, they were persistent *and* determined to wind me up even further.

Hoping that my caller would push off, I lowered down

the TV to listen, but instead of silence the doorbell buzzed another two times. Scared at the sheer doggedness of the person outside, and annoyed at the idea that if they kept at it they'd wake Daisy up, I sat frozen to the seat. Not knowing what to do I prayed that they wouldn't start banging on the door. With Daisy upstairs I felt extremely vulnerable, so I scrambled to grab my phone again as some sort of security. Looking at the screen, I noticed a new message on it. RAVISHING RORY again. 'What now?' I asked myself.

'It's me outside,' read the message. 'Open up, it's freezing out here xx.' No sooner had I opened the message than I heard a muffled voice come through the letter box. 'Hey, it's me. Open up. I know you're in there. Don't start changing your wardrobe on my account. Let me in.' My brain froze up as I tried to figure a way out of this mess. After all I couldn't possibly let him inside. I looked like shit. But not only that, I had Daisy upstairs in her cot. What if she woke up and needed me? I couldn't take that risk – could I? Not wanting to speak to him, I childishly texted him, 'I'm in bed. Talk to you in the morning.' But, unsurprisingly enough, he didn't quite believe me. 'This is your final chance,' came the voice through the letter box. 'I think my knob is about to fall off with the cold. I know you two aren't acquainted and all, but I'm kinda attached to him. Is there any chance I could at least come in and warm up for a bit? I promise to leave you alone then if you wish.'

Rubbing my head in despair, I dragged myself off the couch and worked my way towards the door. Not knowing what I was going to say, I swung it open to discover Rory still bent over the letter box with a cold, dejected look across his face. 'Did I do something to upset you?' he asked.

'Noooo,' I replied while releasing some pent-up stress. 'It's just—'

'What?'

'Come in.' I pointed towards the living room. 'Hurry up, you're letting all the heat out.'

As he stepped inside it was obvious from his expression that he felt like he had made a very bad decision. I felt awful for denting his ego, but couldn't help feeling the way I did. Not wanting to ruin what we had started to build, I dug deep to stifle my own bad mood and apologized for acting like a weirdo. 'Listen, I'm really sorry, Rory . . . I just . . . I just had a bad day and wasn't feeling very sociable.' I looked at him warming his bum and hands on the radiator and held my breath while waiting for his answer.

'No, I'm sorry,' he answered coldly. 'I forgot how bad you were with surprises. It's my fault.' As I searched for a plausible excuse for my erratic behaviour, Rory broke in on my thoughts by asking, 'Is there something I'm missing here? Last night there were sparks. What happened tonight?'

Knowing that he deserved an explanation, I hummed and hawed before choosing my words very carefully. 'Listen, Rory. There's things that you don't know about me. Things that I can't explain to you right now. They're not necessarily bad things – just things. We all have secrets, I'm just not at liberty to share mine with you right now. Have I lost you yet?'

'No. But if you're looking to go that route I think you may be going the right way about it.'

Struggling to find the right thing to say, I did what any other woman would have done in that situation, and kissed him. At first he tried to resist, but putting on my best lip service, I could slowly feel his mouth, then face, then shoulders relax into enjoying the moment. Bringing my hands up to cup his face, the contours of his cheeks and bearded jawline lured me closer. Although I knew better than to be entertaining him in Maura's house with Daisy upstairs, his distinctive manly smell made me weak. We must have kissed solidly for about five minutes before Rory broke away and asked, 'Do your secrets involve any other lovers?' His eyes searched mine to check for sincerity.

'No,' I answered truthfully.

'Any warrants for your arrest? Any highly contagious diseases? IRA connections? What are we talking here?' Despite originally being angry, it was clear that with the heat and some endorphins finally running through his system, he was beginning to thaw out physically and psychologically. He might have been interrogating me, but he was now doing so with a quirky smile across his face.

Sensing a playful moment, I joked, 'Maybeeee.' But on seeing his reaction I quickly set him straight by saying, 'I'm sorry. That's not funny. The answer is absolutely NO to any of your last suggestions. I'm sorry I can't divulge any more than that right now. You're just going to have to trust me that I am a good person – and realize that whatever mysterious veil I might be casting over myself, I fancy you an awful lot.'

'How much?'

I then did my best to put on a Michael Caine English accent and teased, 'A lot. Not a lot of people know that,' and smacked another wet kiss on his lips.

Not noticing the time slipping past, we must have spent at least an hour locked smooching, and without saying another word we went from kissing up against the radiator to a collapsed state of semi-undress on the floor. Although this wasn't how I wanted our first time to be, I couldn't help my urges, and braved pulling off my baggy sweatshirt – I figured the lacy see-through bra underneath was hotter than my outerwear. Appreciating the intention, Rory purred at the sight of my almost naked breasts. 'You are magnificent,' he cooed, as he gently brushed his stubbly beard across my chest, down over both my breasts and further south across my tummy. 'I have to ask, though . . . where is everyone tonight?'

'A movie. Maura and John have taken the kids. But I'm sure we have at least another half an hour before they make it home. That should be enough time. Shouldn't it?' He looked at me as if I had just asked him to leave his grandmother in a cold car overnight, and I backed away from him in a moment of confusion. 'Did I say something wrong? By the look on your face, you'd think I'd asked you to do something immoral.'

Looking at me with a seriousness that suggested I had fucked up once again, he asked, 'Is this really how you would like our first time to be?'

The best reply I could think of was an honest one. 'No, but as a woman who feels limited in her options, could I ask you to turn a blind eye to convention and go with the flow?'

As a smile rippled across his face, his cheeky manner returned. 'Half an hour, you say? Well, we have several options to choose from tonight. Would you like the Rory Baxter special, aka "The Works", which takes a full half-hour? Or could I tempt you to a "Mini Special"? That includes everything contained in "The Works" but takes place over the course of a supersonic fifteen minutes. Or lastly, there's "The Quickie".'

'Really, what's that?'

'Well, it's probably the most practical option in this particular situation.'

Trying to control my giggles, I asked, 'Why's that now?'

'Because it involves me doing this . . .' Wasting no time, he quickly lowered his mouth towards my neck and began caressing it with powerful kisses. I let out a little moan of passion. Clearly liking what he heard, he temporarily lifted his head back to smile and say, 'But that's just for starters. Then I get to do this . . .' and returned to his work, where he performed some expert caressing down from my neck and across my chest, which he had already exposed by gently popping my breasts out of my bra.

With my senses alive again, every touch of his hands and mouth felt like they were breathing new life into me. By now Rory had full control over my body and I no longer wanted to fight him. I groaned with pleasure as he slid down towards my stomach, the gentle bristles of his beard reminding me of our naughty encounter at the nightclub, and he continued his descent southwards without any further commentary. Massaging his hands across my hips and slowly around to my bum, he was in the middle of pulling my pyjama bottoms down with the tips of his fingers when I heard a knocking sound outside the front door that sounded like the kids. I grabbed his hands – 'Hang on!' – and at that moment the front door opened to an almighty ruckus of kids screaming and parents barking orders.

Thankfully, in the extended time it took the gang to disrobe their wet coats and place their winter wellies up the stairs in their usual formation, Rory had quickly helped me to cover up and we had repositioned ourselves on the couch with just seconds to spare. We made a valiant attempt to look comfortable, but the truth was obvious – at least to Maura and John anyway. If only I'd had a camera to capture their surprised faces. But after collectively welcoming the group with a 'Hi guys!', a wave of panic enveloped me as I realized one of the kids might call me Eva. I didn't have to worry, though, as the sight of a large bearded man in their living room was enough to turn them all mute. After their initial charge into the place, all three of them abruptly backed up into their parents' groins for safety, with little Jack doing some obvious damage to John in the process.

Taking charge of the situation, Maura ordered, 'All little people upstairs and into their PJs,' while John turned on his cool-parent charm and stuck out his hand.

Showing respect for the man of the house, Rory stood up and nervously shook it. 'I've kept your seat warm,' he joked, signalling to John to sit down. 'I was just on my way off now.'

Though John said there was no rush, I decided to seal the deal. 'No, it's fine. Rory was just going. Weren't you?' A confused look shot across his face again, but I knew if I didn't act fast, there would be no getting rid of him for the night. 'Look, I promised I would help Maura get the kids down. You don't mind, do you?'

Not prepared to make a scene, Rory graciously backed down and agreed, 'That's a good idea. Sure, like I said, I was heading off now anyway. Good to see you again, John.' Gathering his crumpled coat off the floor, Rory dragged his feet out to the hall where he started pulling grumpy but playful faces. 'Has anyone ever told you before that you drive them crazy?' he asked me.

Lifting up his jumper to quickly kiss his belly I teased, 'A few.'

Anxiously, he pushed me away, laughing. 'Stop it. Don't be starting something that you can't finish. I'm already frustrated enough as it is. You're killing me here, girl.'

So I reached up to kiss him on the lips and promised him, 'It'll all be worth the wait. You just have to have some patience, unfortunately.'

And, surprisingly, he agreed. 'You're right, mystery lady. I'm loving the danger and the intrigue that's been going on. But when it's the right time we'll know. Now go on and help Maura, and don't forget to tell that little lad how lucky he is having such a sexy woman putting him to bed – I'd steal his spot any night.' As I leaned in to kiss him one last time, Rory looked around before swiftly lifting me up, pushing my legs around him for balance, and through my haze of giddiness told me, 'I'm going to Rio next Monday for a week. When I'm back can you make a window to see me?'

'A week?'

'Yeah, sorry. I'm there to film some prostitution ring. It's meant to be pretty grim. So when I get back, I'll be needing me some good lovin'. Hopefully, if you're up for it, you'll be the woman to give it to me?' Before I got an opportunity to speak, he pinched my leg, making me squeal with laughter.

Of course, that only alerted the children to the strange activity, causing both the girls to appear at the top of the stairs, asking, 'What's going on?'

Sensing that I was sailing too close to the wind, I immediately shouted back, 'I'll be up in five minutes to read you a story,' and wriggled for Rory to put me down.

Pushing him out the door I waited till he was halfway down the drive before quickly flashing him my boobs from under my sweatshirt. 'I'll call you, OK?'

To which he gave me the thumbs up and mused, 'I hope so, as you are now my mysterious Irish colleen. There's a lot I need to find out about you.' Turning at the gate, he continued, 'Well, there's a lot I need to uncover, anyhow.' Happy in himself, he blew me one last kiss and then disappeared off into the cold sleeting rain. As happy as a cat with nine lives, I returned inside, grinning from ear to ear.

Feeling like I had a noose around my neck, I arrived into Sir Charlie's on Saturday night determined to complete my mission in one final eight-hour shift. From the point of view of the bouncers outside the club, I was just walking up the streets towards them, chatting into my phone. But of course my filming had begun, and I was talking about them and had them on camera as I approached. As luck would have it, they were the particularly dodgy-looking ones that had been on the door the evening I overheard the two guys in the toilet complaining about Craig withholding their drugs. If there was some way I could catch them acting inappropriately again, my job here would be done. Distracted by the already long queue of scantily clad women behind their red ropes, neither of them took much notice of me hanging around possibly longer than I should have, ensuring that I was able to capture their faces and voices on camera.

Once inside, I could see Craig holding court, and got a devil's glare from him as I walked past his post at the manager's station. Determined not to show any weakness, I smiled back at him and kept on walking, all the while thinking to myself, *I'm going to get you tonight*. With my hidden camera safely in place and fully charged, I stepped out on to a floor which was heaving with Saturday-night partygoers. I felt ready to take on the world as I hummed along to the tune 'Bulletproof', and prayed that I myself wouldn't have to be. I was doing this to secure my future – Daisy's future – and when I was finished we would go back to Dublin with a fat cheque and return to our old life.

Deciding to be proactive and see if I could make friends with the doormen, I prepared them some of their favourite 'special coffees' and trotted out to get acquainted. Despite the fact that I was brandishing hot toddies I didn't exactly receive the warm welcome I was hoping for. After a few grunts of acknowledgement they turned their backs on me and I was left with nothing else to do but return inside. Once there, I was cornered by Craig. After a barrage of questions – including, 'What were you doing outside?' and, 'What weight are you now?' – I managed to fob him off with some generic answers. Knowing that I wouldn't get anywhere being his hate-figure, I chose to ignore his grumpiness and tried to turn on the old Valentine charm. Did it work? No. He barely showed a smile, not to mention his dental work; instead he informed me that a large party from a fashion show would be in around midnight, and that I needed to be on top of my game.

Cursing him, and creeped out by his nasty obsession with his female employees' weight, I went through the motions of serving my tables, and after asking one of the other girls if they could babysit my station, I went for a ramble out the back to see if I could locate any dodgy dealings. Although a couple of the chefs were playing cards, smoking roll-ups and drinking shots of what looked like whiskey in one of the storerooms, I kept moving with a wink and a smile, as I was in pursuit of much bigger wrong-doers.

Not knowing what I was looking for, I began to walk in the direction of Craig's office and was astonished, yet quietly thrilled, to find it open. Of course I didn't know what I might find or where to look now that I was in, but I felt a good place to start might be his filing cabinets. Right enough, between the sheets of invoices was a half-empty bottle of vodka and a large Bank of England bag of coins and rolled-up notes. Lifting them both up for the camera in my hair to properly view them, I made a little joke that if we had been living in Chicago during the Prohibition era I might just have bagged me a crime, but I quickly replaced them both and continued with my search.

With nothing else in the cabinets, I tried his desk, but all of the drawers were locked. Rummaging around in coin boxes and on shelves for keys, I was out of luck. Nothing was going to be found on this search – except, it turned out, me. Hearing a noise from behind, I turned to find a small, extremely camp-looking young twenty-something stand-ing in the doorway.

'What are you looking for?' he asked, his pencilled eye-brows arched.

The truth slipped out before I had even consciously processed it: 'Coke.'

'Excellent!' He grinned. 'Did you find any?'

10

My snooping had been discovered by none other than Craig's ex-boyfriend. Luckily for me, the split had been acrimonious. I played along with Matti's desire to bitch about what a shit Craig was, and how, 'He should know better than to dump the best shag he ever had!' We bonded briefly over hating men and needing coke, and returned downstairs to a now even-busier floor, where Matti blended into the crowd, yet thankfully kept well away from Craig or any other staff members.

Assuming that Matti was the one that the guys I'd overheard in the toilet had described as Craig's 'bitch', I wondered if Matti could have been dumped by Craig in an effort to protect him? If that was the case, Matti sure as hell wasn't doing himself any favours by hanging around. Unfortunately, I already had too many unanswered questions buzzing around my head, and there was no room to add my worries about Matti to the list just yet. So, although I kept one wandering eye on his whereabouts, I got on with the job at hand.

By 1 a.m. the place had begun to resemble a tin of sardines, with the room full of skinny models draping their long, lean limbs all over the furniture. Instead of delighting in Saturday night fever, all the faces looked sullen and miserable – and intent on getting wasted. Everywhere you looked people were sucking on straws as they drank vodkas or glasses of white wine. Thinking back to my own underage drinking, I figured they were using the straws in a clear attempt to get the alcohol into their systems quicker, and like a concerned mammy I just wondered: with their zero-sized waists and zero body-fat, where the hell was the booze going to go?

Needing once again to focus my worries, I decided that if they didn't care what state they were getting into, neither should I. I concentrated instead on feeling slim and fabulous, and being on the ball when it came to my tables. 'Welcome to Sir Charlie's. I'm Alice, let me know if I can be of service.' It was only as these words slid off my tongue for about the fifth time that evening that I realized I was saying them to an oddly familiar-looking face. The one and only Ed Black had slipped on to one of my tables, and was looking even more gorgeous in the flesh. Famed in the tabloids for his one-night stands with actresses, pop-stars, TV presenters – but never models – he was the biggest fashion designer to emerge out of London since McQueen and McCartney, with a profile akin to that of the art world's bad boy, Damien Hirst.

There was a short exchange of words between himself and another male friend before the boys ordered two *pints* of Jack Daniels and full-fat Coca-Cola. And within seconds of me turning to the bar to get their order I heard the words, 'Nice arse,' coming from behind.

Doing my best to sound sassy, I swiftly turned back and joked, 'Thank you. Such a shame it couldn't fit into any of your designs, though,' before continuing off to the bar.

As the night grew on, so did the banter between Ed and his pal Joshua, and it was becoming increasingly obvious why Ed never shagged any of the lacklustre models in his entourage, as all they seemed to do was complain about not having enough drugs. They were unrelentingly sickly and grumpy. Meanwhile, I couldn't help being a little starstruck by the celebrity designer and his mate. So I began slagging Ed off, and saying things like: 'You're the black hole that sucked talent up and spat it back out again.'

Suddenly, after one too many of his models had asked me for coke, I found my moment of clarity. At first I'd batted off their interruptions as much as I could, feeling they were getting in the way of my socializing, but now I finally copped the opportunity they were giving me to incriminate the bouncers. Slipping outside, I politely asked one of the hard guys standing next to the head of security, Jake Lewis. 'Listen, I'm really sorry, but Ed Black is at my table with a load of models, and they keep asking me for coke. They're saying they're gonna leave soon if they don't get sorted. I'm not sure what the story is, but I just thought I'd pass it on.'

Staring at me without any sort of reaction at first, the hard guy finally said, 'Leave it with me. Tell them there's been a delay and we have some on the way.'

Fighting the urge to kiss him or scream with joy, I calmly replied, 'Sure.' Then I skipped back off towards my monstrous models and told them, 'Good news, girls. There are some supplies on the way.'

Overhearing me, Ed's pal Joshua let out a cry of 'Hallelujah', and gaiety was once again restored to the beautiful people. By 3 a.m., though, the posse of half-collapsed models had nearly met their limit, with only their normal-looking mates, most probably make-up artists and hairdressers, keeping them animated. Watching his flock disintegrate before him, Ed leaned over to me and asked, 'What's the story on the coke? I can't stand the stuff, but unless I get something into these bitches, I'll be celebrating the launch of my new collection on my own.'

Telling him I'd make some more enquiries, I headed back outside, and this time called Jake over to speak with me. Apologizing for interrupting him, I told him about the situation inside and asked if he could help, hoping that he would use the words 'cocaine' and 'I will supply' in the same sentence. But he just asked me to send Ed or Joshua out to him so he could deal directly with them. Back at the table I did what I was told, and, without missing a beat, Joshua jumped up and declared that he was going to sort this out. Within minutes he had returned. 'Stand up, everyone, and grab your coats, you've pulled. We're going back to mine now.'

As if they were just puppets on a string, the dead models awoke and rose up tall, pulling themselves and their matching grungy duffle coats together. Ed asked for the bill, and on my return with it had another order for me. 'You're to get your coat, too. You're too much fun to leave behind.'

'You'd never be able to handle me. My chunky ass is too juicy even for your black hole. And I've to hang on here, anyway. I won't finish my shift for another hour, at least.'

Not accepting this, Ed summonsed Craig to tell him, 'We need to kidnap this woman. My sanity depends on it.'

Thankfully, Craig was still avoiding Matti, who, remaining at the bar in a rage of jealousy, had quite blatantly started snogging another young man. So I knew Craig wouldn't have heard about me searching his office. In fact, he was actually pleased that I had made an impact on an important VIP like Black. He showed the broadest smile I'd ever seen and cheerily said, 'Take her. She's all yours.'

Curious, I asked, 'But what about my station?'

Craig just shook his head and answered, 'Go and enjoy yourself. Don't worry about a thing.'

As Craig dismissed himself to go and check on the transport, Black told me to put £250 on the bill for my 'excellent service' – and hurry up, as they'd be waiting outside in a car for me.

I was putting on my coat when I suddenly questioned why the hell I was going to this house party. Sure, it would make for a great salacious story to tell Parker and Lisa over a couple of glasses of vino tomorrow evening, as by then I would be nursing my hangover with a cure. But hadn't I captured enough footage on my camera this evening without needing to frame more people for drugs? Or had I? Still wondering whether to stay or go, leave the camera in or take my headpiece off, I was in the middle of checking myself out in the mirror to see how all the electronics were holding up when Heidi, one of the other waitresses, popped her head around the corner and bellowed, 'Your chariot awaits you. Ed Black says to hurry the fuck up!'

Making the decision to go and enjoy myself, but leave the camera in just in case, I grabbed my stuff, waved goodbye to the staff – hopefully for the final time – and rushed out the front door to be ushered into a black Hummer limo. The two boys cheered as I arrived, though the models groaned with disapproval, and I realized that this wasn't going to be an easy crowd to win over. I was just beginning to curse my judgement when one of the girls at the other end of the car asked, 'What's the story with the charlie, Joshua? Did you fucking get sorted or what?'

Sitting in beside him, I remained silent as he replied, 'Jake has sorted it, babe. He's personally delivering it to my gaff. Said something like there was too much heat around the club tonight, so they couldn't hand it over. So talk yourself down from that ledge, babe, you'll get your snow very soon.'

Trying to talk myself off a ledge – a ledge of excitement at the thought of getting my documentary finished – I started to bounce around in my seat to the music of Beyoncé, and began singing along to my own version of the lyrics, 'Well, if you liked it then you shoulda stuck your finger up it . . .' Despite hating the idea of socializing with a mere mortal, even the snottiest of models cracked pretty soon, and before the song had itself finished, the entire limo were singing along to my new version.

We pulled up outside an old three-storey Victorian house that resembled a derelict-looking squat rather than a party palace fit for professional mannequins. Clearly a regular haunt for this crowd, it seemed that I was the only one to think the place looked like a shithole. Navigating my way around old sofas and piles of full black bin-liners as I walked up the garden path, I had to suppress screams of horror when I thought I saw a rat run out from behind a bush. The inside of the house offered a completely different set-up. Superbly finished, it was a tastefully decorated and elegantly restored building, absolutely in keeping with the period. Grand paintings loomed large on the walls, giant grandfather clocks ticked, and antique coat- and umbrella-stands stood proudly in the hall, as if waiting for the arrival of Sherlock Holmes.

Full of questions, I held my tongue as all the girls filed into one of the back rooms, where some nondescript dance music was promptly put on and everyone began lighting up cigarettes. Not quite comfortable in my surroundings, I tried to blend in by asking, 'What do you have to do around here to score a drink?'

An animated Ed Black replied, 'Scoring *me* is always a good start!'

That rippled in a collective slagging from the models, who teased, 'Ah, you're all right, we're not that thirsty!'

I found the side of a leather sofa to drape myself across, and did my best to look content with my own company. Soon enough Joshua arrived holding a basin of bottles, which included everything from vodka and champagne to some dodgy-looking cans of cider. As another girl arrived with armfuls of glasses, I cheekily offered my professional services to open the champagne, and teased that if I drank enough I just might manage to open it without the use of my hands. Claiming that he had seen that done before on a trip to Bangkok, Ed ordered that I start drinking immediately, and was just in the middle of telling Joshua the details when a stressed-looking Jake Lewis burst through the door. 'You're some bastards,' he declared. 'You lot are about as subtle as a puff at Gay Pride!'

'Shut up and get your arse in here,' snapped one of the models. 'I need me some baggies.'

'That's no problem, Janice.' Jake smiled. 'You just need to show me some readies. There's no more credit for you. I've told you before, and now I'll tell you again: I'm not carrying you any more. I'm doing a spring clean through all my old tabs, and you, my lovely, are top of my list.'

The room fell quiet as everyone assessed the stand-off

between Janice and Jake. There were calls of 'woooo' that cut the tension, and one model, thinking she was hilarious, chanted, 'Fight! Fight! Fight—'

Ed Black interrupted, 'Easy does it, guys,' and ushered Jake back outside the door. Then he asked softly, 'How much are we talking here, chief? Maybe I can fix you up.' After a few short words outside there was a loud screech from Ed: 'How much?' Followed by, 'She can fuck off. No way, man.' Back in the room, Ed screamed over at the model who'd reached her credit limit. 'What the fuck do you do with it, Janice? Sprinkle the stuff on your cornflakes?'

Visibly embarrassed, Janice picked up her bag and ran out of the room past both Jake and Ed, cursing them both as she went by. Showing no loyalty at all, the rest of the group sniggered with laughter at her humiliation and proceeded to make their own deals with Jake. As Ed settled himself on the chair next to me, I overheard him whisper to the girl across from him, 'Fifteen K.' And to whoops of laughter he added, 'She can go fuck herself with that sort of bad debt. She'd be a decrepit old woman before she'd worked it off. And her ole saggy ass would be no good to me then, that's for sure.'

Doing my best to smooth over the friction, I resumed my expert champagne-opening skills, and in a bid to entertain Ed pretended to aim the cork at each of the models' heads, as if I was going to let it go like a shotgun. As Jake started to dole out little clear plastic bags of cocaine, I did my best not to stare, continuing to crack jokes with Ed and the comatose model sitting beside him. Clearly anxious after seeing what had happened to Janice, all the girls riffled through their tiny handbags and offered up £80 for each of their packages. And then, with the same ease that I'm sure they felt stepping out on to a catwalk half-naked, they immediately emptied rolled-up notes out of their purses and used Visa cards to chop up the 'good white'.

Ed made it so clear he hated the stuff that the pressure to dabble was off me, and I could save face. In typical Irish self-deprecating fashion I joked, 'I'd like to hang on to the few remaining brain cells that I have, thanks. Unfortunately I was lumbered with more fat cells than brain cells, so I have to protect them as best I can . . .'

Ed kindly jumped to my defence and whispered, 'You're more woman than any of these bitches, honey, so don't feel the need to put yourself down.'

Unsure if he was making a move on me, I played the mate game rather than being flirty, and although I knew I now had all the evidence I needed to end the documentary, I decided to hang around a little longer and let myself have a little fun. As loud me-conversations began over what fashion campaigns or shoots each of the models had coming up, I watched as the madness in the room increased and their eyes widened in a crazy, unhappy way. It was then that I felt strangely comforted. As I looked around the room I thought to myself that while I might not be a size four, if this was what these so-called beautiful people called happiness, they were more than welcome to keep it. Feeling like a voyeur at some reality-TV experiment, I started to enjoy watching the addicted. While they wiped their noses on the hems of their skirts, their sleeves or – as one poor unfortunate did – on a curtain, I wished that Parker and Lisa were with me to witness the drama, and that they'd brought some popcorn and cheesy nachos with them!

Although I was having fun, not even the free champagne and the ringside seat could fight off the tiredness. Finally unable to ignore my exhaustion, I finished off my drink and, trying to be as subtle as possible, picked up my coat and bag and edged away from the sordid party without telling anyone I was about to leave. Just as I approached the front door the doorbell rang, bringing both Ed and Joshua into the hallway.

'Where do you think you're going?' asked Ed, leaning against the living-room door. 'The conversation in here is getting pretty dull, I know. But if you go I might just have to attack myself with a blunt instrument and give myself a lobotomy to put up with this crowd. Please don't go.'

Flattered by his request, I laughed back, 'Ah, I'm sure you'll survive,' before pointing towards the door and suggesting, 'Maybe this could be your saviour now?' Not wanting to open the door to any more drug-dealers, I stepped back and allowed the man of the house to greet his new callers. Preparing to slip out inconspicuously once the coast was clear, I was surprised to see both of the sexy barmen, Blue and Harry, from Wednesday night at Sir Charlie's. They were accompanied by some other equally hunky guys.

I had to think twice about my decision when they came out with, 'Don't go now, darlin', we've just brought the party with us.'

Against all my better judgement I buckled, gushing, 'I suppose I could stay another half hour.'

Easily another hour or so later, I was back in the living room dancing on the furniture and playing a nonsensical game of Who Can Gyrate Their Hips the Most? with Harry. It was all juvenile and fun until a couple of the girls got into a debate over who had the most sticky-out nipples, and decided to expose their breasts to prove their point. Although I was no Pamela Anderson myself, I had to struggle to stop myself shouting, 'Turn around, we can't tell who's pointier by looking at your back!'

I was saved from the embarrassment when one of the guys loudly joked, 'Which one of you two girls gets the best reception for BBC 1? Maybe I should give them a tweak and see?'

As the room laughed, a few of the lads playfully jostled as if to form an orderly queue to take turns tweaking the buttons. The jokes turned to gags like, 'I'd been searching for the perfect place to hang my coat,' and, 'They certainly look like my kind of ear plugs!'

Calming my inner diva, and returning to sitting rather than standing on the couch, I found myself cushioned into Harry's shoulder without realizing how I had gotten there. Knowing that I shouldn't be in such a compromising situation because I was now dating Rory, I drunkenly reasoned that my roving cameraman was far too nice to be believed, and that after I told him the truth about me, he'd be running out the door anyway before I got a chance to explain myself. With those stupid thoughts in my head, and the memory of being painfully dumped in the past, I decided that I would pucker up to the gorgeous Harry when he lunged, and even whispered the words *carpe diem!* just before we kissed.

Although I went with it for a couple of minutes, I soon pretended that his hands were tickling me so I could pull away. Despite being incredibly handsome, even more so than Rory, to be honest, he was without question one of the worst kissers I had ever come across: wet, sloppy, and most annoyingly slow and weak with his tongue movements. I almost felt like I wanted to throw up because an image of kissing someone's granny kept flashing into my head.

I'd kissed a girl (and I really had) with more power and strength in her little toe, never mind her jaw, and I knew the universe was sending me a message. I read it loud and clear: in no way was I meant to be kissing any boy other than Rory – well, definitely not this one, anyway.

Doing my best to ease him off me with some random jokes, I was doing well until Harry started prodding at my hair with his finger, and questioned what the hell had I stuffed inside my wig? For a split second I allowed him poke about at my hairpiece before quickly remembering that I was still wearing my hidden camera. Unable to push his strong hand away, I first crumpled on to the ground to get away from him, and then scrambled to my feet, claiming I didn't feel well. Seeing that my coat was stuck under the bums of another courting couple, in a split-second decision I chose to abandon it and just grabbed my handbag and ran out the door before he could assess the situation further. But it was too late – Henry wasn't drunk enough not to realize he'd spotted something. He ran out after me, shouting, 'What are you hiding in there? Are you a fucking undercover copper?'

Knowing that my cover was blown, I unbolted the door and fled out into the dark. I had no idea where I was running, but I was sure I didn't have time to hang around and work out the best route home. I just avoided the streetlights and prayed that I'd be lost in the darkness. I could hear Harry calling from the garden, but he didn't seem bothered to come out after me. Maybe he was busy rounding up a search party, who knew? All *I* knew was that I wasn't prepared to take any chances. My getaway needed to be fast. And I wasn't going to make it easy for him to find me if he did come hunting.

With my heart pumping out of my chest and my throat feeling like it was being cut by the cold air rushing through it, I added to my misery by removing my shoes so I could run faster. Figuring the consequences of being caught by a gang of lads who handled drugs would be a lot worse than any damage that could be done to my feet, I jogged as fast as I could with my shoes and handbag in each hand and chanted to myself, 'I'm going to be safe. I'm gonna be safe. I just got to keep . . . running . . .'

Several minutes down the road I heard a car approaching fast from behind me, so I quickly ducked behind a garden wall and waited with bated breath. As it slowed down just by where I was hiding, I was sure that I was about to be caught. I didn't pop my head up to check and see if I recognized anyone in the car and thankfully it moved on, leaving me whispering to my guardian angel, 'Thank you, thank you, whoever or wherever you are.'

My body was now shivering and my teeth chattering with the cold, and I knew that I had to keep moving to be in with a fighting chance of getting back to safety. So, after feeling my hair and deciding that my camera was still safe enough to remain there, I cautiously slipped back out on to the road, and started running again like my life depended on it. Fighting the negative thoughts that were racing through my mind, I tried to keep thinking positively, and as the streets remained empty and quiet I joked with myself that the exercise would do me good, and that if it was celebrity-spotting I was after, this was probably the best time to bump into a few of them, because they'd probably be out jogging at this early hour, too.

As my body neared breaking point, I happened upon a petrol station. Like the North Star, its neon lights shone bright, and gave me the extra energy I needed to keep me going. Of course, once I reached it, I found its glass doors were shut. But after some pleading with the young guy on the other side of the hatch, I eventually got him to open the doors, though he said, 'If you come in, you'll have to buy some shit . . .'

I limped past the piles of morning newspapers, feeling like a misplaced hooker who'd just escaped from a human-trafficking ring. I knew I looked bloodied and bruised, but kept smiling in a positive way, hoping that it would distract from my dishevelled appearance. Then I asked if he could phone me a cab, and if he served anything hot? He told me I'd have to wait ten to fifteen minutes for the cab, and that hot dogs and coffee were the only HOT things in the place – adding, 'Apart from me, of course!' Trust a hormone-filled teenager to find a woman hot even when she'd been almost run into the ground!

I was just about able to work the coffee machine, so I made myself a cappuccino and left it sitting for a few moments to cool. Unsure what else to do, I went fishing for my mobile in my handbag, almost dropping it on the floor with my misconnecting frozen fingers. The coffee was still too hot to hold, so I put my phone down beside it on the counter and cupped my hands over the steam, relishing the heat. Although it took me a couple of stabs to take my phone off keylock, when I did it read: 1 New Message.

Like a beacon of hope, RAVISHING RORY flashed up on my phone. Nervously laughing at the ridiculousness of his title – and vowing to change it in the morning, if I ever got out of this nightmare alive – I opened it up to read the words, 'Hey sexy! R U missing me yet? Just arrived in Rio. Weather too hot. Wish I was back cuddling with you xox.'

I swallowed the lump in my throat and tried not to let my eyes fill up. Until my taxi came, I was still in danger, and I couldn't afford to let my emotions get the better of me. I needed to remain alert and on my guard. The last thing I wanted was to have any more champagne secrets, and tonight had to spell the end of them.

The young man working in the station was smiling at me – he found my dishevelled, semi-naked state understandably amusing – and it was an effort to avoid his eye. So I hid myself in behind the coffee machine, warily watching for the taxi and fiddling with my shoes. I tried to get them back on, but I had too many cuts and grazes. I suddenly realized that my tough-girl act might make the petrol-station guy laugh, but I'd pushed the boundaries too far. I had infiltrated a posse of drug addicts and their dealer. Did I really have the nerve to hand over the incriminating evidence I'd collected? Could I live with the worry of shopping them all? What about the guilt if I didn't? Most of all, what would happen to Daisy if I was caught by Harry – or worse – Jake Lewis?

Thankfully, I did make it home safe. When I arrived in the door Maura was already up, and looked at me with alarm. Without the energy to explain what had happened, but just enough to let her know I hadn't been hurt or attacked, I slumped against the kitchen table. Keeping any conversation for a later stage, she ushered me into the front room with supplies of blankets and a hot-water bottle. Ordering me to lock the partition door from the inside, she gave me one of her long motherly hugs and told me to get some sleep.

'We'll talk when you're ready.' She smiled, then left me and my body to rest.

★   ★   ★

By Monday morning and after several soaks in salty baths, I had thawed out enough to feel almost human again. I hadn't spoken to anyone about my ordeal yet, not even Parker or Maura, but the one person I knew I had to speak to was Bradley. Not wanting to be overheard, I went to the local park on my own, claiming I was just popping out to buy milk and bread. I wasn't sure how this conversation was going to go. But I sure as hell knew that it would involve a bit of shouting.

I settled myself on a quiet bench, and it took me several attempts before I actually dialled Bradley's number. To make sure I forgot none of the facts or details from the weekend, I had jotted out all my thoughts on three pages of notepaper, which I held in my hands as I dialled. Trembling as much as I had when I'd been hiding behind that garden wall the previous morning, I angrily blurted out, 'You nearly got me killed,' the second I heard his voice at the other end. Remembering the fear I'd felt the day before and filled with anger, I must have ranted at him for five minutes solid.

Finally he asked, 'OK, can I speak now? I never meant to put you in danger. As you know, the drugs side of the documentary was only something that gradually grew in importance, once we started investigating Sir Charlie's. And you did agree to do the undercover work, didn't you? You were happy to take all that money . . .' He went on like this until I finally calmed down enough to talk without cursing or screaming.

'OK, we need to strike up a deal,' I told him. 'I've got what you want. But I'm not sure I want to hand it over.'

'What do you mean?' he asked nervously.

'I've got Jake Lewis on camera dealing cocaine—' Before I finished my sentence I could hear Bradley at the other end of the phone whooping with joy. Doing my best to crush his moment of triumph, I continued, 'But I'm not prepared to just hand it over.'

Silent for a few moments, Bradley slowly asked, 'And why is this?'

'*Because I'm worried for my safety*,' I replied, as forcefully as I could.

Realizing that he had to do some more damage limitation with me, he quickly adopted a soothing tone, 'Why don't you come into the office today and we'll talk it through?'

Knowing I'd be in a weaker position on his turf, I firmly told him, 'No,' and kept my spare fingers crossed that I'd stick with that answer.

'Ah, Eva, come on,' he pleaded. 'It's really not as bad as it seems. We might not even use this footage in the final edits.'

Infuriated by his patronizing tone, I quickly interrupted with, 'Don't try and kid a kidder.' I was fiercely angry at his attempts to sway me. 'I'm not thick, Bradley. Scared, yes. Stupid? Maybe up until now. But I'm telling you, I'm going to need a lot of persuading before I'll give you any more film.'

Once again, there was nothing but silence down the line, as Bradley decided how he should play me.

'Eva, I realize you had a scary time of it on Saturday, but—'

'Don't you "but" me, Bradley Brady . . .' By now I was wired, so I went on in a shaky voice, screaming, 'Don't you dare call me Eva. As far as you are concerned, my name is Alice, and you better not tell people any differently.' Feeling a wave of terror grip my body I let loose. 'I am fucking terrified for my safety, and that of my daughter. What good will money be to Daisy, if her mother has been shot dead by a friend of Jake Lewis? Well? Can you live with that on your conscience? Well, can you, Mr Producer?'

Feeling myself starting to hyperventilate, I went no further, and cut the line in a rage.

He rang back immediately, but I couldn't bear to answer it for fear of the things I might say, or the things I might be told. Instead, I ran towards the nearest large tree and flung myself on the ground, crying like a toddler having a tantrum. I was so angry at myself for having been sucked in by the glamour of the money and the prospect of being a TV star.

I couldn't forgive myself for not researching the project carefully and not asking more questions at the start. And also for being naive enough to think that this undercover work was something I would be able to handle. As I kicked and scraped at the dirty ground, the discomfort of the muck filling up my fingernails added to my aggravation. I had been stupid before, but never as reckless as this.

I must have crouched, crying, in the shade of that tree for twenty minutes before the exhaustion of the previous night, and the sheer fatigue of crying, wore me out. I didn't know how I was going to get myself out of this mess, or if it was even possible to do so. But the sight of a woman pushing a buggy in the distance reminded me of my responsibilities to Daisy. I knew I had to change the situation from being a case not of *if*, but *how* I could get us out of danger. Picking myself up off the ground, I vowed that I would never end up in a ditch, or have to hide behind a brick wall in the middle of the night, ever again. To make that happen, though, I would have to stop lying and start sharing more. Did I have the strength to do that?

11

After much texting and planning from Rio, on Thursday evening my big date night out with Rory at a TV awards ceremony finally came around. I was hyper with the excitement, and when he opened his mouth and said, 'Wow, you look a million dollars!' I knew all the effort I had gone to was worth it. Indeed, after a lengthy six hours preparation to make myself camera-ready, the end result made me feel like a plastic princess from the outside in.

As if I was on a mission to go to hell, now not only was my life a fraud, but my skin was covered in Fake Bake, my hair was plumped out with fake hairpieces, my eyes weighed down by Cheryl Cole fake lashes, and my miniature breasts were bolstered by, humiliatingly enough, a pair of sports socks, as I'd forgotten to buy the chicken fillets I needed to whoosh me up. Lisa had been my best bet for a magnificent ballgown at short notice. I picked one out of her wardrobe via Skype, and she very kindly couriered it over to me with the threat that I HAD TO get laid that night, and HAD TO tell her all about it. Otherwise I wouldn't ever be allowed to borrow another thing off her again, as, according to her, dresses like this particular one deserved only nights of romance and lust. I was probably a tad too short to be wearing a full-length champagne-coloured gown. The diamond-encrusted skyscrapers that Lisa had also packed for me did help in making me taller, but they weren't so useful in helping me walk very far – or fast!

Rory was unable to keep his hands off me from the time I fell into the taxi, and his pawing wasn't helping me get to grips with my new diva look. 'Stop touching me,' I cried a couple of times, but my pleas for mercy went unheard.

'You can't tell me to keep my hands off the goods,' he teased. 'You specifically told me earlier in your text that you had gotten all dressed up just for me. Those were your words, so get used to it. You are my property tonight, my plaything, and thank you for doing such a good job for me.' I spent the rest of the taxi ride to the venue trying to fend off his lingering kisses, in a vain attempt to keep my lipstick intact. Although I put up a good fight, I didn't protest too much. I was just so happy to be with him, and loving having him to myself. If anything, my only wish was that Parker and Lisa could be around to see me looking so good. Before I left the house I had taken some nice photos of me with Daisy in a cute princess costume I had picked up in Camden Market and, after her, no one else really mattered.

Although Rory had initially wanted us to walk up the red carpet together in front of all the photographers and autograph hunters, I convinced him that we would only be humiliating ourselves in doing so, as we'd probably get pushed out of the way by Jedward or the Cheeky Girls. As a serious camera man, and as a very important waitress, I wasn't sure that our fragile egos could take the embarrassment. So, instead, he brought me around the side and up the back entrance (joking, 'It won't be the last time I do that') before whisking me into the inner sanctum of London's high fashion parade and a celebrity-spotter's heaven. No matter where I looked, there were recognizable faces to be seen. Jamie Oliver, Louise Redknapp, Ant and Dec, Gok Wan, Myleene Klass, Loyd Grossman; everywhere I looked, famous faces were laughing and air-kissing and generally being fabulous.

Two complimentary glasses of bubbly and several con-versations later – with couples Rory didn't introduce me to because he claimed not to know the wives' names – and it was time to move towards the ballroom and find our seats. After queuing to see the floor plan, I felt giddy at the sight of seeing 'Rory Baxter Plus 1, Table 6.' Praying for a fun table, Rory and I scanned down the list and found we were sitting next to someone called Gavin Taylor. 'I don't know him,' sighed Rory. 'And Mae Durkan, don't know her. Oh, hang on, this should be fun. They've put Tanya Cruze and Issey Blaze at our table together. Those two hate each other. They had some catfight on a plane in Spain or something. I actually think it was to do with who had the bigger boobs. Can you imagine if they kicked off tonight? Talk about ringside seats.'

Struck down with panic, my voice did its usual disappear-ing act, so I just shook my head feverishly as if to reciprocate the excitement, and distracted him by pointing towards the loo. Almost tripping to the floor as I tried to escape, it must have taken me at least three hundred baby-steps to cross the five yards across to the Ladies. Once inside, the only thing I could think of doing was to ring Parker. He would be the man with the answers. He would be my rock of sense. He would be – 'Fucking engaged!' I hadn't meant to verbalize my frustration, but the words seemed to vomit out of my mouth, causing the entire gaggle of lip-gloss junkies to turn around from their prized spots in front of the mirrors and stare in my direction.

With a brief, half-hearted apology, I skulked into a free cubicle and tried to gather my thoughts. Maybe Tanya wouldn't recognize me. After all, she hadn't in Sir Charlie's. But I was no longer in control of the random images that ran through my head – visions of me running out the door with my heels stuffed into my tiny clutch bag faded out to a visual of Tanya and Issey wrestling me to the floor and pouring bottles of red wine all over my beautiful borrowed dress before declaring to the room that I was the scumbag that ruined their lives. I'd been thinking of this award ceremony as a welcome relief from the worry about Sir Charlie's. Now it had all returned, even worse than before. Despite trying to get through to Parker several more times, I had no luck, so I decided to readjust my padding, keep my Irish accent subdued, and hope for the best.

Pushing past all the over-perfumed and over-coiffed Danni Minogue and Jordan wannabes, I re-emerged into the crowd. By the time I tracked down Rory he was buzzing like a true social butterfly and doing an impressive job of working the room. I watched him air-kiss the ladies and bear-hug the lads – everyone he talked to seemed genuinely happy to see him. For a moment I questioned whether I was good enough for him. After all, I was the queen of deceit, while he was Mr Popular.

Not able to handle the idea of countless introductions, I played the 'sore feet' card and asked if we could sit down at our table. We were the first to arrive and I immediately started searching for the name cards. Sure enough, just to add to my hell, both Tanya and Issey had been seated directly opposite me. Despite there being a large candelabra centre-piece between us, I made the quick decision that if the girls were sitting slightly to my left, instead of opposite, I'd have a greater chance of ignoring them. Doing my best to hide what I was up to, I asked Rory to go to the bar for me, so I could change the seating arrangements without fear of him asking too many questions. But my request did nothing but open up a whole new range of questions.

The first was, 'Can you not drink the wine on the table?' The next, 'Can you not hang on for a waiter?'

And then, while Rory debated whether or not he'd have a fighting chance of getting served even if he did go to the bar as, according to him, blokes never got served, a glamor-ous couple approached the table and sat down, leaving me no option but to smile and say hello, and forget all about changing any of the name cards.

Pouring a hefty serving of white wine into my red wine glass, I got the oddest look from Rory as I proceeded to knock it back in one. 'Steady on there, gorgeous,' he said. 'We've got a long night ahead of us, and I've loads of colleagues that I'm dying to show you off to. Let's not give them reason to start telling any Paddy jokes, all right?' Acknowledging his plea, I stopped gulping, but only managed to leave a drop in the bottom of the glass. Giving him my best puppy-dog eyes, I apologized, and with a quick kiss on my nose he was swiftly sidetracked by a couple of guys sitting down at a nearby table. I shooed him away to go chat to them and burn off some energy.

As the tables began to fill up and the stage just in front of us became cluttered with beefy blokes in black jeans and tees moving microphones and teleprompters around, I prayed that the girls, who still remained at large, would be no-shows. By the time the show kicked off, it seemed my prayers had been answered, as neither one of the now former-WAGs had turned up to occupy their seats.

As the host, JT Collins, took to the floor to welcome, 'All the liggers and everyone else from the meeja business,' I could feel a weight lifting off my naked, shimmering shoulders, and I began to relax into the fun of the evening. With Rory, my proud date, by my side, my panic dissolved away and once again life felt good. I liked being his girl. Although he hadn't actually used the term 'girlfriend' yet, I certainly felt that I was, and hoped that he would be calling me that by the end of the night.

After a fairly inedible starter – allegedly a crab cake – JT took to the stage again and told everyone to, 'Hush up, please, as I've four very good reasons for you to give me your attention.' As suggestions like Westlife and Take That were shouted from around the room, JT giggled with excitement. Pleading for some quiet, he explained: 'We're talking bigger than Westlife.'

The crowd cried out, 'Wooo.'

'Yes. And we're talking bigger than Take That.'

The crowd 'wooed' again.

'And, combined, they're bigger than Katie Price. Put your hands together, people, for Tanya Cruze and Issey Blaze.'

The audience went wild, and I began to feel like I was the front-seat passenger in a car crash waiting to happen. The lights from the stage flickered with such intensity that I found it hard to breathe, and before I had a chance to hyperventilate, the girls emerged from opposite sides of the stage and walked towards each other as if they were going into battle. As they stopped, just inches away from touching, the audience fell silent and dramatic *X-Factor* music bellowed from the speakers. JT spoke over it in his best *Star Wars* voice, 'They said they were enemies. They said they were in rehab. They said they were finished. But they were wrong.' As the room hummed with excitement JT coughed before saying, 'But they never predicted a reconciliation. Girls, take it away!'

And then as the audience whooped and screamed with joy, the girls leaned slowly forward, embraced, boob to boob, and locked lips in a full-on snog. The huge video screens at either side of the stage closed in on their glossy mouths as the girls drew back, smiling, and then went for it again. Unable to control his enthusiasm, Rory punched the air and screamed, 'There is a God!' Then he quickly resumed his seat and kissed me on the nose. 'Sorry, hon. But that's the way to open a show.'

As the dramatic music continued, and the girls' smooching became wetter and deeper, JT took up his commentary again and teased, 'What do Britney and Madonna know about kissing? Now *that*, people, is a girl-on-girl snog with authenticity!'

After the girls finally parted, the pair of them bounced their barely covered, well-enhanced boobs over to JT and asked, 'Did ya like that?'

Trying to keep a straight face, through the screams of hecklers, JT replied, 'Yes. That was a lovely show of, emm, friendship. Is that what you might call a traditional WAG greeting?'

'Nah,' Issey answered. 'We're not WAGs any more.'

Tanya then chose her moment to cut in and channel Beyoncé with some 'Single Lady' lyrics of her own – 'Any single ladies in the audience? Put your hands up, girls!' – lifting Issey's arm up as well as her own.

While JT temporarily lifted his own up in the air and shared in the joke, he quickly resumed his composure and thanked the ladies for sharing their new status, and asked them to announce the first winner.

'Thanks, JT,' beamed Tanya, as always the more assertive one. 'Both me and Issey were delighted to . . .'

'. . . kiss and make up tonight,' gushed Issey.

'Ha! Ha! And the winner of this year's Best On Screen Kiss was . . .'

As the girls used their stage performance to grab as many headlines for themselves as possible, the terror I had experienced earlier seized hold of me again. Rory's eyes were still firmly fixed on Issey and Tanya, so he was unaware of my mental anguish as I twisted and turned in my seat, trying to work out how to avoid a confrontation. With the heat rising, I was checking all the nearest fire exits when a man from behind our table leaned over between Rory's shoulder and mine and bellowed, 'Hey, pal, brace yourself for the silicone invasion! You're one lucky bastard!' Within a few short moments the girls had left the stage and were seated at our table. Despite giving a frenzied wave to all of us, me included, their attention was obstructed by the legions of well-wishers and horny blokes that seemed to be magnetically pulled towards them from other tables.

Although my heart was pounding, it slowly became apparent that my fear of these women was similar to my irrational fear of spiders. Just because they were close, it didn't mean they were going to spring over and bite me. And as the evening continued and the girls revelled in their tabloid triumph, the tension in my body eased. Although I couldn't exactly say I was enjoying myself, I did take some pleasure in the subtle and the not-so-subtle PDAs that

Rory was showing me. Clearly appreciating the time I had taken to look the part, he made the effort to put his arm protectively around my shoulder, to shower me regularly with kisses, and to order me my own bottle of champagne – in between texting his mates at other tables, that is, and giving me a running commentary on who was supposedly having affairs and who was already falling over drunk.

As the night continued and the awards for 'Best Sex Scene' and 'Readers' Poll Best Torso' were announced, Tanya and Issey's frequent trips to the toilet left them looking increasingly messed up. After starting a wager with a fun couple sitting next to us, Rory was set to pocket £50 if both glamour girls managed to keep their nipples under wraps, and another £50 if they lasted the night without another catfight. But by the time JT said his own inimitable goodbyes – thanking the chairman of the magazine on stage by enthusiastically grabbing his bottom and pretending to snare him in a manly snog – Rory was out of pocket £100, as both girls got their nips out for a passing photographer, an event which led directly to a series of increasingly violent arguments over who was attracting the most attention, and who was going to try and bed Gerard Butler. Happy to hand over the cash, Rory gushed, 'Some girls are just cheap entertainment.' Then he turned to me and cooed, 'Whereas you, my gorgeous, are simply high class.'

By the time we'd finished the last of our champagne, most of the other guests had departed for the bar already so, with flowers from the place-setting in my hair, we merrily headed that way so that Rory could, as he put it, 'Finally get a proper drink.' As we joined the tailback, Rory bumped into a guy whose name he actually *did* remember. He called him Slash, without elaborating further than that. The two boys started laughing and joking like they were long-lost brothers. There was a bit of whispering, and some coded talk, which from what I could make out seemed to be about another woman, possibly an ex of Rory's. But when Slash took an all-too-long look at my bum, Rory protectively complained, 'Hey, take your eyes off my lady's trunk, thank you very much.'

Taking it all in his stride, Slash offered a half-apology. 'Sorry, buddy, but it's gotta be noted, your lady has got junk in her trunk.'

Giddy from the bubbles, and not wanting an argument to break out, I whooped, 'Yes, I have! But the only man getting his hands on this junk is my man, Rory.' I kissed him to break the tension. Then I remembered Lisa's threats, decided to be bold, and suggested to Rory, 'Let's forget about getting another drink for the moment. Why don't we find a broom closet or a storeroom to get naughty in?'

Surprised, he asked, 'Really? Absolutely. Any ideas where?'

Looking back into the ballroom, I signalled towards the stage and said, 'Wanna try backstage? There have to be some free dressing rooms by now. Everyone is out here in the bar.'

Not needing to be asked twice, Rory playfully slapped my bum and started to whistle loudly as he led me back into the now emptying venue. Passing the last of the stragglers, Rory chuckled in a giddy manner. 'You have a very naughty mind. But I like it. I like it a lot!'

As we arrived over at the edge of the stage it was obvious that we had to take a chance, and try to slip behind the curtain where the celebrities had been coming out. Looking at Rory, I asked, 'Are you game?'

After a quick look over his shoulder, he replied, 'You are my dream woman. Let's go!' As we slipped behind the velvet curtain Rory couldn't help but let out an excited giggle. Like an experienced burglar, I shushed him to stay quiet and gripped his hand even tighter. I told him to stand tall, and, if we were stopped, to offer the excuse that we were collecting some borrowed dresses. So we continued to tip-toe through the cables and around giant kit boxes until we reached a long corridor that had a row of closed doors. We ran down to the first door, but hesitated when we heard a group of people talking inside. The next two were both occupied, too, and it wasn't until we reached the final one that we heard the sweet sound of silence. Looking like he'd just won the Lottery, Rory cried, 'BINGO!' As he opened the door, we were greeted by nothing but darkness.

Feeling for a light switch, I found one and flicked it on, but Rory quickly switched it off again. 'What are you doing?' I asked.

With a naughty plan clearly in mind, Rory told me, 'Be quiet. Wait and see.' I bumped into chairs as I shuffled inside, and Rory shushed again as I let out hearty cackles of laughter. He masterfully manoeuvred me around, positioning me on what felt, in the pitch dark, like a sturdy make-up table. Standing somewhere in front of me, he began slowly to lift up my dress and expose my legs. My laughter gone, all I could hear was his deep, controlled breathing. In the cold room his breath warmed my chest as he leaned over to kiss my small, but now heaving, breasts. He had to grapple with my dress, but managed somehow to ruche it up around my middle. The waist was corseted, and despite his best efforts the rest of my body remained tightly bound by smooth satin. He stuffed the overflowing material into my hands, saying in his husky voice, 'Hold that up.' Large, strong fingers pulled at my G-string, slowly edging it out from under me, and slipping it softly down over my thighs and off past my toes.

Since dirty-talk wasn't exactly a specialty of mine, I struggled to find the perfect words to enhance the moment. Choosing to keep it simple, I whispered, 'Come here and let me feel your rock-hard dick,' and hoped that that would turn him on. Of course it did.

Letting out a quiet laugh, Rory muttered under his breath, 'You are one sexy minx. You are so fucking hot.'

As I thanked him, and applauded his great taste, I tried to adjust my eyes to the gloom, but I could barely see what Rory was doing as he banged about in front of me. It was the sounds which gave him away. From the rustle of belts, zips and buttons it was obvious that he was undressing himself, and I felt exhilarated with excitement at the arrival, at last, of our first time.

Not wanting to ruin the moment, but not wanting to get caught out either, I gently asked, 'Rory, by any chance do you have any—'

'Of course,' he interrupted. 'I didn't think we were going to get the opportunity tonight. But I bought a fresh pack of condoms today, just in case.'

'Aren't you the presumptuous one?' I teased, as I quickly slipped my sports socks out from under my dress and into my handbag for safe keeping.

'Well, surely you can't blame a guy for dreaming about this gorgeous body, now, can you?'

I was just about to answer him back when I felt him lifting my breasts above the top of my dress, so that my nipples were exposed. They hardened immediately in the cool air, and stiffened further as he softly cupped his mouth around my left breast. I felt an immense release of energy as I pushed my chest automatically in the direction of his touch. Circling his tongue tantalizingly around my nipple, he moved up to kiss my neck, before dropping down to kiss my inside leg, and then moving further and more insistently up inside me. In the dark I couldn't see a thing, and, feeling like I was blindfolded, I groaned with the sheer pleasure and fantasy of it all. With my other senses heightened, every touch, every kiss, every time he put his fingers inside me and every time he circled my clitoris, seemed to take on a greater intensity than I could ever remember having felt before. It sometimes took me ages to orgasm, but tonight I was screaming with pleasure and laughing with joy in what seemed like minutes. Furious with myself for coming too quickly, I apologized and pushed him from me. He refused at first to lift his head away when I pleaded, 'Get off me for a minute.' When I changed tack and asked, 'Can I please touch your dick?' he happily retreated.

He licked his lips and told me, 'Fuck, you taste damn good.' Turned on again, I reached forward and grabbed hold of his balls first, and then worked my way up to his erect dick. This was my first time to touch it and . . . *Oh-my-God*, it felt huge! I let out a tiny whimper of delight, and Rory's body shuddered as I stroked him. 'Eas-y there.' He choked. 'I'm sorry . . . I'm not sure how long I can hold on for.' I wanted to taste him, but Rory had other ideas: 'Please, let me put myself out of my misery.' He groaned. 'I've needed to fuck you for so long now!'

Wanting to feel him inside me, I was more than happy to let him in. 'Come on then,' I goaded. 'Fuck me. Fuck me hard.' Hearing the telltale rustle of a condom wrapper, I positioned myself close to the edge of the table and, unable to wait any longer, begged him, 'Come on. Fuck me. Fuck me now,' as I hustled the loose swathes of my dress safely behind my back. I had only just prepared myself when I felt Rory lift up my bum and pull me forward on to his waiting cock. I was still wet and highly sensitive, and the feeling of him entering me was powerful and almost overwhelming. 'Oh-my-God!' I cried again, remembering how much better it felt to have sex with someone you really cared about.

'Come on, baby,' whispered Rory. 'Come with me. Come with me again.' We soon found our rhythm, and bumped and ground together, going from steady, to fast, to finished in a matter of minutes. It wasn't the most amazing sex I had ever had, certainly on record the shortest, but I was happy since I had been pleasured first. And he was happy with a weight lifted off his mind. Buckling slightly on to me as he finished, he apologized for his poor performance, but blamed me entirely for being, 'Such a crazy, cool, sexy bitch.'

Teasing him, I joked, 'You're right, I am,' before fumbling to find his lips and give him a big celebratory kiss.

Needing to fix himself up, Rory asked, 'Do you mind if I turn on the light?' He allowed me just enough time to hide my modesty. When I said I was ready, Rory flicked the switch, almost blinding me in the process. Instead of anything subtle, full fluorescents beamed on, along with a full complement of old-fashioned bulbs around the mirror I was leaning against. As Rory grappled with his trousers, I rooted in my clutch for my compact, to check out the full extent of the damage to my make-up. Trying not to stare at Rory as he pushed himself back into his suit, I was distracted by the tragedy that was now my face. With red lipstick smeared across my skin and bleeding up over my top lip, bare rosy cheeks, and formerly smoky eyes now just bloodshot and panda-like, it was hard to know where to start. Begging him to turn the lights back off, I winced as Rory shuffled back over to me and kissed me on the nose. 'Don't be stressing, sweet cheeks. You're the best-looking girlfriend a guy like me could ever dream of having.'

I liked how that sounded. 'You said your girlfriend. Am I your girlfriend?'

Not missing a beat, Rory put his hands on both my shoulders, pulled me close to face him and whispered, 'I hope so.'

Hardly believing my ears, I continued, 'You never said anything, so I didn't want to assume.'

He just laughed quietly and continued stuffing his shirt into his trousers and fixing himself in the mirror behind me. 'Alice, are you crazy?' he asked. 'I think you're incredible. I was so proud to have you on my arm tonight. If you want me to ask you I will. OK, then, so will you be my girlfriend?'

After the stress of thinking I was going to be attacked by Tanya and Issey, followed by the euphoria of our backstage fumble, I wasn't sure if I wanted to laugh or cry. Along with these mixed emotions, a wave of guilt flooded over me. What was I doing with this guy? It was obvious that our relationship was flourishing – we'd now even had sex, albeit briefly – but things had started to get serious. Rory was not a one-night stand, and he deserved to be treated with more respect. Maybe it was the drink talking, or just the post-sex calm, but I suddenly felt the urge to come clean. 'Rory, I need to talk to you about something.'

'OK, girlfriend, hit me. What do you want to tell me?'

'Mmmm, I need to know what you think about lying.'

Trying to look sober, Rory pulled a serious face and said, 'I can't abide it,' in a faux-regal voice. 'Why do you ask?'

'Come on, I want you to focus for five minutes, please. We've had loads of fun tonight. But I need to know what you think about fibbing.'

Doing his best to show interest, Rory said, 'I sorta think it's the same as lying, really. Don't you?'

'Umm, not really.'

Not giving up the joking, Rory put on his royal voice again and asked, 'What is it you are trying to tell me, girl-friend? Spit it out, young wench. I'm in need of another drink.'

Bottling out, I made a weak joke to distract him, and made a promise to myself to tell him about the real me tomorrow. Or at least as soon as both our hangovers were gone. 'OK.' I smiled cheerfully. 'It's the moment of truth. I'm not sure how well I hid this from you, but I'm not a natural blonde.'

'Ha! Ha! Now what do you really want to tell me?' Rory was straightening himself up and looking concerned instead of flippant. 'Come on, what's bugging you?'

Although I truly wanted to set the record straight, I reckoned that the truth was not a good idea after several bottles of France's finest vintage bubbles. So I threw him a bone and faked it again. 'I think I told you I was thirty. I'm not, I'm thirty-three and my thirty-fourth birthday is next month. Do you think I'm a hideous old maid, now?'

Taking a moment to assess my statement, he replied. 'Nooo. I don't remember you saying how old you were, but of course not. I'm thirty-five, so I believe that makes us perfectly matched.'

Once again out of the woods, I breathed a sigh of relief, but also felt a nauseous wave of shame that at this point in our burgeoning relationship I was still able to keep champagne secrets.

As we headed back to the bar for final orders we must have looked like love's young dream to any passers-by. Despite everything, things were working out perfectly. All I needed to do was expose myself as the lying, cheatin' bitch that I had become, and everything would just be dandy. Well, that was the plan, anyway . . .

12

'OK, Lisa, give me some advice. I need to be cool, calm, sexy – in control.'

'Sounds like you need some Xanax.'

'Eh, no, thank you. I'd also like to have a personality as well. Come on, this is a big deal for me here. This is the first time I'm going to see where Rory lives. What if it's a dump? What if he has creepy hoarding issues?'

'What, like collects locks of hair from celebrities, or saves his urine and shit?'

'Eh, not quite. What weirdos have you been palling around with lately? I was thinking more along the lines of knives and weapons, or maybe phallic-looking kitchen utensils. But now that you mention it, I'll be extra careful while looking through his fridge for apple juice.' I giggled. It was so great having a silly conversation with Lisa. It took my mind off the ever-present terror about Sir Charlie's.

'Yeah, never really got into collecting, myself,' mused Lisa.

Teasing, I joked, 'Except for blokes?'

'Ah, they don't count.' She laughed. 'Though I did once date a guy who collected murderabilia.'

'What the hell is that?'

'Works of art produced by serial killers, I discovered.'

'Really?'

'No, honestly, it's true. They were all paintings and stuff. As far as I can remember he had pieces by Charles Manson and John Wayne Gacy.'

'Was he not a cowboy?'

'Ha! No. A different John Wayne.'

'Jesus. That's a bit grim though, no? Were you not worried about the psychological state of a guy who collected art made by serial killers?'

'Not really. He said they were just investment pieces, I believed him. Though, looking back, he was big into asphyxiation.'

'Fair enough. What's he doing with himself now? Do you still see him?'

'No. He lived with his mother, as far as I can remember, which I thought was a bit creepy, especially considering he was in his forties. But he moved away, something to do with a sewage problem under his house. I think it stank badly. I never heard from him again.'

'Wow, the one who got away, eh?'

'What?'

'Nothing, you fool. Enough about your lunatic conquests. We could be here all day discussing them. I'm nervous. I need a pep talk, so hit me! Come on, what should I be thinking? What should I be saying? What should I be wearing?'

Typically, the last was the question to grab her attention. 'As little as possible really. Maybe just a fun fur coat and no knickers? That's sure to get any party going.'

'OK, strike the last one, please. We're not filming a cheap

porno. I need to know the etiquette for first-time house-visit banter. Do I bring a plant? A pot of stew? Should I ask for a guided tour? What? I'm freaking out here.'

Sensing that Lisa had moved the receiver away from her ear, I knew my behaviour must have sounded psychotic.

'Hello? Lisa? Can you hear me?'

I waited a few moments before I heard a rustling at the other end of the phone and then, 'Have you come back down to earth yet?'

'I'm sorry, Lisa, it's just that I'm really starting to fall for this guy, and, many obstacles aside, I think I might be able to make a go of this one.'

But Lisa had been down this road one too many occasions before with me. 'That's great, love. But try not to marry this one. Not before the summer, anyway.'

Trying not to be offended, I bit my lip. 'I'll do my best,' I said, and then did a good job of answering my own questions. 'Bottle of wine? Be myself and generally go with the flow?'

'Sounds about right,' agreed Lisa, before pulling her old trick of saying, 'Hello? Hello? The reception . . . is really . . . bad. If you can hear me . . . I'll call you later!' And with that, she was gone.

In the taxi over to Rory's apartment images of what I might be greeted with flashed through my head. Was he going to open the door to me in nothing but a novelty pair of elephant pants? Or maybe he'd fancy himself as a bit of a Hugh Hefner and don a smoking jacket and cravat? Thankfully, all such sordid thoughts were quashed once I got there. He was dressed casually in jeans and a simple grey tee, and had trimmed his beard and hair in an obvious attempt to look groomed. In a way I preferred him scruffier, but it was still sweet that he had gone to the effort for me. Not sure whether to go flash and buy champagne, or play it low key with beers, I had bought both at the off-licence, and stepped through the door looking like an alcoholic who needed to get pissed before she could have sex. Mind you, in a way that was partly true. Even though we had been intimate, booze had been a big factor in our last encounter, and walking cold into his apartment was extremely daunting, even for a diva like myself.

As he proudly ushered me into his living room, I soon began to feel more at ease. Although it had a definite bachelor feel to it, with several large photographs of him in combats with a bullet-proof vest, posing with his TV camera, it was inviting and comfortable; and from the general air of cleanliness and display of brand-new candles dotted around the room, it was clear he had gone to some effort to create a setting in which to woo me. Playing the perfect host, he took my coat, plus my heavy bag of booze, and asked me to sit down and make myself comfortable while he went off with them. On his return he handed me a drink. 'One of my specialities. This is a Baxter own-recipe Mojito. Now, excuse me, if you will, while I finish off some final preparations in the kitchen.' I offered to help but was quickly put right. 'No way,' he demurred. 'In approximately five minutes, I will be all yours for the night.'

'I love a man in control,' I whispered, flirting back, and received a kiss on the lips for my efforts before he disappeared off once more. Feeling like one of the contestants off *Come Dine With Me*, I quickly stepped up my snooping and began sniffing around his bookcases. Lonely Planet guides rested beside life stories of comedians like Peter Kay, as well as more serious biographies and luscious photography books. I had just taken out *The Great LIFE Photographers and Photojournalism* and started flicking through its glossy pages when Rory raced back into the room holding an extremely large clay pot and dumped it on the dining table in the corner, which was already fully set for two.

Seeing my amusement at the sight of his red polka-dot oven gloves, Rory said defensively, 'They were a present from my mother!' before slipping them on to a chair and making his way over to me.

Not wanting him to think I was laughing at him, as it was a rare treat to have any man cook for me, I waved the book and asked, 'Are you in it?'

With a disappointed face he sighed. 'No, not yet,' he said, before giving me a cheeky wink and smiling. 'My greatest work is yet to come.'

Not sure if he was hinting at his personal or professional endeavours, I asked, 'So, do you think of me as work, then?'

Rory said swiftly, 'No. I think of you as purely pleasure.' But it wasn't the answer I was looking for, and the expression on my face evidently reflected that.

'Oh, don't look sad,' Rory pleaded. 'I didn't mean that in a bad way. I just meant that I'm only just coming into my prime professionally. I've so much that I still want to achieve. But I also know that I've a great deal to look forward to in my private life, too.' He looked me straight in the eye till he saw me blush. 'There she is. Listen, it's very early days with us, and I don't want to come on too strong and frighten you off, but I'm smitten by you. And, well, I hope that we can make a go of things here. Is it OK to say that?'

Not expecting such commitment, I felt myself go weak

at the knees, and it was a few moments before I could find the words, 'Of course it's OK to say . . . I mean, it's more than OK.' As I looked into his dark green eyes, I could see a twinge of disillusion. Angry at myself for not responding better to his plans, I quickly kissed him and explained, 'Sorry, I didn't mean to sound so down in the dumps. It's just that I've had my heart broken before, and, well, I'd prefer it if you didn't make big statements unless you plan on following them up.' I put my hand over his mouth, as more words felt that they needed to pop out of mine. 'If I'm honest, I'm gonna put myself out on a limb here and say that, yes, I'm also a smitten kitten. I think you're amazing, and now the idea that you cook? Well, you're starting to come across as too perfect. Which is a worry, because I'm not. And, well—'

'Hold it there, please,' interrupted Rory. 'Stop.'

'Stop what?'

'Stop panicking. There's no need. No one calls me amazing until they've tasted my food. Then, by all means, you can give me a five-star rating.'

Understanding that this was far too deep and meaningful a conversation to have with a sober head, I let Rory kiss me again on the lips as he held me lovingly. When he pulled back he gave me an adorable smile and simply said, 'Let's just sit down and have something to eat. No pressure, OK?'

Nodding in agreement, I quickly changed the subject. 'It smells gorgeous, by the way. What is it?'

'It's a lamb dish. I hope that's to your liking?'

'I'd eat the leg of the chair, I'm that hungry.'

'Good stuff. Well, this is a favourite of mine. I hope you like it. I used to go out with an Indian girl who was an amazing cook, so I stole all of her best recipes.'

Still slightly nervy, I teased, 'I'm sure that's not the only thing you stole from her!'

But instead of giving a defensive reply, he came over all dewy-eyed, and smiled. 'Nipa was great. She taught me a lot.'

Curious if she'd broken his heart, I cautiously asked, 'What happened?'

'She died a couple of years ago now, in a road accident. Nipa was a motivational speaker. She was on her way home from a talk one evening when the car she was driving collided with a wall. They reckon she fell asleep at the wheel. Hopefully, she never knew what hit her.'

Totally surprised, I apologized for making light of his ex, but he seemed to take it all in his stride.

'It's OK. She was a Hindu. She believed in reincarnation. I do, too. So I know that she's around somewhere, happy and living life to the full.'

'Wow! That's a really positive way of looking at things.'

'Is there any other way to look at life and death?'

'No one close to me has ever died. A girl once did after being at a house party that Parker had a couple of years ago, and I found that quite hard to deal with. None of us knew her − she just arrived and then suddenly got sick. But that was nothing. It must have been so tough for you, to lose a girlfriend like that, in such a tragic way.'

'It was,' he admitted. 'But life goes on, and I believe that she still watches out for me.'

Chancing a joke, I asked, 'Is she in the room now − like, a fly on the ceiling?'

And, seeing the funny side, Rory laughed before saying, 'Her name did mean "one who watches over". Whatever about now, I'm hoping she's not hanging around later. Well,

I'd hate her to have to watch some of the things I have in mind for . . .' He let out a cheeky laugh. 'But seriously, I do feel that she has taken care of me in some way. Look, I've gotten myself into a few sticky situations when out working, and I just felt that there was someone looking after me.'

'I understand.'

'Hey, I wasn't trying to intimidate you.'

'Gosh, might be a bit late for that. I'm just hoping she approves of me, and doesn't poison me with her curry.'

'Come here to me.' Rory chuckled. 'You've no ghost to live up to. Nipa was human, too. She wasn't saintly. But maybe she found you for me? She wouldn't have wanted me to be lonely.' Seeing that he needed to put the fun spirit back into the evening, he put on a spooky voice and teased, '*Yes, you are the chosen one! Waa, haa, ha, ha!*' And as he tickled me, my worries started to lift, and my inner diva began to return. I was never going to be able to compete with a dead woman, so why bother trying? If he was speaking from the heart, maybe she did matchmake us? It wasn't exactly the most conventional of get-togethers after all. In the immortal words of Doris Day I just had to accept that whatever will be, will be . . .

Although Lamb-à-la-Nipa was a little bit spicy for my Oirish palate, it did give me a thirst, which in itself helped me relax and forget my inhibitions. Not wanting to bring up any ex-partners, either his or mine, we talked work: mostly his adventures across continents vast and dangerous, as well as some of my hopes for the future. As always when I got misty-eyed, I spoke about writing a book, and how I would love to do a scriptwriting course, and it was only after I forgot myself and mentioned working for *YES!*

magazine that I remembered that Rory only knew me as a waitress from Sir Charlie's.

'You're a journalist back in Ireland?' he interrupted, looking surprised. 'How come you never mentioned it before now?'

Doing my best to fob him off, I said, 'Oh, it's just a sideline thing, really,' and kept my fingers crossed that he'd forget all about it. Of course he didn't. Being a man who had worked in war zones and doorstepped criminals, he wasn't the type to not be curious, and he wouldn't let it drop.

'So what sort of stuff did you write, exactly? Are we talking beauty, fashion, true life?'

'Hardly!' I laughed. 'Just silly things, really. The odd movie or theatre review. A bit of red-carpet stuff. Nothing very important. It didn't rate compared to your photography, so that's why I didn't mention it. Honestly, it was just a brief thing. I'd rather you forgot all about it.'

Perplexed, Rory grabbed his mobile from the end of the couch and declared, 'Well, let me be the judge of how insignificant you were at *YES!* I presume they have a website, yeah? Let's Google that now, and—'

'Oh! Stop!' I pleaded. 'Please don't. I bet you, I won't even be there.'

'Really?'

'Yeah, I can't imagine I'd be credited anywhere on it.'

'OK, here we are. *YES!* magazine. Ohhh, very sexy website, there's Lunch With Lucy. Fashion, with some very badly dressed, over-accessorized he-slash-she and . . . No, there's no Alice. Oh, that's a pity, isn't it? I can't see you here.'

Jumping up to kiss him and distract his attention from any further research, I laughed. I said, 'I told you so,' before snatching his phone off him and throwing it back across the couch. Ignoring his pleas to be handed his phone back, I instead gave him my seductive eyes and whispered, 'It's getting late, are you not getting worried about the time?'

'No, why?' asked Rory. 'What time is it?'

Trying to keep a straight face, I whispered again, 'I think it's time you took me to bed.'

'Ohhh, do you now, madam?'

'Yes, I do, sir. And while there's a time and a place for after-show party sex, there's also a time for good, old-fashioned bed-bonking. This is that time.'

'But what if I said that I would quite like to make love to you tonight all slow and sensual?'

Liking where this was leading, I continued, 'Well, firstly, I'd ask: where would you start? And then, secondly, I'd ask: when can you start?'

'Well, my Irish rose, I can simply answer both of those questions in one go, by doing this . . .' Then, taking me totally by surprise, Rory swept his arms around me, picked me up and walked with me to the bedroom like he was a groom carrying me over the threshold. It made me feel all girlie, and I whooped with joy as he talked me through his plan of action. 'I'm gonna strip you. I'm gonna lick you. I'm gonna taste you. And then, when your body doesn't think it can take any more pleasure, I'm gonna start all over again!'

The second he threw me on the bed, I lifted my loose jersey top over my shoulders and started to wriggle out of my tight skinny jeans. By the time I was down to my well-thought-out and coordinating black-lace bra and thong, Rory had kicked off his jeans and tee, had kindly removed his socks, and was down to his crisp white boxer shorts, which were bulging promisingly in all the right places.

'I'll show you mine, if you show me yours . . .' he teased, throwing me the glad eye. Taking the lead, I cheekily flashed him a nipple. Laughing with the frustration, Rory declared, 'You might want to play hard to get, but I certainly don't,' and he pushed down his boxers and threw them straight at me. As they slapped me in the face so did his fresh, musky scent, and tingles instantly shot around my body. I showed my appreciation by keeping the pants over my face and cooing, 'Mmmm. Delicious.' Before I had a chance to look out from under them, Rory had straddled me, and begun to slowly push my shoulders back down on to the bed. Since Rory didn't remove my blindfold, neither did I; instead I just relaxed and allowed him to circle my body with his hands and his mouth, while anticipating his next moves in my mind.

In preparation for the night ahead, I had waxed and shaved every inch of my body, before tanning and polishing off my skin with a bronzer. Giving myself the best chance of looking cellulite and stretch-mark free, I felt as confident about my body as I was ever going to, and with that in my head I knew that I was going to have fun. Although there was a faint hum of music coming through from the living room, we were doing a pretty good job creating our own sounds. Both of us were groaning with desire, each of us needing and wanting this time together. This was a completely different experience to the last time we were intimate. It was comfortable, and there was no sense of urgency. Just as good as I remembered it, his cock had a powerfully solid feel as it rubbed off my stomach and across my thighs.

Despite having played the submissive role up to now, I all of a sudden felt the need to take control, so in a fit of passion

I threw off my cotton mask, demanded that he roll over, and jumped on top of him like a feral alley cat. Clearly happy to go along with any of my suggestions, Rory's face beamed with joy as I swished my hair across his body and then, with a bit of effort, began to masturbate his dick between my breasts. Being only a B cup it wasn't the easiest of tasks, but from the reaction on his face, I seemed to be doing an impressive job. So I kept pushing myself, and stroked him up and down, up and down, keeping my eyes looking up at his the entire time, watching his responses and, of course, striving to make it more intense with every thrust. Worried that I could be starting to chafe him, I kneeled away for a second, and quickly knotted my hair back off my face in a bundle.

Looking concerned, Rory asked, 'What's wrong?'

But all I offered back was, 'How wrong is this?' as I placed my mouth fully around his now bright pink, throbbing dick. He released a wave of noise as I almost reached the base of his shaft with my lips. I tried to get to the bottom, but I couldn't – he was literally too big for me to swallow. He tasted good, though. It had been a while since I had had a cock in my mouth, and there was something extra-erotic about his. It looked nice – it was clean and tidy, and the little hair he had was well-trimmed and stayed where it was meant to. If you ignored the ghost of a dead ex-girlfriend, who was probably now reincarnated as a wasp and sitting on the wardrobe watching us in a jealous rage, this guy had everything I was looking for.

For a split second I thought about stopping what I was doing, lifting my head up and blurting out my secrets. That way I could make him promise to forgive me. Let's face it, men would promise *anything* during sex. As Rory's panting and grunting became louder and more powerful, I brought my mind back to what my mouth was up to. With Rory close to climaxing, I didn't want to lose momentum. I continued to run my tongue around the head of his penis, while firmly massaging him in a faster and rougher fashion. I had to make the decision: would I swallow? Or would I chicken out and let him cum over my chest? Thinking of all the effort he had gone to for me during the evening, I decided to give him the full diva treatment, and stayed with it. His body began to spasm and shake, and I watched his eyes and face crunch up as if in pain. As I worked his cock into the side of my cheek I suddenly felt his entire body tremble, almost violently, and my mouth began overflowing with his spunk. Trying to seem in control, I did my best to swallow as much as possible, which was fine as it wasn't foul-tasting. Carefully whipping any excess leakage away with my hands, I left his body mess-free and Rory seriously impressed!

'Fucking hell,' he whooped, as he ran his hands over his beard, up over his eyes, and up through his hair to punch the air. 'You have been sent from heaven, I tell ya. No one told me Catholic school taught ya that!'

Basking in my glory, I snuggled up to cuddle with him, and nestled in under his arm, while twirling the small hairs on his chest with my finger. I was just getting settled in when Rory pushed me back a little and said, 'And now for your turn.'

Despite my pleas of, 'I'm fine. I'm happy to cuddle,' Rory leapt up off the bed.

'Hold that thought,' he said. 'I'll be back in two seconds.'

Not sure if he was going to return with a ten-inch dildo,

a gimp mask or even a butt plug, I was relieved to see him brandishing a squeezable jar of maple syrup. 'What's that for?' I asked playfully.

'It's for you.' He smiled proudly. 'I'm gonna lick it all into you.'

My confidence was instantly knocked. I covered my crotch with my hands. 'What's wrong? Do I smell?'

'Don't be silly. Look, would I do this if I thought you tasted bad?' With that he pushed my thighs apart so he could slowly slide two of his fingers up inside me. Only to remove them and stick them in his mouth, cooing, 'You taste, mmmm, finger lickin' good, baby. This maple syrup is just for fun. So stop your worrying.'

Liking his sense of adventure, my own naughtiness returned, and I began to bounce around the bed pulling different poses and asking, 'Would you like to get saucy here? Or maybe you'd like to get saucy over here?' Rory had to chase me a little to pin me down, but eventually he got a firm grip on my legs. Settling myself in a comfortable position, I found it hard not to scream with the giddiness. Dizzy with the idea of having my privates smeared in pancake sauce, I joked, 'My boobs might be small, but at least this pancake chest of mine was good enough to do the business earlier, remember?'

'Oh, I'm still remembering.' He smiled. 'And for that I am extremely grateful to you and your dirty mouth. But now the only resemblance you have to a pancake is that I'm going to flip you over like one – on to your front.' As he spoke he manoeuvred me on to all fours, pushing my shoulders down on the bed. This left my ass exposed in the air, and without any further talk Rory pulled apart my cheeks and began oozing lashings of thick maple syrup all over my behind. Feeling dense and cool straight from the cupboard, the sauce almost sizzled over my hot, sweaty body. As my excitement began to build, I pushed my head under a pillow, and opened myself up as much as possible to allow Rory to devour me.

'You're already sweet,' he whispered. 'Now you're sticky and sweet.' And with that he nuzzled his nose and tongue in close, and began licking and rubbing me, arousing me in his own sloppy and unique way. With previous lovers the loud squelching noises might have made me squirm with embarrassment, but that was not the case with Rory. Even though it usually took me about ten minutes to orgasm with oral sex, this time I was screaming for mercy within a couple of short minutes. Although I was disappointed that I couldn't last longer, a big part of me was content that I was able to fall into his arms again afterwards and hold his skin close against mine.

As he slid in beside me with the face of a child who had licked their plate clean, I pretended to slobber over him like a puppy, and the two of us laughed out loud with joy at such a successful make-out session. Unable to wipe the grins off our faces, we continued to giggle like teenagers for ages, until our body heat began to cool, and we needed to climb under the covers to keep warm. As much as I wanted my body to remain tangled up with his all night, I knew that I couldn't stay much longer: Maura had told me she had errands to do first thing. Even if she hadn't, I couldn't let the kids witness me staggering in the door as they sat at the breakfast table munching on their porridge!

I needed an exit strategy, but I also still needed to find the motivation to leave him. As we huddled under the covers, he tenderly played with my hair and rubbed my shoulders to keep me warm. We resumed our conversation from dinner earlier, and our chat about life and the pursuit of happiness went on late into the small hours. Eventually, though, I could sense that Rory was getting weak with tiredness, even though like me he was fighting it to make our date last for as long as possible. Making the brave move, I finally announced, 'OK, that's it, folks. The party is now officially over.'

As if he already knew the answer, he asked sorrowfully, 'Will you stay?'

'I can't. I'm sorry.'

'Why, does Maura refuse you admission if you're home too late?'

'Ha! No, it's not like that. I've just got things to do in the morning, that's all.'

'You can use my toothbrush if you're worried about morning breath.'

'You are so sweet to think of me, but, no, that's not going to swing it. Listen, next time I'll stay. I promise. Now call me a taxi, please. This Cinderella needs to get home.'

'Hmmm, OK, just this once. But if you want to be a fairy-tale character, I might just have to make you my own Rapunzel by locking you up here in my little castle. And then you'll have to let your hair grow really long if you want to escape.'

'Well, maybe I won't want to escape. And, maybe, I might want to stay here for ever? How would you like that fairy tale?'

'Sounds like the perfect happy ending to finish off my other happy ending . . .'

13

'Grab your dancing shoes, baby . . . I'm bringing sexy back. Yeah!'

'Go away, it's the middle of the night.'

'It's gone nine o'clock.'

'Exactly. I'm gay, and I'm grumpy anything before noon. You should know that.'

'I do, but I thought it would be worth suffering your mood to give you some good news.'

'OK, I'm sorry, I'll start over, if you please . . . And, good morning to you, Miss Sex, Drugs, Camera, Action. What has you so perky at 9.15 a.m.?'

'That's better. Well, I'm very happy to announce that I'm coming home tomorrow morning. Daisy has her appointment with her specialist, she got a last-minute cancellation at the Blackrock Clinic, and, wait for it, Michael even paid for our return flights home. So, where you gonna take me tomorrow night? I want dancing, I want drinking, I wanna make gossip!'

'Oh-my-God! You can't come back tomorrow.'

'Eh, not the reaction I was hoping for. Why not?'

'Because I was supposed to be having a surprise night of romance with Jeff. I have a hotel booked. Facials, champagne, the lot!'

'And it was going to be a surprise?'

'Yeah.'

'Well, that's cool, then.'

'Why, exactly?'

'Cause he won't get upset about what he doesn't know about. Take me on your surprise date instead. Come on, please? You know you wanna.'

'But what about Jeff?'

'Buy him a big ball of feckin' wool and he can make love to that for the night. Oh, come on, please, please, please? I'll love you for ever.'

'Steady on. I'm allowed to slag him. You're not. Jesus, of all the weeks, Eva. Let me see. How about the three of us go?'

'Three is kind of a crowd, Parky.'

'Well, then, let's rope Lisa in, and it'll be just like old times. How does that sound?'

'Dangerous and exciting all mixed into one. Yay! Thank you. I'm sorry for gatecrashing, but I've missed you.'

'Mmmm, not that much, I reckon, judging by your most recent text message about *Roar-y*!'

'Indeed, my interests have been captivated by another man, that much is true. And he's even told me he's smitten, so I think I might have found me a keeper.'

With that, I could hear Parker falling about the place with laughter at the other end of the phone.

Giving him some time to settle himself, I asked, 'Have you finished? When you have, you can tell me what's so funny.'

'You, ya mentaller,' squealed Parker, through more sniggers.

'Why, because I haven't told him the whole truth, and—'

'You mean ANY truth.'

'OK, so there are a few holes in my life that I haven't filled in yet, but we're still at the getting to know each other stage, so—'

'You're delusional, Ms Valentine. You have to tell the man. And soon. It's not fair on either of you if things are going as well as you say. Hello? Are you still there?'

Not liking having the obvious pointed out to me, I let Parker hang on the phone for a bit. I wanted to tell him to shut up and mind his own business, but I couldn't. He was right, but like an ostrich I had stuck my head in the sand. I still didn't want to face up to the reality that I was going to have to tell a man who was mad about me that I was a liar. Biting my tongue, I chose to ignore Parker's last comments and asked, 'Will I ring Lisa, then?' I hoped he'd move on from the issue as well, because it was still too early in the morning for him to speak, never mind argue.

Parker took the easy option and simply replied, 'Yes, please.' With so much left unsaid, he rushed me off the phone, claiming he needed caffeine, and I was left with just my guilt and too many unanswered questions floating around my head.

As I sat alone with my thoughts, I asked myself how high the chances were that Rory would forgive me. And which should I tell him about first: my false name, undercover work or Daisy? And, of course, then there was the Tanya and Issey story as well. Oh, and the small matter of possibly being hunted down and murdered in the near future.

Wishing I could turn back time to that first moment he had asked me, 'What is it that you do?' I imagined myself telling him that I was a divorced single parent, and that I wore a hidden camera in my hair to expose drug-dealers and petty criminals. And then I imagined watching him scrunch up his face, excuse himself to the toilet and walk off into the distance – for good.

Travelling with Daisy was a dream. You often saw stressed-out mothers screaming blue murder at their kids to sit in buggies, but I never had that problem. There was never an occasion when I needed to raise my voice, or use bribery or make threats. Daisy just wanted to be near me, and would travel to the end of the earth with a smile on her face once I, her mammy, was holding her hand.

On the Aer Lingus flight home I must have seen and nodded at five or six people that I knew from Dublin, and all of them seemed to smile back at me with a strained look on their face. As paranoid thoughts started up in my head, I put the funny looks down to my new blonde do, and assured myself that not everyone was aware that I was a cowardly cheat. Besides, it was such a relief getting away from England. After a perfectly uneventful flight, our cases were some of the first few to emerge out on to the carousel, and we were just breezing out to the taxi rank when my luck, and my good mood, suddenly changed.

'Hiya, Eva,' screeched an all-too-familiar voice from behind me. 'Honey, it's Anna, how are you?'

Trying not to look too disappointed, I turned around to see an old – or should I say former – friend from the social scene, Anna. Once upon a time we used to be partying pals, back in the days when I was still hanging around with Maddie. Although Anna could be great fun, she had always had a dangerous gossiping tongue, earning her a nickname, 'Reuters', that she shared with the international news agency. Of course she eventually told one too many secrets out of turn, and had since been shut out of the inner circle by Parker, Lisa and myself for safety reasons. But since we had never officially told her to take a long walk off a short pier, her brass neck allowed her to ignore the obvious and poke her nose into our worlds whenever she got the opportunity. 'Hey, Anna. What has you at Dublin Airport so early?'

'Oh, I've been working for a small independent radio company lately, and, well, they think Tiger Woods is landing into town today to play golf at the K Club, and I'm here to try and get a few words out of him.'

'Wow! That's exciting.' I pretended to show interest, but she didn't even listen, just ploughed ahead, looking for gossip as ever.

'So you're back in Dublin then, yeah? And this is your daughter? Oh, she's . . .'

Not looking for a deep conversation about Daisy's condition, I interrupted her then by saying, 'Yes, she's great, thanks. We're home for the weekend. A few things to do, and then it'll be back to London.'

Instantly I knew I had opened up a can of worms by mentioning London, and she straightaway began firing intrusive questions at me. 'So who are you working for over there?'

'What do you do?'

'Are you seeing anyone?'

'Oh, and did you know Michael and Maddie have split up?'

Stunned by her questioning, I was just about to ask her, 'What the hell?' when Ronan Keating and his wife Yvonne walked past us at a quick pace, with several newspaper types running after them.

Catching Anna's eye, a frustrated-looking photographer complained, '*He's* the fucking celebrity golfer!'

Trying to hide my amusement, I teased, 'That's not much of a scoop, really, is it? "Ronan Keating arrives into Dublin" shocker!'

Shooting me an evil glare, Anna asked her photographer friend, 'Are you sure?' To which he nodded and replied, 'He told us inside he's here by invitation of Michael Smurfit, and is heading to the K Club to play golf with him this afternoon.'

After a tense few minutes – Anna temporarily lost her cool and I had to ask her not to curse so much in front of Daisy – I offered to share my taxi into town. I didn't necessarily want to breathe the same toxic air as the woman, but I couldn't pass up the opportunity of hearing all the latest dirt on Michael and Maddie. I had only spoken to Michael the day before to get details of the specialist at the Blackrock Clinic, and he hadn't given anything away about things being rocky with himself and Maddie. But then again, why would he?

Once we were all safely strapped in we asked the driver to take us to Ballsbridge first, so we could offload Anna, and then I simply told him, 'We'll have another stop after that,' so I wouldn't give any further information away for her to use. During our ride across the Liffey I learned that the depression that Maddie had suffered after the baby had come back, and that she hadn't been working much lately. I was curious to know if Anna had heard of Michael cheating on Maddie, as he had blatantly flaunted his philandering ways in front of me during a chance meeting when Maddie had been pregnant.

However, all Anna would say was, 'There've been as many transgression rumours as there have been around Tiger Woods. But I'd hate to pass on any gossip unless I knew it as fact.'

Fighting the urge to send a smug text to Michael, I tried to focus on our daughter and all the questions I would need to ask the specialist. After some more idle chat about various folk from the social scene, I waved Anna off and told her, 'It was great to see you.' Which, amazingly enough, didn't cause nausea, as she had truly shortened the journey and distracted me from the appointment ahead of us.

Having never been to the Blackrock Clinic before, I felt like we had stepped into a plush hotel rather than a private hospital, and that for once Michael had finally done right by his child. Despite the comfortable surroundings, however, there was no way of disguising the professionals for Daisy. She was always nervous of strangers, and the sight of a table full of medical equipment – the syringes in particular – sent her over the edge. Her terrified whimpers were heartbreaking. Somehow finding the strength of a child three times her age, she struggled to break free from my grasp, and no amount of singing her favourite nursery rhymes was going to pacify her. Once the blood sample had been taken, we were both exhausted and full of anger. Daisy of course vented her rage at me for putting her through such torture. Meanwhile I cursed Michael over and over in my head for all the pain he had caused us both.

On the plus side, Daisy's specialist had seemed hopeful that Daisy's tests would come back negative. Since Daisy had been through some operations before without any sort of complications, the specialist reassured me that this condition would probably have showed up before, and that from just a quick, surface examination she seemed to be thriving.

Neither a 'star patient' sticker nor a sticky lollipop would prove a long-term fix for the damage Michael might still bring about, and if the gossip was true it seemed we weren't the only family he had now abandoned. It was hard to figure out my feelings about such a split. Was I happy? Probably a little, though for all the wrong reasons. But while I still harboured a lot of anger at my former best friend Maddie for stealing my husband away from me, I still loved her and missed her, and knew that Michael couldn't have gone unless he had wanted to leave.

Feeling a little giddy in the taxi back to Terenure, en route to my parents' house, I texted Michael, asking if by any chance he wanted to see Daisy. Of course his reply came back, 'I'm busy today,' which left me let down once again, and even less inclined to cope with my mother's usual welcome of abrasive questioning and generally grouchy demeanour.

By three o'clock I had reached my limit with her. So, handing her £200 of the Queen's money, I told her to order the sofa bed from Cost Plus Sofas that she'd been dropping hints about, and asked if I could go out for a few hours to see my friends. Leaving Daisy happily cuddling on the sofa with my dad, I ran out the front door like a teenager escaping detention and hopped on the first bus that passed that could take me into town. Even though I had only been away just a short time, the journey past all the old landmarks was a nostalgic one, especially when I began to notice the many shops and pubs that had closed down since I'd last seen them.

I had planned to meet the gang at six o'clock and head to the Shelbourne Hotel, but hadn't mentioned it to my mother, who would have hit the roof and done her usual complaining along the lines of, 'I am not an open babysitting service. You can't just walk in here and abandon your daughter with me . . . blah . . . blah . . . blah.'

The best plan would be to text my dad later giving him the news that I was going to stay overnight, and then he could deal with the grief. Thankfully her irritability didn't bother him. He had the ability to zone her out and ignore what she was saying, while nodding, supporting and calming her at the same time. It was this trick that enabled him to still happily live with the woman, otherwise he would have gone potty years earlier. He would quietly joke that their marriage was his prelude to sainthood, but we all knew that he loved her very much despite her shortfalls, and that he depended on her completely. To an outsider they might look unhappy, but in fact, in their own way, they were both deeply contented, which goes to prove the theory that there is always someone for everyone.

By the time I'd arrived at George's Street, I stepped off the bus a new woman. Deciding to leave all my emotional baggage on the 19A, my swagger returned as I hit the fresh air, and I was determined that no ex-husband nor grumpy mother was going to keep my spirits down. To avoid suspicion, I had only left the house with some necessary toiletries, so with time to spare and money in my pocket I headed straight down the George's Street Arcade and enjoyed some leisurely clothes-shopping in a couple of my old favourite boutiques.

With several too many bargains under my arm, I skipped off to the Shelbourne to change in the toilets and beautify myself, and then cosied into a corner of the Horseshoe Bar with a glass of white and a couple of glossies, including *YES!* magazine, for entertainment. I had barely flicked past the perfume and luggage adverts at the front of *YES!* when a text from Rory beeped through on my phone, reading, 'Hey sexy. What U doin?' With a big smile across my face, I texted back, 'Drinkin & relaxin. Wot U doin?', taking a large gulp of my wine with the excitement. Several texts later, I had established that Rory was stuck on a motorway due to bad roadworks. He texted that despite the traffic, 'I'm almost overwhelmed with that Friday feeling!' Curious as to what he was so excited about, I asked, 'Should U not B pretending to be sad, now that I'm out of the country?' His reply, 'But I'm in YOUR country!' nearly made me collapse off my seat. Not trusting my eyes, I read his text over and over before biting the bullet and ringing him. His phone had barely rung once when his smooth voice answered, 'Hell – lo?'

'Are you serious? Are you in Dublin?'

Sensing that I was prickly rather than overjoyed, he answered slowly, 'Emm, yes. Is that OK?'

'But what are you doing here?'

'Ehhh, well, I came to surprise you. *So surprise!*'

Needing another mouthful of wine, I decided to take a big gulp while deciding how to answer him.

'I thought you'd be happy,' Rory said. 'I'm only here for the night, but I thought it would be nice to hang out with some of your mates. Would you prefer if I turned the taxi around and headed back home?'

Realizing that my hot boyfriend was about to be

seriously offended if I didn't offer up some positive words of encouragement, I blurted out, 'Don't be silly. This is great. I'm in the bar at the Shelbourne, so I'll see you when you get here.' Panicked, I immediately rang both Lisa and Parker and left frantic voice messages telling them to call me Alice when they got in, as Rory had turned up in Dublin unannounced. Fearing the worst, I imagined all the possible dangerous situations we could encounter while hanging out in Dublin, and ordered a double vodka and 7 Up to calm my nerves.

By 5.50 p.m. I had received texts from both Parker and Lisa telling me to stay cool and that they'd be in within the hour, and had my breath taken away as Rory walked through the door brandishing a massive bunch of red roses. Looking like a Hollywood heart-throb, he strode straight over to me, making everyone in the small bar turn to look, and getting down on one knee asked, 'Please don't be angry with me. I just wanted to spend time with you. That doesn't make me a bad person, does it?'

Slapping him over the head with one of my magazines, I told him, 'Get up before you make an eejit out of yourself!' and kissed his adorable face with enthusiasm, to show him that I cared. This was undoubtedly one of the most romantic gestures a man had ever made for me. Was this guy for real? After he complained that his lips were going to chafe, I agreed that my own chin was becoming raw from the bristles on his beard, so we stopped kissing and I asked, 'And what if I hadn't answered my phone?'

'Well, I suppose I would have just looked up the phone book,' came his reply. 'And started ringing all the Maguire families.'

'Oh.'

'But we don't have to worry about that now.' He smiled. 'I'm here, so let's celebrate.'

Two glasses of champagne later, Parker arrived into the bar with big hugs for both Rory and me, and apologies for running late. Rory had just offered him a glass of champagne when Parker pulled a serious face and said, 'I've a favour to ask.' As my heart sank and my eyebrows arched in Parker's direction, I could see his lip tremble with giddiness, 'Would you mind if we all have dinner up in the Princess Grace Suite tonight? It's just it would be a waste not to use it, and it would give us all a chance to get to know Rory better, without the intrusion of other people.'

Feeling a wave of relief, I jumped up and kissed Parker, told him it was great to see him, and ushered them both upstairs, handing Parker the bucket of champagne and Rory my bags of clothes before they had a chance to speak. Moving as quickly as possible, before anyone else I knew could say hello, we climbed the stairs, or in my head the steps to safety, as Parker and Rory made friends again over football talk. Arriving into the beautiful suite, we were greeted by Jeff and Lisa with a very zealous welcome of, 'ALICE! How are you? And RORY, how wonderful to see you!' I gave Lisa a gentle kick to her shoe to remind her not to wind me up, and she immediately toned down her voice, as did Jeff, and we all made ourselves at home, surrounded by plush comfort and walls that would never talk!

Like nervous contestants entering a Big Brother house, we mooched about: moving books on the bookshelves, tapping the antique clocks to see if they worked, and running fingers over the expensive curtains and marble fireplaces. With Rory in the room and my identity and history largely unwritten, there was an underlying unease between my friends and me: I was terrified that they'd slip up and say the wrong thing. And they were probably wondering what stories they could tell without dropping me in the doo doo.

As the evening relaxed and the champagne flowed, I started talking about seeing Anna earlier that morning. And as we all collectively shared a laugh over her disappointment at seeing Ronan Keating instead of Tiger Woods, I remembered a picture message I had on my phone about how Tiger had loads of expensive cars, but now he had a hole in one. I handed it around to show the gang. My phone had only just reached Rory's hands when it loudly beeped with a new message. 'Oh, oops – there's a message here from your dad,' said Rory, as he frantically fiddled with some buttons.

'Oh, God. Don't worry about it. Just leave it.'

Frozen to my seat, I watched almost in slow motion as he pressed the retrieve button on my phone, concentrated for a second and read aloud the words, 'Everything A OK. Leave her 2 me. Have a fun nite!'

With all eyes on me, I just about managed the words, 'OK. Thanks. He's talking about my mam. She wanted me to stay in, and, well, ah, it doesn't matter.'

Breathing yet another sigh of relief, I told the guys, 'We'll be back in a minute,' and dragged Lisa into the bedroom for a private chat. As soon as we were hidden away on our own, I asked the obvious nervous girlfriend question. 'Well, what do you think of him?'

And, playing the dutiful best pal, she replied, 'He's great. It doesn't matter what I think of him, anyway. Once you like him, I like him.'

Frustrated by her careful reply, I thought about berating her, but then weakly said, 'Thanks,' and returned to the group while she used the bathroom. Although I didn't always understand Lisa, she did generally have her reasons for odd or evasive behaviour, so I let it go and decided that whatever she thought about him would eventually come out in the wash. What did come out to that bedroom five minutes later, though, was a woman looking for devilment. 'OK, everyone,' she said. 'Let's have a game of truth or dare.'

Clearly intrigued, Parker asked, 'Excuse me, what did you say?'

'You heard me, and so did you, Ms Alice. Truth or dare. Let's play it. This party of ours needs a little spicing up. You can't bring your new boy all the way over to Dublin and have him leave thinking we're all dry shites!'

While I tried to pick my jaw off the ground with the shock of Lisa's suggestion, Parker and Jeff chimed together, 'I'm game,' to fits of giggles, followed by Rory giving the thumbs up, which of course left everyone looking at me again.

Coming across a tad defensive, I snapped, 'What are we? Fourteen again and looking for a cheeky snog or a grope of someone's nipple?'

Instantly claiming her moment, Lisa whipped up her top, exposed her gorgeously pert breasts and cried, 'Did some-one mention nipples? Yes, please, I'd love a grope.'

Totally ignoring my opposition to the whole idea, everyone fell about the place laughing at Lisa, before Parker collapsed to his knees, cupped her breasts and explained, 'These are works of art. I don't know why us gay men love boobies. But we do. We just love boobies.'

Not in the least bit shocked, Rory winked at Lisa. 'Boobs are great,' he said. 'And we've clearly got a work of Michelangelo hanging in the room with us here tonight.

But I think I'm more of an ass man myself.' Quick as a flash he gave my bum a loud smack, and I screamed with the fright. 'Yep. Definitely an ass man.' He grinned. 'Now, that is the truth!' He planted a big kiss on my lips.

Starting to see the funny side of things again, I thanked Rory for his public display of affection, and turned to Lisa. 'Please cover up as Parker is beginning to drool on the expensive rug. And we all know what comes out of his mouth can be quite acidic.'

A little disappointed by my request, Lisa popped her girls back under her top, saying, 'That was quite nice, actually. Thank you, Parker, you've a lovely grip,' before pressing on with her party plans. 'Let's use this empty Moët bottle to play spin the bottle. OK? The neck gets to ask truth or dare? And the bottom end gets to choose their poison.' Without waiting for another reply, she swiftly made a space on the coffee table and spun the bottle around with an excited look on her face. With all eyes on the bottle, my shoulders tensed up as it stopped between Lisa and me. 'Oh, fancy that,' cooed Lisa, thrilled with herself. 'Which would you like, Alice? A truth question or a dare?'

Knowing that I couldn't possibly leave myself open to any confession, I snapped back, 'A dare, please,' while trying not to spit fire in her direction.

Chuckling to herself, she asked, 'Are you sure you wouldn't like an easy truth question, hon?'

'No, a dare will be fine, thank you. So make your call.'

After taking a few moments to ponder the idea, she offered up, 'I dare you to run down to reception – naked – and ask them if you're allowed to smoke in the bedrooms.'

Without even stopping to think, the first words out of my mouth were, 'Fuck off!'

Parker and Jeff started taunting me, 'Ah go on. Ya will, ya will, ya will . . .'

Sensing my unease, Rory stepped up to be my hero, and explained, 'What Alice meant to say was that she'd love to be part of your naughty game, but that she wouldn't like to leave my side tonight, so is there any chance you could please offer her another dare?'

Unable to argue with such good manners, Lisa then conceded, 'OK, fine. Why don't we swap it, and you ask me a truth or dare? Otherwise we'll never get this game started.'

'All righty, then,' I chirped, looking to call her bluff. 'Why don't *you* run down to reception naked?' Of course, her face never flinched at such a request and, without further ado, Lisa stood up, removed her top, much to the delight of all three lads, and proceeded to strip off her tight black satin trousers. As the boys continued to whoop and holler like they were in a strip joint, with Rory joking that he was sure he had a few spare fivers in his wallet, Lisa was about to slip off her almost see-through thong when I cried, 'STOP! Enough already.'

Confused, she blankly looked at me and asked, 'Why?'

'Because, you idiot, otherwise you're in serious danger of being arrested for indecent exposure, and I'd prefer my boyfriend to go back to London thinking we're dull, rather than crazed streakers with criminal records.'

Of course, my sane words fell on deaf ears, though she did back down to some peer pressure by agreeing to keep her knickers on – not that they left much to the imagination. Claiming, 'I've got too much to keep under wraps, and a dare is a dare,' she swanned out of the door of the suite with a catwalk swagger and told us, 'I won't be long.'

With none of us believing our eyes, like giddy children we all leapt off our chairs and went racing out to see if Lisa was in fact heading down the corridor. And sure enough, as we banged heads in the doorway, we caught a glimpse of her evenly spray-tanned bum turn the corner at the stairs. Not sure whether to laugh or cry, I turned to Parker and ordered him to go after her, but he was having none of it. 'You go. And take your little camera while you're at it. You could make another few quid off the back of it.' Thumping Parker in the arm to zip up his loose tongue, I watched as – miracle of miracles – he went mute, and mouthed, 'I'm sorry,' before running back inside for safety.

After several minutes of pleading with both Jeff and Rory to go downstairs and see if she was all right – both of whom refused point blank to rescue her claiming 'nudophobia' and 'catagelophobia' – which were, apparently, the irrational fear of nudity, and of being ridiculed (about nudity) – Lisa arrived back at the end of the corridor like some sort of burlesque dancer, with one hand casually on her hip, and the other waving a box of matches in the air. 'Did someone want a light?' she asked, brazen as ever. ''Cause I got a whole load, and I'm more than willing to use them.'

Not sure if his eyes were deceiving him, Rory turned to me and laughed. 'Now I see where your wild streak comes from. You're a shy bunch, you Irish.' Slightly embarrassed, I apologized for Lisa's lack of shame, but he brushed it off, joking, 'I just feel sorry for you now. How are you going to top that?'

Pumped from her act of bravery, Lisa refused to put any clothes on once back in the room, and instead jumped about the place saying, 'I feel liberated and at one with my body.'

Jokingly I suggested that she might as well treat us all to a freebie lap dance, but no sooner had the words come out of my mouth than she was over rubbing up against Jeff and asking him, 'Well, do you like that?'

While at first we left her to it, using the time to catch our breath and some more much-needed champagne, it soon became apparent that Parker's husband was indeed enjoying the attention from Lisa, and Parker was in no way impressed about it at all. Like a car crash that you don't want to watch, yet can't pull your eyes from, Rory, Parker and myself sat ringside for Lisa's fairly thorough private dance, and watched as Jeff's trousers visibly began to bulge in a place where a gay man watching a gyrating woman should not get aroused. Seeing the anger build up in Parker, I stood up and smacked Lisa on the bottom to try and distract her, and thrust her clothes at her, declaring, 'You're too sexy, girl. Put it away, I almost want to ride you myself!' But, feeling a little emotional at the sight of his husband getting turned on by a woman – the ultimate insult – Parker stormed off to his bedroom without any explanation and slammed the door behind him.

Realizing that she had gone too far, Lisa turned to me saying, 'I was only having a laugh.' But I just stared hard at her and handed her her top again. With an uncomfortable silence in the air, she grabbed her clothes and followed Parker, leaving Rory and me looking at Jeff, whose stiffy seemed to be deflating as the guilt set in. The awkward silence was soon broken, though, as angry shouting began to emanate from the bedroom.

'Do you have any limits? Is every straight man not enough for you? Do you have to take the gay ones too, now?' Thankfully, knowing it was time to suck it up, Lisa kept begging for Parker's forgiveness until the bedroom finally went quiet.

Ignoring Jeff's blushes, Rory turned to me and asked, 'Do you think he killed her?' before the two of us kissed and hugged, and laughed through the madness.

Clearly surprised at himself, Jeff sat in a daze, until I suggested that he probably should go inside and clear the air with Parker. I had to say it to him a second time to get him to push himself to his feet and go in to tell his fella that he loved him and only him. Feeling frisky from the naked energy that had been generated, I turned to Rory and said, 'Don't think me weird, but I'm all kind of horny now. Do you want to slip into the other bedroom next door for a few minutes? I could give you my own version of a Tina Turner.'

Although he nodded and said that he thought it a terrific idea, he stopped me from standing up and asked, 'But first, I've a few truth questions of my own I'd like to ask.'

With a small part of me feeling relief that all my secrets might soon be out in the open, I answered him, 'Sure. What do you want to know?' I kept my fingers crossed over his shoulder, hoping that this wouldn't be the beginning of the end of our beautiful affair.

Staring deep into my eyes, he asked me, 'Have you ever been in love before?'

'Yes,' I replied. 'Once or twice. But I believe that you can have more than one great love in your life. Don't you?'

'Yes,' he agreed. 'At least, I hope so.'

'What else do you want to know?' I asked, giving him another opportunity to unravel my lies.

'I was just wondering if, well, if you're up for a serious relationship or not? It's just that your life is very, well, fabulous, to use a tabloid word, and your friends are extremely colourful, to say the least. I'm wondering what you're doing with me, that's all.'

'Oh-my-God, this is not my life. This here is just a snippet of fabulosity, to quote Kimora Lee Simmons. Yes, my friends are colourful, but I don't live with them. Well, not any more.' As his eyes burned holes into mine, I struggled to keep looking at him. His intensity was almost unbearable, but it was hugely sexy at the same time. 'Look,' I continued, while stalling to find the correct words to fill the void. 'I don't want to just date you. I'm at a stage in my life when I need more. I think we fit. And you've so many wonderful qualities about you that I just want to surround myself with your greatness. Does that answer your question at all?'

As he took a moment to consider his answer, I felt my shoulders tense up and the vein at the side of my neck pulsate. With my foot and loose hand now tapping off the couch, Rory made it obvious that he noticed my stress, and cracked a little smile. 'Hey, sugar tits, why so jittery?' Of course, I collapsed into his chest laughing, and he cuddled me tightly as I did so. 'Yes, Alice, that answers my question. One of them, anyway. I still sense there's a lot you're not telling me about yourself. But I'm happy to wait till you're ready.'

Feeling it was now or never, I lifted my head to meet his gaze again, and said, 'Rory, you're right. There are some things I need to tell you.'

'OK, then, tell me.'

'I . . . I was once married.'

'And?'

'It was a whirlwind thing. I had been knocked down, and he kinda nursed me back to health. He proposed, it seemed

240

right at the time. But after the wedding, he changed. It turned out he had previously had a breakdown, and, well . . . Long story short, it didn't work out, and he left me for one of my best friends. He lives with her now – or at least I think he still does – and they have a child together.'

'That must have been fairly brutal for you,' he sympathized.

'I'm totally over him now, though. So don't think I'm still hankering after a reunion there.'

'OK, I won't, if you say so.'

'I do say so. I've passed at least eight or nine of the stages of a break-up. I mean, I don't think I even hate him now. I'm long past that.'

'So why haven't you made it to stage ten yet? I presume your stage markers go up to ten?'

'Umm, yeah, I suppose they do. I just haven't reached ten because . . . well, I haven't completely forgotten that he exists yet, and, well, that's because we still share—'

'Somebody get me a drink, quick!' came a cry from the bedroom. Rudely distracting us from our heart-to-heart, Parker, Lisa and Jeff came storming out of their room with no awareness of the important and necessary conversation that it had taken us so long to get around to.

'OK. OK. I was being a tit as per usual,' explained Parker. 'Now I've admitted it out loud, we can all return to the fun.'

'Without any grumpy old man interruptions?' asked Jeff.

'Don't push it, straight boy,' snapped Parker, in a less stern voice. 'But yes, fine.'

Rory gave me a long lingering look, clearly intrigued as to what I had been about to say next. I simply shook my head, kissed him gently on the lips, and then turned to the group and asked, 'So, are we all friends again?'

'Yes!' barked Lisa before anyone else got a chance to say otherwise.

'Mmmm, but I suspect some of us are harbouring some secrets,' sniped Parker, while throwing an evil glare in Jeff's direction.

Picking up the gauntlet, Rory mused quietly under his breath, 'Indeed, I suspect some people are,' before turning to me. 'More champagne, my lovely?'

All I could reply was, 'Please. And fewer secrets from now on.'

I waited for a smile, but Rory's face remained frozen.

As he sat up on the couch to top up my drink, he looked me in the eyes and said, 'Let's hope so, *Alice*. I think I at least deserve that.'

14

After copious amounts of booze, and plenty more high jinks from Lisa, the entertainment continued into the wee small hours until I finally gave up the ghost and begged Rory to take me to bed. He didn't put me under any pressure for sex, and I vaguely remembered him tucking me in under the covers in the second bedroom and snuggling in beside me. I wasn't sure if I dreamed him whispering, 'I love you.' But it was in my head, and I liked the sound of those words again. After what felt like only a few short hours asleep, he woke me to say he had to head back to the airport to catch his flight. Initially I thought of begging him to get a later one, but after asking what time it was and being told, 'Eight thirty-five, my lovely,' I knew that I had my own place I had to be. Back at my mother's house, with Daisy.

He was barely out the door when I fled to the shower to cleanse myself of toxins from the previous night. Sure I had lied and told Rory that I was going to have a lazy day, but I didn't specify with who, or where, so I didn't feel entirely horrible about myself as I jumped into action. With bloodshot eyes, I grabbed my shopping bags and just several of my red roses from Rory – that was all I could manage to carry out of the suite – and jumped straight into a taxi outside the Shelbourne asking for, 'Terenure, please.'

Within twenty minutes I was back outside my family home, with only a text from Parker asking, 'What time did you go?' to remind me of what had been. Although I had feared the wrath of an angry mother, I was greeted with a warm smile from my dad and a sloppy wet kiss from Daisy as she announced my arrival with her first sentence, 'Dit's Mam-may!'

According to my dad, my mother had taken up going to Curves every Saturday morning, with her friend Joan from down the road. Much to his delight this allowed him the freedom of watching football on the TV without interruption, and, as he said, 'Enables your mother to burn off some energy at her spinning class.' Happy just to be in her grandfather's arms, Daisy overlooked the fact that she would normally be watching cartoons at this time of the day, back with Maura's kids in London, and cooed up at him lovingly, knowing that the feeling was reciprocated.

Begging my dad for five minutes more so I could run upstairs and change into comfies, I quickly raced up to my old bedroom and slipped out of my stinky clothes. While it wasn't quite the walk of shame that my father had become accustomed to in my late teens, I did feel a tinge of regret, knowing that even a little piece of him might feel disappointed in me for being a floozie. But then, no matter how old I got, there was still something about my old bedroom that made me feel sixteen again, and although I normally hated that, this morning I embraced it, and started singing with delight.

Urgently feeling the need to speak to my big sister, I picked up my phone and rang Ruth's mobile. Within two rings she had picked up. 'Hiya, how's things?' I asked, still full of the joys. 'Fancy a bit of company this morning?'

The reply was a lacklustre, 'Sure. But don't come expecting to be fed. I've nothing in, and I've too much to do in the house to get out to the shops.'

I had expected a more welcoming response, but, wanting to get back out of the house as quickly as possible, I grabbed a smart change of clothes for Daisy and popped back downstairs to ask Dad if everything was OK with Ruth. But, as if he was trying to keep some winning Lottery numbers secret, he defensively replied, 'You'll have to ask her . . . It's not my place to say.'

That sparked my curiosity. I quickly dialled for a taxi before dressing Daisy and gathering up her day bag of bottles and nappies. What could possibly be wrong with my sister that I hadn't been told about? I had only gone to London, not outer space. Surely if there was a problem with her health, or one of the kids, I would have been told? Wouldn't I? Not wanting to arrive empty-handed, I stopped off at the Food Hall on the coast road in Clontarf and bought everything from wine and gourmet sandwiches to magazines for the kids, along with enough chocolate to fatten a piggery.

Although Daisy and I received a rapturous greeting from Ruth's gorgeous kids – Finn, Brendan and Sile – stress was spread all across their mother's face. I knew not to bring up any problems until we had bundled all the children into the front room with their gifts, and Ruth and I had retreated to the safety of the kettle in the kitchen. Deciding to hold any pressing questions until mugs of tea were firmly within our hands and the tin of posh biscuits I'd brought was opened, Ruth spared me from skirting around the issue by blurting out, 'Joe has lost his job, if you must know. And there are more bills to pay than there is money to go around, if you *really* must know.'

Trying not to sound shocked, I told her, 'Yeah, I must know. I'm your sister, and I love ya. So, when did this happen?'

'Oh, more than a month ago, now. I didn't tell you, because I didn't want you to worry. You've enough on your own plate than to be worrying about my crap.'

'Jeeze, sis, that's unfair to you and me. That makes me feel horrible that you can't tell me stuff. I always want to hear your news, good and bad.'

'Yeah, well, Eva, Joe being let go is not exactly something that I like talking about. To anyone. So don't take it personally.'

After a moment of uncomfortable silence, I braved asking, 'Where's Joe today?'

'He's now selling himself as an odd-job man. He got fliers made up, so he's driving around various Northside estates handing them out.'

'Well, that's great that he's keeping busy. Isn't it?'

'Is it, Eva? He's going door to door begging for work, and I'm now cleaning toilets for a few quid.'

'Oh, where are you doing that?'

'The apartments up the road.'

'Listen, as they say, cash is king.'

'Don't patronize me, Eva. I'm in my forties, and I'm scrubbing skidmarks off the toilet bowls of twenty-somethings' ensuites. It makes me feel like a failure. But then I think of the bills and the new trainers that I need to buy the kids, and I feel like flushing my head down the toilet. So do you feel proud of your big sister now? Do ya?'

Placing my mug of tea on the counter, I threw my arms around Ruth's shoulders and gave her a tight squeeze. I hadn't meant to cry, but as I cradled her depressed and weak body my emotions got the better of me, and the tears flowed out of my eyes as I felt her pain and disappointment. 'I'm always p–p–proud of you,' I stuttered.

Of course, once Ruth realized that I was crumbling, she immediately shrugged me off, complaining, 'Stop that. You'll only start me off again, and I've done too much crying about this already.'

Restoring my composure, I inhaled all my tears away and sat down at the kitchen table with my tea. Although I offered up several ways for Ruth and Joe to get back on track, I could see her eyes glaze over and sense her mind praying that I would shut up. So I did. And instead, for once, waited for her to take the lead.

Eventually, after she had fired crisps, cartons of juice and some abuse at the kids, Ruth returned to sit next to me in the kitchen and offered up an apology. 'I'm sorry,' she said. 'I'm just finding all this hard to deal with at the moment. I know there are a lot of other people in a similar boat to us right now, and the world is in a recession, but I didn't think it would happen to us, you know what I mean?'

'I understand. Hey, small mercies, but it's kinda fashionable to be broke these days.'

'Excuse me?'

'I'm just saying, it's trendy to be penniless. Even the rich are poor these days. If ever there was an acceptable time to go bankrupt, it's now.'

Unimpressed with my brand of humour, Ruth looked me square in the eyes and asked, 'Are you finished mocking me yet? If I wanted someone to laugh at me I'd just walk down to the bank and ask for another extension on the mortgage.'

'Why, will they not give you one? Surely you can get that? I thought it was only people who didn't speak to their bank managers and just let their arrears build up that got into trouble?'

'Eva, I honestly haven't got the energy to go through everything with you. Nor should I have to. But let's just say, we had used up all our credits with the bank already. And that was before Joe lost his job.'

'Ruth?'

'Don't even go there,' she snapped, almost gnashing her teeth. 'OK?'

Not wanting to upset her with the kids only next door, I let it be, for now anyway, and agreed to drop the conversation.

'If you've finished with your misguided black humour . . .'

'I have.'

'. . . then tell me all about your adventures in London, little sis. And give me all the updates on this new bloke, Rory. My brain needs a holiday. Cause it's next stop heroin.'

By 3 p.m. it was time to head back to Terenure to avoid the peak traffic, but I was happy to do so, knowing that Ruth's mind had been well and truly distracted with all my tales of espionage and naughty sexual encounters. Mine had, too. Telling her about Bradley and Sir Charlie's had made that side of my life seem less scary, somehow.

Typically, she did what any big sister would do and told me to come clean with Rory, 'Immediately!'

To which I agreed absolutely, and fobbed her off by

promising, 'As soon as I get back to London. You have my word.'

As I waved goodbye in the taxi, I felt a sadness in my heart over two things. One, that my word now meant nothing at all. And secondly, that I hadn't offered my sister any money. Although I had thought about it, I knew that she would have taken such an offer as an insult, and that stuffing money into her pocket would only have made her feel more of a charity case than before. Having had Ruth bail me out on many an occasion while growing up, I knew that this was my time to return the favour. I just needed to find the right way of going about it.

Of course, after hours of excitement with her cousins, Daisy slept the entire journey across the city, which gave me plenty of peace to think. During this time I had decided to enroll Ruth's kids with a model slash talent agency in town and had rung Parker to ask if he could employ Ruth as an assistant anything on his current TV production. Despite saying that he didn't have much work to speak of, he dismissed out of hand the idea of me paying him to pay her, and texted back, 'Don't be stupid. I'll come up with something by Monday or Tuesday. Leave it with me xx.'

While I felt a small sense of achievement that I had at least done something to solve one problem, the guilt over my lies to Rory soon returned. I was still waiting to hear all his thoughts about the marriage to Michael that I'd kept secret. Although he had brushed it aside last night to keep the peace among the group, his opinions were sure to pop up in conversation once we had some time to ourselves. And, of course, the fact that I still hadn't managed to reveal my true identity as Eva, or mention Daisy or my job, remained a major worry.

Tackle one problem at a time, I thought, as I paid the taxi-man and carried my gorgeous but sleep-heavy lump of a daughter up the pathway. This evening I would have to deal with the disgruntled and unwilling babysitter that was my gym-bunny mother. Tomorrow? Well, I would deal with that when it came.

Dinner with my mam and dad was long and painful. By now my hangover-headache had set in, and with perfect timing Mam had begun to question everything! 'What were Daisy's tests for?'

'Why do you have to live in London full-time?'

'Who takes care of Daisy's special needs now?'

'Where do you think you get off just abandoning your poor unfortunate child with us on a whim?'

Her questions went on and on, and just as I was about to reach my limit and blow a fuse my father, the peace-maker, stepped up. He announced he had a cheeky bottle of Bailey's, my mam's favourite, in the front room, and asked, 'Which of my special girls would like a double on ice?'

Grateful for the interruption, I offered to get the ice from the freezer, which meant both of us left my mother alone at the table with the dirty plates and her frustration at not being in control. Several extremely generous Bailey's later, my mother was happily talking about her home furnishings again, while Dad and me battled it out to be the golfing champion on the Wii.

It was only when I was retiring to bed that I remembered I had left my mobile in my jacket upstairs. It being a Saturday night, I hadn't expected anyone to be in contact, but I was proved wrong when I discovered I had twenty-two missed calls and seven voice messages waiting for me. Although both Parker and Rory had tried to get in touch, the rest were from the not-so-lovely Craig from Sir Charlie's, saying that we needed to talk urgently. I was petrified at the thought of what it might be about, so I automatically rang Bradley to ask his advice on the matter.

Considering it was 11.30 p.m., I hadn't held out much hope of him answering, but amazingly, after a couple of rings, he did. 'Hello there, stranger,' said Bradley sarcastically, sounding a teeny bit merry. 'Looking for something, I presume, or is this just a social call?'

'I'm in Ireland, Bradley, but I've just had a load of missed calls from Craig in Sir Charlie's. Why would he be ringing me? I told them I wasn't free to work there any more. Do you think they know something? Do you?'

'I'm not exactly sure what you mean by "know something". I'm sure they know plenty, Eva. But the question you should be asking is: what do they know about you and your time spent with them at the club?'

Feeling my heart pounding, but aware of my parents in the room below, I just managed to stop myself from yelling. 'Don't be an arsehole, Bradley. Do they know about me? You have to fucking tell me!'

Taking his time to answer, Bradley eventually revealed, 'They might. Letting someone find a camera in your hair probably wasn't the brightest thing to do, but—'

Feeling like I was losing my mind, I barked, 'But what? But posting you the footage was, you mean . . .'

'But nothing, Eva. My intelligence is patchy. I only hear bits and pieces. It's probably best if you stay in Ireland for a bit, though. Just as a precaution.'

'Precaution against what, exactly?'

'Surely you don't need it spelt out for you, do you?'

'Say it, Bradley. I want to hear YOU say it.'

'OK. Your safety could be at risk, Eva. For now, I recommend you keep your head down and stay away from London nightlife. I can't imagine that sounded any easier coming out of my mouth, but you wanted the truth, and now you have it.'

Complaining that he was in a bad reception area, and that he really needed to get back to some birthday celebrations, Bradley hurried me off the phone and coldly finished by saying, 'I'll speak to you Monday. Goodbye.'

Feeling like I was standing at the mouth of a volcano, trying to balance and not to fall in, I sat wavering on the edge of my bed as a million thoughts raced through my head. Turning into a version of my mother, I began to question everything. Like: why the hell hadn't Bradley warned me? Maybe he had been setting me up all along? Or maybe he was going to throw me to the lions to save his own skin? That night I ignored Rory's 'Goodnight Irish rose' text and cried myself to sleep, with the mother of all headaches banging across my temples.

The following morning I walked to church with my mam and dad for the first time in decades – now a mother myself, yet still a sinner. While I wasn't sure whether or not I was still a believer, I needed to walk into a house of God and seek guidance. I wasn't sure where to turn to next, so I reckoned church was as good a place as any. As I sat surrounded by hundreds of little old spinster women, laden down with rosary beads and Catholic guilt, I pondered what had brought them to this place: why they were lonely, and why they were seeking help from a higher being. Had they also lied to good men and chased fame and fortune in a dangerous and unforgiving city? Was this to be my fate in another thirty or forty years' time? As I stared into the eyes of a nearby statue of the Virgin Mary, I found neither solace nor redemption, but instead saw a mirror version of myself on the wall. After all, she looked as sad as I felt. And she bore a child whose destiny she was unsure of. Never before had I compared myself to a biblical figure. OK, maybe Judas? But Mary . . . never.

Temporarily drifting off into a sad place, I was thankfully snapped back to reality by the grace of my daughter. Content in her own little world, she was kicking her short chubby legs with excitement as she repeatedly kissed her soft cuddly teddy and chuckled to herself. She was the picture of innocence. I couldn't help but lean forward to her buggy and give her another kiss myself, which of course made her yelp, and my mother complain for us both to be quiet.

As I turned back to look at my mother, all I could see was the anger in her face and the creases that mapped out years of disappointment. Although I never intentionally wanted to hurt her, I couldn't bear being around her another minute, so, saying, 'Shhh yourself!' I gathered up my bits, turned Daisy's buggy around, and made to leave.

'Where do you think you're going?' whispered my mother sharply.

A feeling of giddiness had returned, and I felt the urge to shout, 'HELL!', but chose, instead, to mutter respectfully, 'I'm not sure yet. But outta here.' And I continued towards the door without any further explanation.

Despite feeling a tad lost, as I had no game plan about where to go, or how to get there, I did enjoy being mistress of my own destiny. And, of course, I knew that I had immediately to sort things out with Rory if I was to stand any chance of sharing a future with him. So I got on the phone to Ruth and asked, 'Is there any chance you could take Daisy for the night? I have a bit of business to take care of overseas.'

'My rates are cheap,' came her reply.

'You pay for what you get, I reckon. Sounds like a deal.'

By 9 p.m., after a hastily booked flight, I was back in London and in the arms of my lover. Cuddling on his couch with a glass of champagne in my hand to loosen my tongue, I didn't want to spoil the moment with the horror story that was my real life, but I knew that I had to go for it.

'Listen, Rory, I'm sorry.'

'Sorry for what?'

'A lot of things, unfortunately.'

'Oh gosh, this doesn't sound good. Talk to me so . . .'

'Well, there's actually two things – no, three things, as well as my marriage – that I want to talk to you about, and haven't told you about before.'

'OK, it turns out that there's actually something I want to say to you, also. But you start first.'

'Oh, Christ. Rory, I'm so sorry for lying to you but—'

'Spit it out, Alice.'

'OK. OK. Firstly, my name is not Alice. It's Eva. Eva Valentine.'

Rory's face looked emotionless, and he just said, 'Go on.'

Feeling my body tremble with the fear, I continued, 'And I'm a mother.'

'A mother?'

'Yes, to a wonderful little daughter called Daisy. She has Down's Syndrome, but is the most perfect baby you could imagine.'

'Wow,' whispered Rory. 'But you never said.'

'I know, I feel horrible about myself. It's just gone on so long, and, well, I didn't want to lose you, and things just sort of snowballed, and . . .'

'What else?'

'Mmmm, OK, I haven't just been working as a waitress in Sir Charlie's, either. I've been working as an undercover reporter in there, and, well, I've had to wear hidden cameras in my hair and all sorts. It's a long story, but it's for a TV documentary for TV4 and it'll be out in a couple of months or so.'

'Really?' screeched Rory, with a sudden burst of animation.

I was suddenly confused. 'How come that got the biggest reaction?'

'Oh.' Rory smiled sheepishly. 'It's just I already knew your first two confessions. I wasn't aware of that last one.'

'What do you mean, you didn't know about the last one? You knew my name wasn't Alice? And that I had a daughter?'

'Yep, pretty much.'

'How? Why didn't you say?'

'Hang on a second, those were your secrets. I was just waiting for you to tell me in your own time.'

'But how did you know?'

'Good ol' Maura. She told me most of your background ages ago, and made me promise to say nothing until you found the right moment to tell me yourself.'

'And you're OK with that? About Daisy and everything?'

'Actually Daisy and I had a little chat.' Rory picked up his phone, fumbled with it for a few moments, and then handed it to me to reveal a picture of him and Daisy together. 'Look, here we are making friends.'

Holding the phone in one hand, I held my mouth with my other, and tears streamed unannounced down my face. 'But. How did this happen? How long have you known?'

'Oh, ages now. I just called over to the house one morning when I thought you were in and, well, Maura answered the door with Daisy on her hip. She offered me a coffee, and filled me in.'

'Why did she do that?'

'Because she was worried about you. Worried that you were digging yourself a hole – which you were, by the way, but you're incredibly lucky.'

'Why?'

'Cause A, I prefer the name Eva. I think it suits you much better; B, I love children. I was only being defensive when I spoke about kids before. And C, I dig your mystery job and I look forward to rating your camera work. On TV4 no less. Very impressive. Who do you think you are – me?' Laughing through the tears, I made a terrible mess of my sleeve as I tried to mop up my face. But for some reason he never stopped smiling. 'So, what's the story with this husband of yours that you haven't forgotten about? Is he liable to come through these doors on a white horse and steal you away again?'

'Ha! No chance. Using the word loser is probably a bit strong. But you've more decency in your little finger than he has in his entire body. He has no interest in seeing Daisy. That hurts me sometimes, but she's probably better off not knowing him. At least she'll never miss him when he runs off again.'

'Sounds like you're both better off without him – *Eva*.'

'Wow! My name sounds very sexy when you say it.'

'Does it, Ev-a?'

'Yes, it does, Roar-y.'

'Hey, don't try and sidetrack me with sexy talk. You've just confessed to lying to me every day since I met you. That's not good. How do I know that I can trust you?'

'Because I've told you the truth. You know everything now.' I suddenly remembered about my not-so-friendly drug-dealing colleagues, but chose better of telling him. He had enough information to process already. I'd just have to gently slip that into casual conversation another time.

'But who's to say you won't lie to me again? Is this just standard for you?'

'Absolutely not. Things just got out of control. I had to keep my real identity secret to start with, and then I was having so much fun with you that I, well, I was afraid to ruin things. And then . . .'

'What changed?'

'Oh, God. Lots of stuff. But I don't really have the energy to go into it any more at the moment. Mainly me, though. I changed. So do you think you can forgive me?'

'There's no need.' He smiled. 'You've nothing to be forgiven for. Just don't lie to me again, please.'

'OK. That's a deal. Hey, didn't you say you had something to tell me?'

'I'm not sure. Did I?'

'Ehhh, yeah, you did. So come on, then. Do your worst. I've spilled. Now it's your turn. Though please don't tell me you're leading a double life with a family in the country, or you have a terminal disease. I don't think I could handle those.'

'OK, then. I won't say anything.'

'Really?' My heart skipped a beat with the fear.

'No. Only teasing. What I wanted to tell you was, well, that I love you.'

'You do?'

'I believe so.'

'Even with all my madness?'

'Probably because of all your eccentricities, Eva. So how do you feel about that?'

'Wow! I didn't expect you to say that tonight.' I was just about to explain why, when tears started exploding out of my eyes again with the relief.

'Hey, hey, hey. Stop that,' ordered Rory with a worried face. 'I was shooting for a possible blow job,' he joked. 'I wasn't trying to make you cry.' As he made me laugh again, I let out a loud snorting noise which startled both him and me. Pulling back from me slightly, he teased, 'Ohhh, lovely, who let the pigs in? We've a Babe in the house.' Then he cuddled in close to me again, and asked, 'Well, do you think you love me?'

Doing my best to quickly smarten myself up, I wiped away some black streaks of running mascara and dried up my nose before whispering the words, 'I love you, too. That's what has changed. I want to share my life with you. All of my life, Daisy included.'

Before I got a chance to say any more, Rory clasped his big hands around my face and kissed me passionately. As if the floodgates had opened, there was so much I now wanted to tell him, but it would have to wait. There had been enough talking done already tonight. What was needed now was some heartfelt, genuine love-making. As he unlocked his lips, he signalled to our champagne and told me, 'Grab the glasses. I think we need to take this inside to the bedroom.'

I stood up, and caught him giving me a serious stare. 'So no more secrets from now on, you hear me?'

'What about champagne secrets?' I asked with a giggle.

'No way, no more champagne secrets, either. Maybe just a few champagne kisses instead.'

15

'Let's just do it, Eva. Right now, before you talk yourself out of it. Are you with me or not?'

After a night of mind-blowing sex, followed by a morning of exhausting love-making, coffees and far too many mind-numbing questions from yours truly asking, 'Are you sure you can handle taking on someone else's kid?' Rory had frogmarched me to a nearby tattoo parlour. There we had picked out a simple image of a daisy for us both to get inked on our ankles. I wanted to get my existing 'M' tattoo altered, and Rory wanted his to be matching.

'It's not quite a wedding band or ring of commitment.' He sighed. 'But a daisy is made up of a circle. And a circle is a symbol of eternity, since it has no beginning or end. So let me show you how much I love you and want to look after you and your daughter. Come on, get that gorgeous ankle of yours up on the table and let's do this.' Finding him hard to resist, I did what he said, and kept my fingers crossed for better luck than with the last man I did this with.

While it possibly would have been a better plan to tell Rory about my worries about the drug-dealers *before* I let him get inked, like everything else I had confessed, he seemed to take it all in his stride as we sat over a late brunch.

'You sure know how to get yourself into a bind, don't you? Don't worry, I know people who know people. But I think first I need to meet with this guy Bradley, just to get the size of him. He might need some leaning on. What do you think?'

'I agree. At first I thought he was a friend, but now I'm worried he . . . well, I'm not sure where I stand any more.'

'On a sore ankle, I'd say, if yours feels anything like mine,' he teased, while poking at his new tattoo. 'I have never felt more like a girl in my entire life.'

'Hey, watch yourself, Mr Not-So-Macho. You never heard any yelps out of me.'

'Yeah, well, you regularly go through the torture of leg waxing.'

'True.'

'And you've given birth.'

'Also true, but having a tiny daisy tattooed on your ankle doesn't come close to that sort of pain. So be grateful you're a man. You'd never survive!'

After temporarily deviating off course from official matters, and making several nearby businessmen a tad uncomfortable with our public displays of affection, we eventually untwined ourselves long enough to hatch a plan to meet Bradley and get some answers. Several unanswered phone calls to Bradley later, he eventually called back and agreed a rendezvous at a neutral location in the suburbs.

Our meeting was in the lobby of a run-down old hotel, with ageing, fed-up staff who didn't seem to care about themselves, never mind anyone else. It was the perfect place to be public, yet anonymous. I just wished I had had a camera to record Bradley's face when, after initially thinking he was just meeting me, he saw Rory sit down and hold my hand. Bradley looked so startled, Rory might as well have been holding a gun.

After assuring him that Rory was just there to listen and observe, I fired off a number of questions of my own, demanding I get answers to all of them.

'I need you to guarantee that you will not give away my true identity. Not to any other contributors. Not to anyone else in your office. Not on the credits for the programme. Can you do that?'

'OK.' Bradley nodded.

'Who do you know inside Sir Charlie's? Who gives you your "intelligence", as you call it?'

'I can't say.'

'Why not?' interrupted Rory, leaning forward towards Bradley, who looked more than a little intimidated. 'This is important information, man. We need to know that you are a genuine guy. Cause right now you're not coming across as one.'

'Listen, I don't know who you are,' said Bradley, squirming in his seat. 'But I don't need to answer to anyone – to you, or to you, Eva.' He turned pointedly to me. 'You were hired to do a job, and once you finish the last voice-overs your final payments will be made. Simple as.'

Feeling Rory's grip on my hand tighten, I chose to speak up before Rory did. 'Look, Bradley, I agree that I was hired to do a job. And if anything, I did it a little too well for my liking. What started off as undercover work on petty criminals developed into something far more hardcore, don't you think? And that was a danger I believe you knew about from the start, but failed to let me in on.' Feeling Rory's large hand clench again, I nudged him back and continued, 'I just need you to protect me now. And keep me informed of anything and everything. Do you understand?'

'Yes,' replied Bradley sheepishly. 'But I don't think you have anything to fear, really, once you shut down your UK mobile and move back to Dublin. There's no way you can be traced.'

As Rory and I shared an angry look, I asked Bradley, 'That's it? I've got to go into hiding, while you possibly go on to win an award for being the brainchild behind it all? That doesn't seem right. Why do you get the accolades while I become the recluse? I was the one out there putting myself in danger. How come you're not scared for *your* safety?'

'Why should I be?' asked Bradley.

'You're using my footage, right?'

'Yes.'

'Then you're the producer of a programme that exposes drug-dealers and people who use drugs. Doesn't that put you in danger?'

'What's your point?'

I was just about to explain my point when my new body-guard leaned forward towards Bradley again and told him bluntly, 'Eva's not going anywhere. If any trouble comes her way, it'll be passed on to you. Got it? Just because you didn't have the balls to go in yourself, doesn't mean this wasn't your doing.'

'Listen—'

'Listen, nothing. You know more than you're letting on. But I can tell you now, if anyone lays so much as one finger on a hair of her head, they'll be answering to me. Have I made myself clear?'

Visibly shaken, Bradley made his excuses and was out the door in a flash. Fear aside, I had been a bit turned on by Rory's masterful bad-boy act, and looked around to show him my appreciation only to see a very different man sitting beside me. While seconds previously I had had Vinnie Jones on my team, Rory was now reduced to a quivering Paul Burrell character, claiming, 'That was kinda fun. But I think I just scared myself there.'

With plans to catch an evening flight to Dublin to be with Daisy, Rory and I spent the rest of the day back at his place, wrapped in our own figure of eight on the couch, plotting and discussing how we could make our relationship work. That night I finally went to sleep with a clear conscience. My ankle was still throbbing a bit, and my head was dizzy from the amount of decisions I would have to make – or had already made but couldn't bring myself to say out loud just yet. Despite all this, I was happy. In fact, the happiest I had been in the longest time.

The next morning I bounced out of the bed. Once I had examined my ankle I set about putting my To Do list into action. Parker had thankfully come back to me with some shift work for Ruth as an assistant to the director on a TV movie he was doing, so excitement was well and truly in the air for the Valentine girls. The only bonus for the man of the house being out of work was that he could help out with the babysitting. While role-reversal was not quite his thing, Joe's best defence was humour. 'Looking after kids is woman's work,' he teased. 'And everyone knows it takes a bloke to do woman's work properly. Just call me the Gordon Ramsay of home-help.'

Off to her new job, nothing could faze Ruth, but with a firm warning she told him, 'If there's not some restaurant-quality grub on the table, I'll fucking turn into Gordon Ramsay myself and fucking throw a tantrum.'

Although I felt like my life needed to be based in London, I had to put my daughter's safety first. So Rory and I decided it would be best if Daisy and I stayed in Dublin for the short term. As a result, looking for a flat was my first priority of the day, as was getting in touch with Daisy's old child-minder, Alice. I would have preferred to squat in the comfort of Parker's palace at the Docks, but I knew Ruth's house was the best option for now. Daisy would be happiest in the company of her cousins. Plus, I would get an immediate babysitter until I got the real Alice arranged, with the added bonus that I could now legitimately hand Ruth money for bed and breakfast without her having to feel embarrassed.

Unfortunately, as the day crept on so did more than a twinge of sadness over the fact that I was making plans to move back to Dublin without the man I loved. He was texting me constantly, but my old paranoia kept reminding me that a woman out of sight was a woman out of mind. And no matter how many times he wrote the words 'I love you' I would keep asking myself: why does he love me? I'm just not that lucky.

Safely rooted back in Dublin with Ruth and family, and finding myself obsessing again, despite a long and memorable goodbye from Rory, I sought help from the one mean person I knew who could drag me back to reality – Parker!

'You want me to go where? The Northside? Are you kidding me?'

'Shut up, Parker. You're originally from the Northside, remember?'

'Vaguely. But I drive a CL-Class Mercedes. That's

probably worth more than the houses over there. Do you think I'll be safe?'

'If you keep talking like that, no, as I'll be the first person to smack you. Now shut up, and hurry up. That fabulous Merc of yours needs to drive me to several potential homes this evening, so when can you get here?'

'Ohhh, Eva da Diva is back! Yes, ma'am. Let me grab my driver's cap and I'll see you in about an hour.'

'An hour?' I screeched.

'You're too easy.' Parker chuckled. 'I'll see you in twenty minutes, girlfriend.'

After the promise of automobile grandeur, I was a tad disappointed to see a small silver Yaris pull up outside Ruth's house. 'What happened to my great limo?'

'I left it on set. And borrowed this off one of the crew. Does it suit me?'

'Sure it does. All you need to do is put a blue rinse in your hair, age another thirty years and you're set. Parker, 'fess up, who did you get this car from?'

'The dinner lady.'

'Ahhh, I rest my case.'

Two hours later I had seen more than enough depressing rentals, and ordered Parker to drive us to the Yacht for a glass of something alcoholic. 'I could cope if these ads were honest, but they say "family-sized bathroom" and "requires slight upgrading", instead of "comes with a bucket in a closet" and "needs to burnt to the ground to be fumigated"!'

'You could come live with me, ya know? Until you got things sorted in London again.'

'No, I can't. As lovely as that thought is, your place is a total hazard for Daisy, and, well, I'll need my own space for when Mr Lover Man comes over.'

'So, the secrets are out. And he was cool with every-thing?'

'As ice. But then he knew most of it already. He'd called over to Maura's house in London and met Daisy. She told him all she knew, and then the two of them swore each other to secrecy. The swines.'

'What deceitful bastards,' teased Parker.

'Shut up. But I'm just a teeny bit worried that now my full life is out in the open he'll lose interest in me.'

'Why would he do that? He seems a lot more decent than me.'

'Because I'm no longer the mystery girl. I'm just a mother now, with—'

Parker interrupted. 'You're a MILF. And you were never mysterious. You were just miserly with the truth. In fact you were never mysterious to him if he knew about your name and Daisy. If anything, *he* was the mysterious one. Which, now that I say it, does make a person more interest-ing. I'd almost fancy him myself!'

'So, honestly, what odds do you give me on this last-ing? Two to one? Or are we a long shot at a hundred to one?'

'How the hell am I supposed to know? I only met the fella twice. But if I know men, which I believe I do, I say keep the sex interesting and they'll always come back for more.'

'Any other gems?'

'Yeah, stop being paranoid. Nothing will drive a man away quicker than a paranoid woman. Plus, don't be a nag, and cook him the odd meal. We're simple creatures, really. There's no rocket science to making men happy.'

Cutting short my masterclass, Rory's number flashed up

on my phone. 'Hello, handsome,' I said. 'Were your ears burning?'

'Why, should they be?'

'Yes, I'm having a drink with Parker, and you, unsurprisingly enough, are the number one topic of conversation.'

'How wonderful. I'm in a rush, so I can't stay long. Do you want the good news or the bad news first?'

'Oh, hit me with the bad news.'

'OK, well, I'm off to Spain for maybe a week to film a report on some government minister.'

'So what's the good news?'

'I'll be in Dublin in a couple of hours for the night. I'm checked into the Regency which is only up the road from you, I believe, so I plan on giving you several knee-tremblers before I go.'

My mood switched from anguished to jubilant within seconds and I broke up laughing. The only comeback I could offer was, 'OK, I gotta go get ready. Bye.'

I was just in the middle of ushering Parker out to the car park to drop me back to Ruth's when Rory called again, enquiring, 'Is there something you forgot?'

'What do you mean?'

'Is there something you forgot to say to the man who is flying into Dublin tonight, just so he can worship your body?'

Annoyed with myself, I apologized for my forgetfulness, put it down to shock, and calmly told him, 'I love you. And thank you.'

As we sat back into the old granny car, Parker took one look at my smug face and said, 'Remember this moment when you have one of your stupid turns again. The fella is clearly bonkers about you. So stop stressing the small stuff.'

★ ★ ★

After a later than usual bedtime routine for Daisy, as she was extra-clingy due to a slight cold she had picked up from one of the other kids, I was knocking on the door of Room 160, and listening to Rory inside put on a really terrible Irish accent and scream, 'Hallo? Hallo? I didn't order an escort service. You've got the wrong room.' Despite his fake protest, he quickly opened the door to unveil a luscious trail of red rose petals across the floor, leading firstly into the bathroom, and then all the way to the bed. 'Come on in, my Irish rose. I've missed you.' Smiling from ear to ear I stepped into Rory's little world of romance and forgot any past issues or worries immediately. I also apologized for not having had time to stop off and pick up a bottle of bubbles. Rory said, 'I've had a radical idea. Why don't we leave the champagne tonight? And let's just be together – sober. We don't need alcohol, do we?'

'Radical thought indeed, Mr Baxter. But you're right. We don't need it. We just need each other.'

'And tonight, my lovely, you have me for as long as you so wish. Now can I take your coat?'

'Of course. And you can then take my top, and my bottoms, and everything else underneath,' I teased.

Ready to get down to business, Rory slammed the door behind me and led me towards the bed – which was also scattered with rose petals. 'Too cheesy?' he asked, clearly looking for vindication.

'That's not possible. I love it. And I love you.'

'What a beautiful answer, from such a beautiful girl. May I ask another question?'

'Absolutely. Especially if it involves you asking for more of my clothes to be removed.'

'Well, I was having second thoughts about you staying in Dublin.'

'OK.'

'It just seems too far away for my liking. And I was wondering if you would mind *me* moving to Dublin?' Totally gobsmacked, I was momentarily lost for words, and understandably Rory thought the worst. 'Is that a terrible idea?' he asked with a hint of disappointment.

'NO . . . not really. It's just your life is in London. Why would you abandon your beautiful apartment to come live here?'

'Because it's too far away from you and Daisy. I'm only based in London. My work involves me messing up the environment by flying all over the world. I can as easily fly out of Dublin as Heathrow.'

'True.'

'Then why are you looking so sad?'

'Because – I saw our future together in London. If you come here, we'll never get settled over there.'

'But you've more to give up than me. You've got your family here, and your friends.'

'I've no home, though. You have a home.'

'Yeah, but that's it. I've no sentimental attachment to it. I'd actually like to start afresh, buy a house, make a real family home. And I'd like to do that with you. What do you say?'

'I'd say you've been dropped on your head. But I hope the thoughts remain just the same. Are you sure about this? I'm a crazy lady who hogs the bathroom in the morning, and I've been told I snore—'

'I know. I've heard you—'

'And I'm a hoarder. I collect everything. I must have left

at least six half-empty shampoo bottles in Maura's bathroom. And that doesn't even come close to covering my
night creams and my—'

'Will you stop trying to find reasons not to do this,
please?' bellowed Rory. 'Now, I'm a man of reasonable
means, in the full of his health – in both mind and body –
and I would like to be your life partner and live in sin – for
now. So can I come to Ireland and look after you?'

'If I didn't have druggies after my blood, would you still
want to move?'

'I can't live in a fantasy world of what ifs and buts.'

Trying to make light of the situation I chanced the line,
'In my case, it's no tits and just butts!'

'Yes, ha ha! We'll get to the junk in your trunk in a
minute. But seriously, the reality is, I wanna live with you
here in Dublin. So, for the last time – I need your final
answer. Am I coming over or, as you Irish say, wot?'

At the realization that he was truly serious, I gave his
gorgeous sad face a quick kiss and told him, 'Thank you. I
didn't know how I was going to cope here without you. Please
come to Dublin, and I'll make it worth your while . . .'

As relief settled in, a cheeky glint returned to his eye.
'Really? How so?'

'Oh, you haven't tasted my cooking yet. I'm a wonderful
cook.'

'Good.'

'Yeah, I make a mean Pot Noodle.'

'Nice.'

'And of course there'll be the spooning.'

'Of the Pot Noodle?'

'NO. Of me. We use forks for the Pot Noodle in our
house. There'll be spooning in bed.'

'Oh, could you show me a demonstration of that now?'
Rory smiled as he laid himself down on the bed.

Backing my body in close to his, I could feel his dick was
already hard, and his hot breath on my neck told me that
he wanted a lot more than to cuddle. Gently teasing him,
I flirted, 'See, isn't this nice?' while wriggling my bottom
firmly into his crotch.

'Oh, yeah, I love this . . . spooning. So much so that I'd
almost fancy a bit of forking.'

Stifling my giggles, I asked, 'Did you say forking or fucking?'

As Rory's hands began to wander all over my body, making
me wriggle with excitement all the more, he whispered into
my ear, 'Now that you bring it up, yes, please.'

Deciding that we had done enough talking for the
moment, I turned around to kiss him. Impatient, my hands
began to yank open the belt around his jeans and rip up
his tee and sweatshirt. Reciprocating, Rory started to pull
at my clothes, too, and within a few fumbling minutes
both of us were naked and smiling at each other with the
understanding that we were about to have amazing sex. If
someone had told me earlier in the day that I would have
sober sex tonight, I would have told them, 'No way!' and
necked a couple of cheeky vodkas to sort out my nerves.
But for some reason I had no anxiety as I lay there opposite
Rory. I was turned on even more that this was yet another
first, on our long list of To Dos.

As his large hands cupped my small breasts, I used my
two hands to fondle his balls and his beautiful, large dick,
and we continued to kiss passionately, like a couple in love,
while keeping things nice and slow and steady, as neither of
us wanted to rush the process. Well, I didn't, but Rory soon

made it obvious that he wanted to move things forward at a faster rate, as he suddenly reached his hands down between my legs to push them open, and nibbled his way down across my chin, over all the sensitive spots on my neck, and settled for a time between my breasts.

'These are the best goddamn nipples I've ever had the pleasure of having in my mouth,' he growled. 'I fucking love the way they stand out. They're so tasty I almost wanna bite them off.'

While I thought about joking, 'Please don't!' I chose not to, and egged him on instead. 'Bite me, baby,' I cooed, knowing it was what he wanted to hear. 'Bite me hard . . . *harder!*' Taking my direction, he carefully snagged one of my pert nipples between his teeth and, while dancing his tongue around it, he gnawed down on it gently, which sent shivers shooting around my body, and seemed to set him trembling, too. Trying to motivate myself to be more vocal during sex, I began groaning in response and let out a well-timed, 'Oh yeah, that's good. Yeah, just like that!' as encouragement.

Remembering how good it felt to have his large cock in my mouth, I decided to gently push his head back, and as I crawled further down the bed I gave him my naughtiest wink and joked, 'How's it going there, hot stuff?' Without giving him a chance to respond, I quickly wrapped my moist mouth around his beautifully swelled cock, at which point we became hotel neighbours from hell, as he started howling at the top of his lungs.

I was only beginning to get into a decent stride, also massaging him with my hands as well as my mouth, when Rory stuttered the words, 'Climb . . . around . . . me . . . I want you . . . in my mouth . . . also.' I pulled my mouth off his cock for a few seconds, just so I could ask him to move over and lie on his back, then quickly straddled my body over his and put his dick back between my lips, only to feel the double pleasure of his tongue entering deep inside me and his two strong hands holding my butt cheeks apart. Although I wanted to stop everything I was doing and lie back and enjoy his strong tongue as it sought out hidden pleasure zones, I worked through the ecstasy and continued to give the best head I could. I wasn't going to see him in over a week, so I wanted to give him some sex he wouldn't forget.

As fingers explored and tricks were turned, our drenched bodies began tensing and pulsating together, and I could feel Rory stop for a moment to say, 'Come with me baby . . . come on . . . come with me . . .' I could have prolonged the moment, but I intensified my rhythm in masturbating Rory, and focused my mind on the good work he was performing on me, too. Within moments our bodies were twisting and contorting in unison, as the pleasure we had been offering each other reached its climax. Feeling myself come just moments before Rory, I almost jumped into the air to pull away from his mouth with the intensity, nearly stopping the flow of his own orgasm. He wasn't thrown off, though. His whooping and hollering soon came as my mouth filled up with his warm, salty spunk.

As soon as I had tidied up my face, I threw my exhausted body down beside him once again, and joked, 'I think we should make a habit of eating in more often. Don't you think?'

Not missing a beat, Rory joked back, 'Be careful what you wish for. I could easily turn into a werewolf and we might never leave the house again!'

*   *   *

The next morning poor Lisa had to endure several painful situations. First, a trip to her dentist, followed by a visit with me to a play centre for Daisy, where she had to listen to screaming kids playing in the ball pit while also getting an earful from my loved-up self on how Rory was my 'Mr Wonderful'. Tormented beyond reason, Lisa kindly allowed me to wax lyrical about the curls in his hair, the shape of the muscles on his legs and the smell of his neck. 'It is cheesy. Not in a funky way, but in a delicious melted-cheeseburger sort of way.'

'I get that. Francis tells me I smell like garlic.'

'What, your breath?'

'No, my skin, apparently. But when I told him I don't even eat garlic he says he does, and that every time he does it he thinks of eating me!'

'Lovely. So does that mean yourself and himself are back on track? Whatever happened to that phone-sex fella you told me about – did he start hitting all your wrong buttons?'

'The less said about that sex pest the better.'

'Why?'

'It doesn't matter. I'm putting you on an immediate info-diet. You'll be much happier when spared the details.'

'All this talk of food has made me hungry for knowledge. Why so stingy with the gossip? Feed me!'

'Because I'm not always a good judge of character . . .'

'Understatement . . .'

'Ssh. I make mistakes. But I learn from them.'

'And?'

'We eventually met and he tried to strangle me – and not in a pleasant way.'

Shocked, I blurted out, 'There's a nice way?'

Unimpressed with my inquiries, Lisa defensively bragged, 'Yes, there is actually,' before rooting in her handbag to find her mobile for distraction.

Not wanting to upset her further, I smoothed over the moment by encouraging her to talk about herself again.

'OK, keep your knickers on . . . So tell us about Francis. I thought he had been kicked to the kerb?'

'Nah. He'll always be part of my life, on and off. Along with the threat of cancer.'

'Oh, how are you feeling? Are we talking about the big C?'

'Sorry, no, we're not. I just had a moment there. It's because the dentist mentioned how shocked he was to see my teeth so brittle and weak. Which led to me crying about my cancer and—'

'Oh, Lisa, I'm sorry.'

'Oh, Eva, don't be. He sent his assistant on some wild goose chase and then we ended up shagging in his dentist chair.'

'For real?'

'Yeah.'

'Wow!'

'Hmmm, he offers quite a good service. I should give you his number.'

'Eh, no thanks. The only banging I want to get at the dentist's is the plaque off my hard-to-reach back teeth. I find it difficult enough to stay in the chair when he starts prodding me with his little scraper. If he was to come at me with anything else, I'd surely run a mile.'

'Hmmm, maybe? But that guy definitely knows how to give a girl a good drilling.'

'And does he charge extra for that?' I teased, on noticing Lisa's mood become sad again.

'Are you kidding?' screeched Lisa, snapping back to her usual self. 'I was so fabulous that that bastard owes me and all my phone book a lifetime of free root canals.'

After receiving one too many dirty looks from a neighbouring mother, we eventually pulled Daisy out from underneath the multicoloured plastic balls — which was no easy feat as she most definitely didn't want to go — and headed back to Ruth's in Lisa's cramped, very un-family-friendly Audi. We were almost back at the house when a text message from an unknown number beeped through on my phone. 'Hi Eva, it's Maddie. I heard UR back in Dublin. Can we talk? xx.'

'Who is it?' asked Lisa. 'You look like you've just seen a ghost.'

'I have. It's from Maddie. She wants to talk to me. Is this a set-up? Have you been speaking to her?'

'No.'

'Are you sure?'

'Quite positive.'

'What the hell does she want?'

'Didn't you say Reuters mentioned that she was depressed, and that Michael had left her?'

'Yeah.'

'Well, it's probably something to do with him. Or maybe she just wants to see you?'

Defensively I blurted out, 'Well, I don't want to see her. I've nothing left to give her.'

Treading carefully, Lisa said slowly, 'Well, maybe she just wants some time to make amends.'

'Excuse me?'

'It's been a long time, Eva. A lot of water under the bridge. You were best mates. You were much closer to her than you ever were to me.'

'Ah, Lisa—'

'Don't be soft. It's OK. I know you still miss her. So why not give her another chance? If she's no longer with Michael, well, you've more in common with her than ever before. Don't you think?'

Grumbling under my breath, I complained, 'She's a stupid cow—'

'Hey, listen, we've all had our problems with foot-in-mouth disease. But forget mad cows. You two are just simply mad!'

Furious that Lisa was comparing me to the woman who had stolen my husband, I snapped, 'And how exactly do you make that out?'

'Well, you're both MAD.' She chuckled. 'You're Michael's Abandoned Divas. You can't argue with that.'

Breaking a half-smile, I looked back at my mobile, only to feel a shooting pain at the sight of Maddie's name on my phone. I did miss her. But I wasn't sure if I missed her enough to forgive and forget. Lisa was right, though. We did have so much in common now, as we both had a child by Michael, and, if his track record was anything like it had been with me, she was probably struggling to support herself without any help from him. Now I was more financially secure than ever before, and I had Rory to support me emotionally. Knowing this, and remembering how I had felt after Michael had left me, I quickly replied to her text. Although Lisa tried to sneak a peek at what I was typing, she was still driving, and the busy traffic wouldn't allow her to get a proper look.

'What did you say?' she asked excitedly. 'Were you nice to her?'

'Oh, yeah,' I replied sarcastically. 'I asked her did she want me to babysit for her Friday night.'

Frustrated, Lisa barked, 'Oh, stop being such a tit. What did you say?'

'I just said, "What do U want?" That's all.'

'Ouch.'

'Too frosty?'

'A little. But that's to be expected.'

Just then another text beeped through from Maddie. It read, 'I don't want to talk via text. Can we meet? It's over with Michael. I miss U. I want us to be friends again. Can I make it up 2 U?' As I coldly read it aloud to Lisa, I immediately felt conflicted. While one part of me wanted to call her straightaway and make plans for cocktails, another large chunk wanted to scream abuse at her, and tell her to go rot in hell! I was about to eradicate the chance of either happening by deleting her number when a strange sense of confidence filled me, and I texted back, 'I'm staying at Ruth's in Clontarf. We could go for a walk along the coast 2day if U want?' And, before I knew what had happened, I had arranged to meet her later that day at the shelter near the shops that was an old haunt for us from years ago. Looking for a second opinion, I asked Lisa, 'Am I crazy?'

'Yes.' She smiled. 'But without a little bit of crazy none of us would ever leave the house. Just look at me. My craziness helped me survive cancer.'

Avoiding the complication of possible interruptions from the kids, both Maddie and I independently chose to leave them at home.

As arranged, we met at the shelter overlooking the sea. Maddie was already there when I arrived. Very eager, I thought, considering I was at least ten minutes early myself. But then again, without wanting to admit it to myself, I was eager, too. Trying to be nonchalant, I didn't say anything until I was sitting down beside her, albeit with several feet between us.

'Hiya. How's things?' I chose to open with a typical Irish greeting, which, although it seemed to ask for an answer, was only ever answered in full by a non-native.

'Hiya,' came the correct reply. And then we sat in silence, looking out at the water for an uncomfortable ten minutes or so, until she said softly, 'I love the hair. You look great blonde.'

Of course, there was so much else that we both needed to say, but it took the distraction of two women pushing their buggies past us to spur Maddie to ask, 'How's Daisy? She must be getting big?'

Quick to answer, I said, 'She's great. Bit of a cough at the moment. But delighted to be staying with her cousins.' I was just about to ask about Maddie's kids when I made a quick split-decision to avoid the small talk, and asked, 'Why are we here, Maddie? I'm too old for any more drama.'

Taking a deep intake of breath, Maddie slid over closer to me and, placing her own hand on mine, softly explained, 'I'm sorry for all the hurt I've caused you, Eva. It eats me up every day—'

'Since when?' I asked, turning to face her. 'Since you stole Michael on Valentine's Day two years ago? Or just since he abandoned you, too?'

Choosing to ignore my question, she replied, 'I didn't

realize you knew. He's taken up with someone else now. She's younger. Less troublesome.'

'Am I supposed to feel sorry for you?'

'No. I feel sorry enough for both of us. I just want . . . I'm just trying to tell you that he's a serial offender. Michael is very manipulative. I didn't go out looking to ruin the marriage of my oldest, longest friend. But I know that's what happened, and that's why I asked to meet you.'

'So you can have forgiveness, or closure, and move on?'

'Yes and no.'

'I've no time for riddles, Maddie. Spit it out or else I'm walking.'

'OK, I just wanted to say . . .' I was hanging on her words when two boisterous young women came screaming with laughter up to the shelter in front of us. Linking arms, they held on to each other tightly as they each in turn play-acted falling down.

'They looked drunk,' I mused. 'Bit early in the day for that.'

'That used to be us.' Maddie smiled, now looking at me again. 'Do you remember the time we went to the cinema to see that Keith Allen movie at the Screen? By the time we'd drunk that naggin of vodka you sneaked in, we thought he was gorgeous!'

'It was just as well we had no more money for booze, otherwise you would have hopped up to the screen and started licking his face.'

'Hey, Eva, you were the one who fancied him first. You said his beard would be perfect for tickling your fancy! I think that's how you put it.'

'Mmmm, I did always like beards, didn't I?'

'You even became one when you fake-married that guy Alistair. Whatever happened to him?'

'Not sure, haven't spoken to him in ages. I assume he got to keep his big house up in Dalkey after he gave his old mother the day out that she wanted.' Realizing that we had begun talking again, I chanced a bit of gloating. 'I'm actually going out with a guy now who has a beard.'

'Really?'

'Yeah, he's from London. He's part-Irish though.'

'Cool.'

'Yeah, he is. He's moving here soon and we're planning on buying a house together.'

'I thought I heard you had moved to London?'

'I had. But I had a bit of trouble there, so I decided it was best to come back.'

'Sorry to hear that. But things are obviously going well if this guy is gonna move back to Dublin for you. It must be love?'

Having made it clear that I had made great strides forward in my personal life, I quit the pleasantries and asked, 'Maddie, why did you make contact?'

'Michael's illness, Eva. It made me think; suppose I was ill? Suppose I died? The point is, I need to plan for that eventuality. For the kids. And, well, I've no one. There is no one apart from you that I would want to take care of them. If I was no longer able to.'

'What about Michael? He's father to one of them.'

'Eva, he's already washed his hands of us. There's no money, very few phone calls. I give him one more birthday, and then I reckon he'll disappear for good.'

'Jeez, Maddie, I don't know what to say to you.'

'You'll think about it, maybe?'

'That's some ask, Maddie. I can't believe you would want me to take your two kids. We haven't spoken in years. What gives you the impression that I would even consider it?'

'I never thought that you would even speak to me again. But now you're here. And while I wouldn't be foolish enough to expect our relationship to just snap right back to what it was before, I've hope that someday we can work things through.'

'And that's it? That's your best shot at making amends?'

'I'm not perfect, Eva. I never was. And neither were you, if I remember correctly. I'm just human. And, well, I've made mistakes. Big mistakes. But doesn't a girl deserve to be forgiven?'

16

'Ruth, I'm not going on a diet just because you've decided you want to be young and gorgeous again. That's not my problem.'

'I am still young and gorgeous – excuse yourself. I just want to be fit.'

'Yeah, right. You're only a couple of weeks working on that movie, and you're already acting like you're the leading lady. Does your husband know that you're going on a diet just so you can fit in with all the cute runners on the set?'

'Hey, hey, keep your voice down. I don't need to justify myself to anyone. Anyway, as your sister I'm taking it upon myself to inform you that crisps *aren't* a vegetable to be counted as one of your five-a-day. Just because you've gotten a man to say he loves you, doesn't mean you can start letting yourself go.'

'Ha! The cheek of you. Didn't you always claim to be a wannabe dieter?'

'Yes, I have been known to be a member of the Monday Morning Club. As in, it both started and ended on the Monday morning. But today is different.'

'Why?'

'Cause you're going to help your big sister. Otherwise I'll just have to start up a Friday Morning Club. Now drink up your prune juice and grab yourself a fresh toilet roll. If this stuff doesn't flush you out, you're not as full of crap as I thought you were. Now get supping.'

After just a few weeks living with my sister we had reverted to our old teenage ways. Hours were now spent experimenting in the bathroom – either backcombing our hair, rummaging through each other's make-up bags or just sitting on the edge of the bath customizing outfits (or as Joe would describe it, 'Butchering perfectly good clothes') with scissors in the hope that we could update and modernize them. This was our adolescence all over again, without the pressure of our dragon of a mother breathing fire down our necks. It was like a trip down memory lane, where we got to bring the best bits about the past into the present, and pretend we had no responsibilities for a while. Oddly, I was finding it far more blissful than any stay at a five-star hotel.

Each evening, when the kids finally went to bed, Ruth and I would race to their computer and log on to our new obsession, Facebook, to trace old friends and uncover numerous perverts from around the world. For a laugh we had taken to sending each other mini-wall posts about our superstar footballer boyfriends. These were of course purely fictitious fellas, as were our relationships with them, but using our overactive imaginations we would dream up all sorts of scenarios, and leave curious messages about being exhausted after shopping or sex! In each post we would announce our arrival or departure from various undisclosed locations in the South of France, mystery locker rooms, and sometimes Miami, where we had travelled to top up on our Botox.

All of this faking about our glamorous lifestyles was just harmless fun to us, and seemed to be generating nothing more than random followers who kept demanding, 'Show us photos lol xx.' It was when a Sunday newspaper repeatedly contacted us and called for our identities to be made public that we started to get a little scared. Eventually we answered the call by posting an *Ab Fab*-style photo of Ruth and I wearing wigs and Jackie O glasses, pretending to be holidaying in Marbella. But we were soon rumbled when our journalist friend posted, 'Dat's not Marbella . . . Dat's Clontarf . . . U FULL OF CRAP! HEY I THINK I RECOGNIZE U . . .' We quickly curbed our tall tales after that.

Ruth's husband, Joe, didn't seem to mind my temporary intrusion into the house. As he put it himself, 'I'm happy to be having an affair with the TV remote and Jeremy Clarkson again. I love my wife. But honestly, hang on to her for as long as you like.'

Despite a mostly virtual relationship with Rory, via text, e-mail and Skype, things were progressing nicely between us, which left me plenty of spare hours to catch up with my folks for quality Mam and Dad time, and with my friends for discussing-Rory time!

Although I hadn't picked up any freelance writing, and the team at *YES!* couldn't give me any work due to recessionary cutbacks, Daisy had received the all clear from her test results, and life in my bubble had become drastically more simple. For the time being, I still had the cushion of money coming in from Brady Reel Time Films, which sadly also served as a constant reminder that possible trouble was only a Ryanair flight away. I was playing ostrich very well, though, and mostly succeeded in sticking my head in the sand to ignore any threatening voices that might enter my head. The only thing that threatened my happiness was the fact that Michael hadn't replied to the text I had sent him about Daisy. Given he was her father, I'd thought that he should be one of the first people to know that her test results had come back negative, but a response never came. I even rang his mobile from a blocked number to check that his number was still live; it was, and I had to deal with the fact that he simply didn't care any more.

While I continued to battle with my feelings of anger towards Michael, Maddie was also doing a good job of keeping that old painful wound open, with regular texts offering friendship and asking for forgiveness. A bit like the old me, she was used to getting her own way, and she wasn't showing any signs of giving up until she had mended our friendship. I secretly suspected that I would buckle soon enough, but in the meantime I was putting up a good fight and making her pay for her disloyalty.

I had always felt that loyalty was one of my best traits . . . well, that had been the case until now, at least, but after reflecting on the events of the last year I came to the conclusion that I, too, had cheated on people, so perhaps I shouldn't continue to act the victim. After all, Maddie was the needy, lonely one – maybe it was time to show her a little warmth and compassion. Making a pact with myself to give her one last chance to make it up with me, I offered the hand of friendship by asking her to go for just the one drink and see how fate would direct us. Unsurprisingly enough, it led us to Keogh's Pub, a favourite old haunt of ours, where one pint led to another and another, and then an argument, which developed into some screaming and tears.

Oblivious to the audience that had gathered around us, congregating with pints and packets of Tayto crisps to watch us as if we were an episode of *EastEnders*, Maddie and I moved from anger to mutual adoration as we shouted and cursed like fishwives. We only noticed the spectators after they began clapping in appreciation when we finally hugged and made up. Although there was a generous offer of free pints from the crowd – to try and make us stay longer – I instead encouraged Maddie to join me for a sobering-up pizza next door, and left our new pals crying for, 'More, please! More!' There had been many promises made that night, including a big one – 'No man will ever come between us again' – and as I looked at myself in the bathroom mirror the following morning, with a full face of smudged make-up, I made a few more promises to myself. The first was to stop making stupid promises that I knew I couldn't keep!

Having made peace with Maddie, I hoped my karma would start heading on a more positive track. To continue this cosmic shift, I made it my mission to mend bridges between Michael and myself, with a view to making Michael a part of Daisy's life – if even just occasionally. Pushing aside my own personal feelings for the man, I decided he should have some sort of visitation rights to her, and though he wasn't exactly looking for any, it was my duty as Daisy's mother to convince him to include her in his world. After a little bit of detective work, I soon tracked him down to a bedsit off Leeson Street, where I visualized him with a pot belly from booze and takeout dinners, caring about nothing more than where his next pint was coming from.

Knowing that he couldn't be strong-armed into spending time with his daughter, nor did I necessarily want him to be responsible for her on his own, I set about a plan to forge a written relationship to start off with – and see how things progressed from there. Although he had been with me in the hospital for her birth, and changed a few early nappies, Michael had abandoned Daisy and me before her three-month birthday, and there were already a huge amount of history-making moments that he had missed out on. So, with that in mind, I started compiling some photographs of her birthdays and Christmases from Ruth's stash, since nearly all my belongings were in storage, and sat down to write my first letter to Michael, as if I was Daisy, starting with the words, 'Dear Daddy, let me introduce myself . . .'

I kept the letter short, describing what presents Santy had brought her last Christmas, and my heart had almost broken by the time I had signed off with, 'Love, your daughter, Daisy, aged 2 xx.' Only a soulless man could resist such a plea, I thought. But if Michael did ignore my letter, I would just write more. Then, next time, I would make a picture using her handprints and footprints. And then I would keep building on the emotional blackmail and start sending tiny locks of her curly hair till he cracked.

With a whole campaign plotted out, I was shocked when Michael did actually reply to my opening move, and some-what sickened that he posted back several photographs of himself on a lads' weekend break in Prague, along with a short non-committal note saying how he hoped Daisy was well and enjoying living with her cousins. I should have known the plan would stir old emotions, and I mentally beat myself up for allowing him to get under my skin again. I hadn't even expected a reply – and I knew better than to hope for something like a cheque for Daisy or the offer of a day trip out – so I felt it impossible to rationalize my venom about his response. But clearly there was still a huge amount of hurt underneath the surface, so after raging for three days I finally found the composure to sit down again and pen another letter – as myself.

This time I used adult words, something not always understood by him. I put the question to him about possibly spending the odd afternoon with Daisy, and although I didn't want her to call him Dad, I did want her to see him as not just a friend, but a family member. Just like last time, Michael soon replied to my letter. Only this time it was with an early-morning text. And it read, 'I can't be who U want me to be. So please don't ask for what I can't deliver. Mx.' Why was I surprised? Yet his words hit me through my heart, like I'd just been shot with a double-barrel shotgun. The pain was immediate and overwhelming, and I felt almost unable to breathe. The failure of Daisy's dad to engage with her somehow felt like my failure.

Poor Rory left me several worried voice messages before I finally felt strong enough to speak to him. Although I didn't want to burden him with my feelings of hate for Michael, I couldn't mask my anger, and ended up screaming down the phone at him for at least ten minutes about what a total shit of a human being Michael was. It was a while before Rory managed to get in, 'I'm sorry, my love. I only just stepped out of my production meeting to see how you were. I really must go back in . . .'

Hating myself even more for annoying Rory at work with my whining, I did what many an Irish person does in a crisis: I put away a couple of bottles of wine and complained, cried and moaned at anyone who would listen. Unluckily for the long-suffering Joe, it happened to be him in this instance, as Ruth was off at work, their kids were all at school, and Daisy was on a random sleepover at my mam and dad's house. My mam was clearly feeling guilty over something and so was offering me some breathing space, which was, to say the least, suspect, but it was clear that she wanted to help me. Because we weren't as close as we both would have liked, this was her way of being kind, and I appreciated that.

By 3 p.m. I was plastered, and swaying from vulnerable victim to rowdy and argumentative pub drunk, and was no way in an acceptable state to greet my innocent nieces and nephew as they arrived home from school. So after Joe had kindly listened to all my man-bashing, he shooed me out of the kitchen up to my temporary bedroom. That is, after I'd left several inches of food debris on the dinner table in my wake, as I embarked on the challenge of consuming my own bodyweight to fill that bottomless pit of grief.

Of course, I quickly fell into a coma sleep the second my head hit the pillow, and didn't wake up till about 4 a.m. the next morning, when an almighty thirst gripped me, and my bladder felt it needed to explode with the disgusting weight of alcohol I had consumed. Although I did my best to pee as quietly as possible, Ruth was waiting outside the bathroom door when I had finished and forcefully ordered me down-stairs with the statement, 'We need to talk.' Surprisingly enough, she didn't give me the big sister speech when we got to the kitchen. Or complain about me eating everything in her entire goodie cupboard. Instead she hugged me and told me that she loved me. 'It's no reflection on you when a relationship collapses,' she comforted me. 'It's OK. And you're going to be OK. And Daisy will be no worse off without Michael in her life. You tried your best for her. Sometimes you just have to walk away . . .'

Having been full of opinions and grievances while bolstered with booze, now I was horribly sober. I listened to Ruth talk sense over a cup of hot chocolate, and as I watched the sunlight begin to filter in under the blind on the window I made her a promise. 'I will try to find happiness and a future with Rory now. You're right, sis, wallowing in Michael's bad behaviour is just living in the past.' I caught a few more hours sleep, and then reached for my phone and called Rory to apologize for my erratic behaviour, and for not answering his many calls and worried text messages. Taking it all in his stride, he too apologized: for having left his superhero jumpsuit at the dry-cleaners, and for not being able to fly over at short notice to hug me and make the world a better place for me.

Of course, just hearing his voice was a tonic. He had a comforting tone, and a way with words that instilled a confidence in me that I strangely couldn't find in myself just yet. Maybe that would change in time? But, for now, I was a stronger person thanks to him. Knowing that he was always at the other end of the phone for a pep talk made me better able to cope with problems that would previously have consumed me and caused devastation and mayhem. For instance, following his practical advice I was going to seek out legal counsel on getting sole custody of Daisy, in the unlikely event that Michael had a change of heart.

With the serious stuff out of the way, my London lover was always quick to snap the mood back to naughty thoughts of sexy lingerie and intimate times we had shared. 'This silly stuff keeps me sane during the day,' he confided. 'I hate being without you. In fact, I miss your skin so much I think

I need to cheer us both up with some special Baxter lovin' – in person.' So, within three days of my Michael meltdown, Rory had me booked on an Aer Lingus flight to London. Although at first he had only said that he pined after me and that my trip over was merely a catch-up, it was when I texted him to confirm that I was safely on the plane that he texted back, 'Wanna help me pack up the apartment so we can speed up my move to Ireland?'

He'd caught me totally off guard, and I let out a squeal of delight which seemed to frighten the life out of a neighbouring nervous flyer. I repeatedly apologized for scaring them further, and my smile continued to broaden, as the idea of getting Rory to Ireland and setting up home with him was equal to winning the Lottery for me. I didn't want him to close off his past completely, as a fresh start was hardly something I could achieve, considering I came with the baggage of a child from my previous relationship. I was excited, though, about helping him box up his life and reopen it again in Ireland with me.

As I stepped out of Heathrow Airport into a black cab, not even the torrential rain that greeted me could dampen my mood in any way. Since the trouble with Bradley and Sir Charlie's the city had felt like forbidden fruit, and I was excited, if nervous, to be back. I hadn't realized how much I'd missed it until the pilot said the words, 'We've touched down,' and I got goosebumps all over my body.

Sure, I was aware of being back on UK soil and frightened of seeing someone connected to Sir Charlie's, but I was also on my way to see Rory to help him sort out his new life, and that just gave me the warmest feeling inside. After a very long taxi-ride in the morning traffic, I handed £65 over to the driver without complaint, and bounced up to

Rory's apartment. I was barely in the door with my jacket off when Rory declared, 'I've a little present for you.'

'Really?'

'I have. Now close your eyes and hold out your hands.'

Obediently, I did as he asked. And as soon as I shut my eyes Rory started to explain, 'The key to a good relationship is—'

'Diamonds?' I interrupted eagerly.

'Sometimes.' Rory chuckled. 'But I was thinking more along the lines of this.' Too impatient to wait for direction, I quickly opened my eyes to find a solitary key in my hands. 'So here you go.' He beamed proudly. 'Keep it.'

Curious as to why he was giving me a key to an apartment he was soon hoping to leave, I said, 'But you're moving out. Why give me a key?'

'This is not just any key. I suppose it's a symbol of how open I am to you. I want you to have access to all areas of my life and my home. And, well, I haven't moved out yet, so my castle is your castle. And, well, it's also a holding key until I can give you the key to our family home. Which, my Irish rose, will happen very soon.'

'Wow, well, thank you, Mr Baxter. I'm a bit overcome, I feel a bit emotional and quite the VIP.'

'Good stuff, I'm glad you're happy.' Rory smiled as he quickly kissed me on the lips. 'Because being a resident comes with responsibilities.'

Sure that he was hinting at sexual favours I cosied up to him playfully, 'Oh, really? And what might those responsibilities be, exactly?'

Staring down at me with his sea-green eyes, he gave me a gentle loving squeeze before making the very unromantic comment, 'Wifely duties, honey.'

Pretending to take offence, I joked in a high-pitched tone, 'Excuse me?'

But he just laughed back, 'Hop to it, girlfriend. Now get in that kitchen and whip us up some lunch. I'm starving!'

While I loved that he was cheeky enough to call my bluff, I put up a mini-protest, complaining, 'I hope you don't think you've bagged yourself some sort of live-in skivvy?'

'Oh, of course not,' came his response, after he had already watched me stick the key in my jeans and walk towards the kitchen. 'But while you're in there, I don't suppose you'd load the dishwasher as well?'

Knowing that he was winding me up, I decided to play him at his own game, and teased, 'Listen here, big boy. The only stacking I'll be doing will be of my naked body on top of yours.'

'Woo hoo! I'm happy with that arrangement. I suggest housework, and get the vision of a bare bum on my belly instead. Are all Irish girls as easy as you?'

Refusing to take offence, I came back out of the kitchen swinging a French bread suggestively, like it was a whip, and joked back, 'Yes. All of us are. Whores, in fact. It's a trait passed down to us from our grandmothers. It was their way of surviving during the British invasion.'

'Oh really?' quizzed Rory. 'Fancy role-playing a British invasion now?'

Waving the bread around again, I asked, 'But I thought you were hungry?'

'Oh, I am,' came his suggestive reply. 'Hungry for some good lovin'.'

That was it. Up to bed we went, Rory flicking on his iPod dock, and to the haunting tunes of Florence + The Machine, we made love several times. In between pillow fights we munched on plain bread, as neither of us had any interest in walking as far as the kitchen to retrieve anything to stick on it. It was one of those perfect afternoons that I never wanted to end. Any outside concerns, such as thoughts of job- or house-hunting, melted away in the warm haven of Rory's arms. Eventually it was Rory's landline, which refused to stop ringing, that dragged him out of bed.

Two work phone calls and a quick shower later and Rory was back badgering me. 'Shake a leg! I thought you were here to help me pack up my old life in order to start a new one with you.'

'I was. But then you sweet-talked me into bed again.'

'Mmmm, come on, lazy bones, it's time to get some work done. I can't believe you're not motivated about packing up all my treasures.'

'Hey, I've seen some of your so-called treasures. Most of it looks like trash to me. As far as I'm concerned, hard work doesn't pay off till far into the future. Laziness? Now that pays off immediately!'

Claiming that I had physically worn him out and so he was unable to lift me out of bed, he chose the tactic of food to lure me back out to the living room. It was a homemade pizza and smelt delicious. 'Plenty of bacon, and extra cheesy!' How could I resist? After too many slices and some gentle goading, Rory finally coaxed me into placing his books and knick-knacks into boxes. While I loved exploring the things that he held dear, and learning what made him tick, it was a large photo album on his bookshelf that really caught my interest. Not wanting to rush in without prior consent, I asked, 'Do you mind if I have a look?'

'Of course. Go ahead.' Not only did he agree, but he also sat down beside me on the floor to navigate me through them, explaining who was who, and when each photograph had been taken.

Having made my way through the college years, and some embarrassing yet hilarious photos of Rory as an awkward teenager – wearing boot runners, and American football tees down to his knees – we worked up through to his adult years, and, inevitably, photographs of him and his ex-girlfriends. But instead of loads of different women, I saw just two. One was a romance in America. The other was the love of his life, Nipa. As I turned the pages, jealousy didn't consume me, but a memory did. Feeling the urge to clarify, I explained, 'I know this woman. I've seen her before.'

As I stared at her photo, I could see why Rory had fallen in love with Nipa. She was adorable. She had the brightest smile, which seemed to light up her whole face. Goofing around in a casual Micky Mouse tee with mini denim shorts, her petite frame was of model proportions, but it wasn't her body that was her most striking attribute, it was her energy. She also exuded a warmth that almost bounced out from the photograph.

'Are you sure, Eva? I don't remember Nipa ever being in Ireland.'

'Nah, I'm almost sure I saw her. I'm good with faces. She's stunning. How could I forget her? It's her eyes, actually. I remember her beautiful eyes.'

Understanding how the female brain worked, Rory chose the diplomatic answer, and joked, 'OK, this is the moment that I stay quiet, otherwise anything I say could be taken down and used against me at a later stage.'

But I wasn't trying to trick him. I was sure I knew this woman, so, straining to remember, I closed my eyes and systematically worked back through all the Indian women I could ever recall seeing. 'No, I'm serious, Rory,' I persisted. 'I know . . . I definitely know. Ah, I've got it,' I finally blurted out. 'I saw her in Germany earlier this year. The day I witnessed Tanya and Issey fighting.'

'You couldn't have,' objected Rory, all serious. 'She's been dead two years now. It must have been someone who looked like her, or—'

'No, it wasn't. She looked straight at me. It was her. She had the same eyes. I know you think I'm mad, but I know what I saw. And it was definitely her. That was the day my whole life changed. That was the day that put me on the path to meeting you. Do you think it's what you said about her name?'

'What, that she watches over me?'

'Yeah. You even said it yourself. Do you think she found me for you?'

'I know I said that, but . . . As a man it's a bit of a difficult concept for me to really comprehend, but maybe? All I know is that she was definitely dead when you were in Germany. But then again, how could I not believe that an angel found you for me? You're perfect. And I'm sure that Nipa would agree.'

Hearing my phone ring from my jacket pocket in the hall, I raced off to answer it, leaving a confused-looking Rory questioning the universe. Feeling rushed, I didn't take the time to check who was ringing first, and was more than just a little disappointed when I realized it was Bradley at the other end of the line.

'Eva, can you talk?'

'Not really, Bradley. I'm kinda in the middle of some-thing.'

'This won't take long. Eva, I've got some news that I think you might be interested to hear.'

'Oh yeah? You sound very serious. How bad is this news?'

'It's fucking terrible.'

I froze. 'Oh no—'

Interrupting, Bradley explained bitterly, 'Craig and Jake have been arrested for possession of Class A drugs with intent to supply. And no one has posted their bail.'

My heart started to beat again, and I asked, 'So what does that mean?'

'You're off the hook, Eva. Lucky for you – but not me – our documentary has been shelved. Their trial could take a couple of years to come up. Who knows? But legally the programme cannot go out until the trial is over. And who the fuck is going to want to watch an old documentary about Sir Charlie's unless these idiots become famous, eh?'

'Ohhh.'

'That's it? I thought you would be happy. You're free now, Eva. I suggest you skip making any further undercover documentaries and stick to making babies or whatever safe little job you would be happier doing.'

'That's patronizing, Bradley. But that's also exceedingly good news.'

'Good news for you, but not Brady Reel Time Films. We'll go bankrupt. Well, that's it. I've no more to say, other than have a nice life. I can't imagine our paths will cross again soon, so—'

'Yes, thank you, Bradley. I won't expect a Christmas card, but thank you for the wild, incredible, life-changing journey that you put me on.' I walked back into the living room and smiled at a still confused-looking Rory. 'You've rocked my world more than you know,' I continued. 'And I thank you for setting me free once again.'

After hanging up I immediately ran into Rory's arms and started weeping. 'It's over, honey . . . I'm free . . . We're free. If Nipa is really watching out for you, tell her thank you. Because finally our tomorrow really starts here today. I never thought we'd get here, and I never thought I deserved a good man like you, but thank you for sticking with me. I can't believe I'm finally getting the happy ending that has escaped me – until now.'

Acknowledgements

We're all experiencing a recession right now, so to continue the cutbacks, here are my trimmed-down thank yous . . .

To my publishers and many editors at Transworld, all the team at Gill & Hess, all the major Irish booksellers – Eason, Dubray, Byrnes and Hughes & Hughes – thank you for all your support over the last few years.

Thanks to my long-suffering agent Ita O'Driscoll for sharing the headaches. To the Irish media, especially the *Sunday World* and *Midday* for all the shameless book plugs. To my fellow Irish authors, such as Cathy Kelly, Patricia Scanlan, Claudia Carroll, Anita Notaro and Cecelia Ahern, for opening the gates for me to follow.

Thanks to my family and friends for the distractions and of course the all-important babysitting! Not forgetting my husband, who bears the brunt of most of my woes – thank you for understanding my long hours. I may sometimes be an absent wife, but that doesn't mean I love you any less . . .

Lastly, my biggest thank you is for all the readers of *Champagne Kisses* and *Champagne Babes* who sent me messages at mad hours of the night through Facebook and

www.amandabrunker.com saying, 'I love your books. When's the next one out?' Your praise fed my desire to create more adventures and allowed me to lose myself in the naughty Champagne world of Eva Valentine. Although I ended up having more sex in my books than in my own bedroom, this Champagne trilogy kept me sane and endlessly entertained.

This book may be the end of Eva's antics (for now) but there's plenty more 'raunch-lit' from Ms Brunker to come. Cheers ☺

Amanda Brunker is an Irish tabloid columnist and a former Miss Ireland. Glamorous and outspoken, she's rarely out of the public eye. Amanda's books have been bestsellers in Ireland, with her début, *Champagne Kisses*, reaching no. 1 in the Irish charts. Find out more at **www.amandabrunker.com**